BOUNTIFUL CALLING

A NOVEL

bancroft press

FRED BURTON

Published by Bancroft Press ("Books that enlighten")
P.O. Box 65360, Baltimore, MD 21209
800-637-7377
bruceb@bancroftpress.com
www.bancroftpress.com

978-1-61088-509-6 (HC)
978-1-61088-510-2 (PB)
978-1-61088-511-9 (Ebook)
978-1-61088-512-6 (PDF)

Cover Design/Interior Layout: Tracy Copes

To all the people in the Marcellus Shale region

locked in unfair fights because of fracking.

Their stories deserve to be told.

CHAPTER 1

Joe proudly carried three prized tickets to the grandstand. For the inauguration of Pennsylvania's newly elected Governor, Jim Cemcast, he'd snared seats for himself and his parents, both of them strong Republicans active in the party for as long as Joe could remember. Joe's dad still displayed pictures of Ronald Reagan in the family's finished basement.

Still, he'd been surprised by his folks' reaction to news he'd obtained entrée to such an important and prestigious event. His usually undemonstrative parents made him feel as if he was giving back in some important way, that he had made good. Such a rite-of-passage needed to be earned, and Joe thought he had, that his fortunes were indeed rising in Pennsylvania's high-level political game.

As Joe and his parents waited for the ceremony to begin, his mind drifted back to his very first visit to the state capitol. It was during a school trip as a student in Ms. Marr's fifth grade class. The 90-minute bus ride to Harrisburg had been unlike any he had experienced. Far from the standard school bus, it was a big, roomy charter with comfortable seats raised high above the ground. Joe looked out the window and felt as if he too was flying, like the birds swooping through the breeze.

The class of 25, all eleven-and twelve-year-olds, disembarked directly in front of the state capitol building, and immediately ratcheted up their exuberance to a degree that threatened Ms. Marr's fragile hold on the assembled group. Normally, Joe would have been right there with his friends, riding the crest between naughty behavior and punishable acts, but this time he felt uplifted by his adventure. This trip, the carrot placed in front of him at the beginning of his civics class, captured his imagination.

On that early spring morning, the air still contained a wintry quality, so the students' pace was far from leisurely. The building they entered was larger and grander than any they had ever seen. Joe felt his own significance diminish as he approached a domed archway protected by assorted gargoyles streaming down and around the façade.

After passing through a revolving door, the class was led to a checkpoint. All of a sudden, Ms. Marr began herding everyone through a metal detector by grabbing students by the shoulder and pushing them forward. A few steps brought them to the middle of the rotunda, an open space leading to hallways and passageways, darkened and removed.

Joe's friends began joking and carrying on the way you would expect fifth graders to behave. But Joe was overcome by the rich mystery of his sensations. The floor was slick and shiny, as if it had just been polished the night before, the waxy smell presenting a smooth, appealing aroma. Joe looked up from the floor and spotted light goblets of various sizes all around, as if to announce a formal ball that could have occurred here hundreds of years before.

The walls contained continuous murals about seemingly important subjects. Phrases describing the journey set upon by our young nation rimmed the perimeters in a font bestowing authority. The four corners contained the words: SCIENCE, RELIGION, ART, and LAW.

Nearby, curving staircases were made of white and off-white marble. The statues and gold-painted doorways perfectly conveyed the same gravitas. Lost to the class, and captured by his surroundings, Joe looked up and up, until his gaze met the canopy directly above him, and then the center, the peak.

As the class moved away, he stepped forward, but he failed to turn his gaze downward, and the slippery floor deceived him. His balance upended, he fell backwards, briefly smacking his head against the stone surface. Ms. Marr ran over to him, both concerned and annoyed. Fortunately, an initially dazed Joe quickly returned to normal. His friends laughed until tears seeped from their eyes. The girls tried not to register yet another instance of a boy's clod-like behavior.

If ever there was a bellwether for the direction a life would take, this was it. For the rest of his school years, Joe could reach back and recall the awe he felt at that moment: the magic of the aged wood, the abundance of marble surfaces that were hard and substantial but at the same time dream-like and inviting, and the colors swirling through the marble like a picture of the Milky Way. But mostly it was the shuttered passageways, the first awakening of intrigue, that stayed with him. The march through his school years began at that very moment.

Today, though he'd soon be entering his fifth year of employment as a state senator's legislative assistant in Harrisburg, Joe still experienced roughly the same emotions when he came to work as he had on that field trip in the fifth grade. The rotunda was a wild, entertaining theater a lot of the time. Bands of concerned citizens, polished lobbyists, cranks, and weirdos were on display most days, everyone promoting their cause as if it was the only cause, the only point of view that mattered or was valid. The state capitol was such a grand building that it could hold all these disparate elements and still retain a sense of order and wonder.

This day, Joe was dressed in his best business attire, as was everyone else in attendance at the inauguration. It was bracingly cold and the sky steel gray, but this only made the well-coiffed attendees more determined and committed to this important event. He looked at his mom and dad. His mom wore a long, bright red coat. His dad's white hair, not unlike Governor Cemcast's, stood out against his deep black overcoat. His parents projected strength and character, and a sense they belonged at this celebration with the state's political and business elite. Joe felt the same. He also felt proud.

They did not have to wait long before Governor Cemcast emerged from the entranceway. The audience stood, anticipating the proceedings that were about to begin. The Chief Justice of the Pennsylvania Supreme Court awaited the govern-elect's advance.

At about this time, when the fruits of long, hard work were about to be harvested, another activity, behind and away from the ceremony, began to make its presence felt. The chants were muffled at first. Joe could hear the couplet, something like, "No fracking. No way. Governor Cemcast must go away!" Looking first at his mom and then his dad, Joe saw a pained expression on both of their faces.

Why now? Joe thought. *Why can't they let it alone for one day?* It was just like any other day at the capitol, but it shouldn't have been. There should have been a honeymoon—for a day, anyway.

The racket did not abate. If anything, it grew louder, even as Cemcast delivered his inaugural acceptance speech. The new Governor seemed unnaturally blind to the demonstrators, and proceeded without acknowledging them, which added to the strangeness and tension of the situation.

The only time the noise lessened was during the singing of the national anthem. The final phrase of the song, "The land of the free and the home of the brave," was met with a whispered, plaintive comeback by one protestor: "WE are the free and the brave." Slowly but steadily, the chant spread among the demonstrators, growing in volume to the point where it would have been impossible for this assembled mass of a few hundred people to get any louder. Joe glanced over at them from time to time, although his father's pointed refusal to look conveyed his strong choice that the protesters should be ignored. Joe imagined the chant causing them to levitate off the ground. They were maybe 100 yards down the esplanade, held back by a protective barrier.

The last time he looked, he saw the back end of a dozen cops on horseback. They were dressed in full riot gear, and were directly in front of the protesters, maybe 30 yards from where they lined up. He wondered what they looked like to those doing the chanting, if they feared for their safety. It was a great photo op for the demonstrators that he knew would soon be widely broadcast.

What insanity! he thought. *What a lost possibility for a fresh start. Not even on this day could the craziness of the outside world be held off. Apparently, there was no rest for those who felt excluded from power.*

CHAPTER 2

Senator Jeff Bain started the meeting by telling Joe he wanted him to organize an important event. Bain's district was located in the coal country of north central Pennsylvania, and the economy had been depressed for as long as anyone could remember. Drive through the few towns dotting this region, and you wonder what held them together. The economic engine that coal once fueled had long been broken. One by one, the small textile industries that provided jobs became victims of globalization, the politics of which left the residents believing it was their own fault for the decline. Senator Bain was not a stupid man, or heartless, but his political acumen was his divining rod—he had recently won reelection for his third term by a sizable margin. He was an acknowledged political leader in the area, and wanted to use his reputation and power to make a difference in the lives of the people he represented.

The senator took up more space than most people. His features, large in every way, were something his peers used to ridicule him during his youth. As he grew into manhood, he sensed his girth caused others to tender him a certain respect. In his political career, he used this to his advantage, shielding the ridiculed boy of the past from his conscious mind.

"I want you to invite every elected county, borough, and township official in the district," Bain began. He was leaning back in his chair. His desk was as large in scale as he was, and made of richly hued mahogany. A lot of planning had gone into the design of this room—it had a sense of permanence; it had been here long before Bain, and most likely would remain essentially unchanged when inhabited by successor politicians.

"Tell them there will be food—a big spread," Bain told Joe. "We're just trying to get them to come in the first place. We'll work out the details later."

He paused, trying to decide how to explain what he had planned to his young aide, who still had a lot to learn about the area he served.

"These people haven't seen real change or had much to get excited about for a long time. Things just keep getting worse, not all at once, but little by little. We're going to give them something to think about. There's no reason for us to be as divided politically as we have been. I've been researching this, and the only way forward is for us to think regionally, act regionally."

Before now, Bain had been guarded with such thoughts. He had secretly been working on them for years. His ability to think strategically had always helped guide his career. But he was not from Philadelphia or Pittsburgh, and he knew that he would probably never rise higher in the state's power structure than his current position. That didn't really bother him; he was satisfied with how far he'd come. But it did refocus his attention, cast his mind back on the people he represented. If this was going to be his life's greatest achievement, he might as well do his damnedest to get it right. And the result of all this pondering was an idea of regional planning and efficiency. It was his chance to lead instead of merely surviving term to term.

"Biggest challenge we'll have with these lugs is to get them to agree to some structure that might lessen their individual control. That's up to me to figure out. But for now, we've just got to get them all together. If you tell them what I'll actually be discussing, we'll have a lot of food left over. So, I want you to be vague—real vague. Just tell them I will be covering some new initiatives I have in mind for the new term. And don't forget to mention the food."

Joe looked up from his notes when he felt the senator's eyes upon him. He had just penned a reminder to find out what textile plants were now closed. He'd also studied the senator, who was showing a side of himself Joe rarely saw. In political terms, this enthusiasm made him vulnerable, and that was a term he rarely ascribed to Senator Bain. This idea of restructuring the political landscape was new and alien to Joe, but that didn't stop him from adopting the senator's excitement.

CHAPTER 3

Bain knew everyone in attendance at the meeting. This was his district and a place he'd made and nurtured all the necessary contacts and relationships. These folks could be counted on to work with him, up to a point, but he couldn't expect them to fall on their swords for him. That was fine. He'd always been careful not to request actions or concessions that would endanger his allies' well-being. But they were his people, sharing his conservative lifestyle and political views. With them, he had weathered many a storm. They would listen with at least partially open minds to what he had to say.

The politicians descended on the buffet as soon as they began to file in. Joe was concerned they would run out of the cold cuts and Swedish meatballs, but after the first and second assault on the food tables, things slowed down. Eighteen of them sat around a horseshoe of folding tables, assembled in the lower level of a recently built township center. Much had been made about this building when it was planned because of the ample parking it would provide. But it was far removed from any dwellings and so sterile and cheaply made that there seemed little reason to make it feel like something better than it was.

When he sensed most had finished eating, the senator strode to the middle of the room. He wanted to get the presentation started before everyone got a little too relaxed. He opened a laptop sitting on a small table and was glad to see the first slide of his presentation appear on a screen on the far side of the room. The title, "Opportunities for Better Governance in North Central Pennsylvania," quieted conversation and focused attention the way a car accident or a sudden natural disaster might. Joe, seated off to the side, thought he detected a couple of attendees scoping out the nearest exit routes.

The senator began by thanking everyone for taking time from their busy schedules to meet with him. He then launched into what he hoped would be the start of a new era in his district, for his people.

"We all know that for some time there hasn't been much good economic news around here. Coal isn't close to what it used to be, and I don't see many people getting rich from the gas they're fracking around here."

He showed several slides that described how the area had declined incrementally in terms of wages, housing, and education.

"More people work at Walmart than for any other employer. Truth is, the citizens of our district don't have much of a chance to make a living wage. There's no manufacturing to speak of. Next to Walmart, in terms of employment, is the hospital. Next to that is anyone's guess.

"And you know the effects this has had. Crime, up. There are kids with nothing to do, no hope. It seems they either move on or get caught up in drugs. Who among you," he asked, his voice rising with emotion for the first time, "hasn't been touched in one way or another by opioid addiction?" Eating around the table ceased. Looks of concern and discomfort replaced the convivial spirit that had preceded it. Each attendee wondered what they had gotten themselves into, if the cost for the meal they had just consumed would be too great.

"We need to do something! We need to start working together. Each and every attempt to move forward falls by the wayside because some municipality won't go along with what is being proposed. Some bruised ego, some loss of control. We all know how that game is played."

Bain's thinly veiled accusations were met with a calculated silence. The computer fan, thus far unnoticed, now roared a loud, mechanical whir, sounding as if it might take off at any second. The senior township supervisor, Mark Walke, chose this moment to respond. His glowing white mane was greased back in its customary style, but his unruffled expression became grim and the redness in his face deepened several shades. Surrounded by his staff, he knew he had to respond to what he saw as a frontal attack.

"So Jeff, are you saying we don't do anything? Or just that what we do is no good?" He met the senator's gaze and they stared at each other for a beat.

Bain had expected this response and, although awkward, everything was going according to plan. It was time to shift into the next stage of his presentation.

"No, of course I'm not saying either of those things. What I am saying is we need to do more, and the way to do that may mean doing things differently. The world is changing. We know that. Let me show you a few more slides and then we can talk some more."

The slides detailed government waste at the state and county level, specifically their county. Inefficiency and overlap were highlighted in all levels of government.

"In another part of the state, a township has been caught with loose zoning laws that a large corporation is trying to exploit. The legal fees to stop the corporation would break their budget. The residents are split down the middle about whether to put up a fight, and the arguments at the township meetings are fierce. No one should be in that position, but the municipalities that all of you govern would be in the same boat if confronted with the same situation."

When he was done, he walked back to the center of the room and turned off the computer.

"This is not intended to be an attack on your character or professionalism. And I am not looking to put anyone out of a job. There will be more than enough work for everyone in this room," Jeff said, giving special emphasis to the final phrase.

"We're glad to know you're not asking us to sabotage ourselves," Mark Walke responded with a curl of his lip, recognizing this was the end of the presentation and that it was time again to start pushing back. "Even, as you say, for the good of the community.

"These ideas sound like big government Washington talk," Mark continued. "That's all well and good, but what exactly would you have us do? You have three townships, two boroughs, and two counties represented here. You expecting all these different municipalities to roll up into one governing body?"

"Yes, that's exactly what I'm proposing. But it doesn't need to happen overnight." Jeff explained how the structural changes could be phased in, how the existing power arrangements could be leveraged and transitioned over time. More importantly, this gave the existing power base, those staring daggers at him right now, time to realign themselves in the new order—that is, if they were still in the work force at all. And this would not be the case for many by the time this realignment was written into law.

"You've been staying up late thinking these things up, haven't you, Jeff?" Mark said, which got a deep, good-old-boy laugh from those encircling the senator, just as he hoped it would. Mark needed to rally his supporters, let Senator Bain know they weren't going to go along with this without a fight.

"But Jeff, we're just simple folk trying to do our job. If I'm keeping the streets clean and garbage collected, I'm feeling pretty good, like I've done my job, the same as everyone else here." Again he reached out to those around him and the response was an audible agreement, a murmur of assent from those not willing to speak against the senator themselves.

"And the people, Jeff…The people elected us to do what we are doing, and have continued to re-elect us term after term. So they must feel like we're doing a pretty good job."

Jeff often used the same logic himself, and it felt just as empty to him now. There was always this dance. One side knew the other and responded in rehearsed fashion, both sides like puppets attached to a single string that jerked back and forth without moving forward. Jeff decided to jangle the string, push the discussion further in ways that some might find offensive. He simply couldn't stand by any more and lead a branch of government that was satisfied with doing the bare minimum.

"But we are their leaders," he said. "They look to us to be forward thinking and responsive to the challenges we collectively face, which means we need to provide more than clean streets. We need to try to help them lead better lives."

The senator looked to each person there. "How about any of you? How would you like to take on a major corporation yourself? And you know that's how it would go down. There'd be no rallying around the township or borough being challenged. It's unfair fights like that I'm trying to avoid."

"That's all well and good," Mark countered. "But, as you know, generally we welcome any businesses. I would welcome most any employer into our township. But that's not the point!"

Mark stood now before concluding his statement, and was eye to eye with the senator. "The point is we like our autonomy and the people like having that personal touch, like having someone, some neighbor they can call if there's a problem. And even if you don't think so, we can fix most of the problems that come our way."

Jeff gave some thought to this comment before responding, "Most of the problems I'm talking about the residents don't see anymore. I walked through the north end of Williamsport this afternoon and counted eight boarded-up buildings. The majority of what is still in use is in disrepair. Most of what I saw could probably still be renovated, but the clock is ticking. I think there's a good chance our towns will turn into ghost towns during our lifetimes. That will be your legacy, not clean streets and collected garbage."

The mood in the room became tense and awkward. Angry expressions darkened the faces of many who took these criticisms personally. Jeff was no longer their anointed spokesman. From all sides, the insults rang out, with little direct reply to the senator's comments. He was cast as the outsider, no more aware of the local problems than big-shot Washington politicians, even if he'd lived among them all his life. They wanted to keep things working the way they had. They referred to it as service, but Jeff felt otherwise. At bottom, it was about self-preservation, even as the community they were elected to preserve was sinking around them. The senator knew he would fail if he evoked their fury, but he could not make the necessary changes without their support. So he would not give up—not yet.

"Let's face it, Jeff," said a voice emerging from the rumble of discontent. It was spoken by the County Solicitor, Sheila DiSanto. Jeff dealt with Sheila often; he trusted and respected her more than anyone else in the room. "There's plenty of truth in what you say. But there is just as much in what those, here, opposed to you are saying. Our communities are in bad shape, probably worse even than what you're describing. We don't need to be told that."

"We can change that," Jeff interjected, but his tone did not convey the air of confidence that it had just moments before.

"No, we can't," Sheila shot back, with a certainty that Jeff's voice no longer contained. "Not now. Maybe not ever in our lifetimes."

"Why not now?" Jeff responded, becoming more and more concerned that a greater degree of truth existed in Sheila's statements than his own.

"That will take a better mind than mine to answer, if there is an answer to be had," Sheila responded after some hesitation. "But I will tell you what

I think. Sometimes you can act on big ideas and sometimes you can't. You try selling this to the people out there and they won't understand. No, that's the wrong word. They understand things aren't going well, alright. It's just that we are all willing to live with the slow decline here, rather than make a leap and do something that could make it worse. The push for fundamental change can't begin with your well-researched facts. People just aren't that logical—they need personal motivation to break their complacency."

"It's our job to put those facts in front of them and let them decide."

"By all means, give it a try. But it won't work. The people are no more ready to implement the changes you're talking about than they are ready to move from this place you find in such decline. But the cities are in even greater disrepair, and most of our citizens aren't farmers, so they can't retreat to the country either. So we stay, and each person sitting here tonight does what he or she can to make things better, to ease the pain. Because that is all that can be done. And if you don't believe that, you're fooling yourself."

The room felt to Jeff as if it was shrinking and the images surrounding him became indistinct. When he moved from his chair to the center of the tables, he had felt as though he was at the center of the proceedings. But now he was aware of a different energy flow. The outer edge, where his audience sat, was where the power had aligned, and he felt like flotsam, drifting along a path he no longer controlled.

"All we need to do is work together to move forward," Jeff said, attempting a forceful tone. But he had lost his conviction, and his words sounded constrained and whiny.

"What will that do?" Sheila pushed onward. "You expect IBM to come riding in here like a white knight and create good-paying jobs for everyone? Or is that yesterday's pipe dream, and have we moved on to Google and Amazon as the new economic saviors? But we both know this won't happen, not here, not any time soon. By the time they're done divvying up the pot in Harrisburg and Washington, there'll be nothing left for the likes of us."

"I am not trying to peddle false hope."

"That is *exactly* what I see you trying to do," Sheila countered. "You know we can't turn this place around just by changing a few policies. So why stir the pot for something that won't succeed?"

The perimeter took over now. A few more comments about letting them alone to do their jobs filtered through. The idea that change was possible had passed, and this made everyone who would have been directly affected very happy.

The meeting ended, as if by some pre-arranged signal they all recognized intuitively. The men and women got up and offered their goodbyes. As to what had just concluded, a collective amnesia immediately took hold—one that would not likely be breached. Jeff, the senior politician and initiator of the meeting, was all but forgotten. He watched the mingling as if from within a fog. Joe, who had remained quiet throughout the discourse, came up to him and asked about breaking down the food supplies. This brought Jeff back from his disappointment. He was glad to use the logistical question as a diversion.

After the meeting, Joe sat across from Jeff in a booth at the Loyalsock Inn. They spoke in clipped sentences while drinking their beer. Joe had no interest in discussing the meeting's outcome. He had never seen the senator lose a debate so decisively and wasn't sure how to act. Joe had a room in a local motel and was looking forward to parting ways with the senator. Then, without warning, Jeff posed a question to Joe.

"So, what did you think of our little brainstorming session?"

Joe had hoped he would not be asked such a direct question, but now that he had, he searched for the right way to respond.

"I can't say they went for what you were proposing in a big way."

Jeff let out a roaring laugh, and Joe let out a sigh of relief.

"Yeah, I guess you could say that," the senator responded with resignation.

Feeling emboldened, Joe replied a little less guardedly. "I just don't know why they had to be so negative… to come down so hard on you. It's like they're saying, 'Yeah, we've got a toothache, but let's wait until it abscesses before we do anything about it.'"

"It really wasn't that bad," Jeff said. "They're under a lot of pressure and are doing the best they can."

"But what you are suggesting made sense. It could help them."

"Yes, it could." Jeff took a moment to collect his thoughts before proceeding, "But Sheila was right, you know. This area is not ready for what we were talking about."

"Why are these people not ready for something that could help?" Joe asked, refusing to see or concede the point.

"I guess because things haven't gotten bad enough yet. That's what Sheila was saying, I think. Don't bother beating your head against the wall. Just hunker down. . . . Make the best of things for now. You'll know when it's time, when the forces are aligned to change things up. There won't be any question in your mind then."

After digesting this, Joe said, "It's too bad there was so much animosity in the room. How do you think it will go the next time you're back here?"

Jeff laughed again, this time with a quiet, knowing quality. "Like nothing happened. They were schooling me, took me behind the wood shed and worked me over a little. That's the way we work things out around here. But we all come back to the same place. Someday I just hope that's a different place."

After a pause, Jeff concluded, "And every time I return, or drive the back roads of my adolescence, I'm filled with a sense of the overwhelming beauty of this place. It gives me a glimmer of hope, and that's enough to keep me going."

They finished their beers in silence before the senator spoke up again, "Been a long day, Joe. Think I'll head home. Thanks for all your help today. It lessened the pain."

The senator rose from his stool with a grunt and gathered his jacket and wallet.

"I think I'll stay behind for a nightcap," Joe said, raising his glass in farewell as the senator waved and turned to leave.

Truth was, Joe was angry at the local politicians for their reaction to the senator's ideas. He ordered another beer, hoping for a change of mood.

As he stewed over the events of the past few hours, Joe's attention was diverted by a commotion at the booth next to his. The waitress was being hassled by one of the guys sitting there. Joe watched this progress until the guy put his hand on her. Joe got out of his seat without thinking, entering the fray.

"Hey, why don't you leave her alone?" Joe said, removing the guy's hand from the waitress's arm. He caught her expression, which was one of surprise. His adversary jumped from his seat and started juking his hand like he was juggling or performing a martial arts routine. The movements so stunned Joe that his combatant could have hit him several times before he could have responded. But this bearded wildman was restrained by a friend who appeared just in time to prevent an altercation. His attitude was, however, equally bizarre. The friend had red hair and beard, and was laughing with all his might. He grabbed hold of Joe's would-be assailant, whose hands still gesticulated in the air, and spirited him away into the crowd. And then they were gone, leaving Joe to wonder if what he thought had happened had actually happened.

"Thank you," the waitress said. "These creeps have been bothering me since they sat down. At least they left money for the bill."

Joe felt unrepentantly manly, a foreign but not unpleasant sensation.

"Glad to help," he said, "That guy was crazy. I was waiting for him to try and take a bite out of me." He paused for a moment before introducing himself.

"My name's Nicole. Glad to meet you," she said after a moment's reflection, her expression now a smile of gratitude.

Joe was surprised how quickly she shed her agitation and replaced it with a bright energy that lifted him out of the dark place he'd been inhabiting.

"You ever see those guys before?" Joe asked, not really caring about the answer to this question but looking for a way to keep the conversation going.

"No, I don't think they're from around here. I'd guess they're city boys in from Harrisburg, maybe even Philly or New York. Up here raising hell. See a lot of that during hunting season. But it being April, I'm not sure what the attraction for them is."

Joe hadn't expected this shift in the conversation, but he decided to go with it.

"I guess you would have to characterize me as one of those nasty outsiders. Up from Harrisburg myself to attend a meeting with the county commissioners from the surrounding areas."

"Politicians are not my favorite people, but I'm willing to consider exceptions." She smiled and he realized he'd passed a test.

"Politician-in-training is more like it. Anyway," he started, pausing to consider his options. "I'm here tomorrow, too. Maybe you'd like to show me some of what you feel needs to be protected from us outsiders."

She smiled distractedly while figuring out how to respond. She had a strict policy about not accepting date offers from bar patrons while she was working. Joe was slight in build but well put together and reasonably handsome, clean-cut in a way you didn't see much in places like this. His head was shaved and his dark beard was starting to become visible . . . but none of this was what drew her to him. He wasn't a brawler, not like most of the guys who fight in bars; he wasn't all amped up the way they get. Instead, she sensed a vulnerable quality, in his eyes mostly, that were like pools of darkness she could dive into if she wanted to, and this is what she let guide her more than his banter. One more thing that registered was that he came to her defense when no one else did, when he had no reason to really.

"Why is it important to you to learn more about what life is like up here?" Nicole asked.

Joe thought for a few moments before responding. "I was sitting in a meeting earlier and there were a lot of different points of view being offered. I didn't really know what I believed to be the truth. That's probably because I'm not familiar enough with the people who live here and the problems they face. Realizing this was a little embarrassing, a little humbling. It's something I'd like to correct."

The vulnerable quality in Joe's demeanor became more transparent while he spoke. His gaze was turned away from Nicole until he uttered these final words, "If you can help me fill in any of these gaps, I'd be much obliged."

Nicole was won over. She couldn't resist his request. In fact, she wanted to see Joe again. "May not be what you expect, but I'll give you the tour and you can decide for yourself."

They looked directly at each other, their smiles becoming a little more relaxed and confident as they made plans for the following day.

CHAPTER 4

Joe and Nicole met at the Loyalsock Inn the next morning at 10:00 AM. It was the time of year when you might experience all four seasons in a single day. The morning was brisk and the sky was clearing, but clouds still blanketed the upper third of the surrounding mountain range.

"Glad to see you," Joe said as he walked towards her. "Looks like we picked a just about perfect day for a tour."

She smiled broadly, which he absorbed like an electric current flowing between them. They were both grateful that this seemed different, more real, than the bar environment. Joe figured Nicole was around his age, twenty-six. In the bar, her hair had been pinned up, but now she let it lay naturally. It was longer than he expected, hanging to her mid back. It was mostly a rich chocolate brown but had lighter tones throughout that looked natural, not salon-generated.

As for her clothing, she'd put on a lot of layers, preparing for changing temperatures and a variety of activities. This included a long, pale-blue country dress with leggings underneath. Under the dress, she wore an ivory-colored turtleneck, a moderately heavy jacket that covered the whole ensemble, and mid-calf hiking boots that completed her attire. Joe felt horribly conventional in his jeans, sneakers, flannel shirt, and jacket. He could blame his outfit on a work-related trip but, in truth, this was what he always wore when not working.

"Yeah, we did get ourselves a good day," said Nicole. "But most days up here are good in one way or another," she added, not aware of the power of this statement. The two fell silent for a moment, enjoying the simplicity of the crisp air and the beaming sun.

"I've been trying to decide where to take you," Nicole began, her thoughts unwinding. "I keep coming back to the small vacation resort my mom and dad own and run. It'll be a little strange bringing you there, but it's the best example I can think of how a small business in this area operates. If the idea weirds you out too much, I totally understand. I can figure something else out."

Joe was surprised but grateful. "Sure, that suits me fine," he said.

"If we still have time after that," Nicole said, "we can take a short hike."

They rode about 10 miles up Route 34 in Nicole's ancient VW Beetle and then went onto side roads Joe had trouble keeping track of. She shifted through the gears with confidence and leaned into the contours of the roads in a way that a driver with an automatic transmission, like Joe, couldn't possibly manage.

The beauty of the surroundings surprised Joe. Most of his family vacations had been to the Jersey shore, the one by the ocean, not Central PA. Country settings like this never had much interest to him. *What was there to do?* he would always wonder. The kids he knew living in these parts—the ones he knew at Penn State—did not give him reason to think differently. But now each winding turn in the road produced a new vista of unrestrained natural beauty, of trees coming into leaf practically abutting the roadway.

"My parents have owned this property for 20 years. My dad always wanted his own business, and when the lodge became available, they took a shot. Summer brings fishermen and families looking for a getaway. Then in late fall and early winter, there are the hunters. My folks also farm a ten-acre plot. Strictly organic. Been that way from the start, before it was fashionable, although I'm glad to see whenever a farmer transitions to organic. They sell some in the local farmer's market and can freeze enough for themselves. They put out breakfast and dinner for some of the guests using a lot of what they grow."

They rounded a bend and a sign for the lodge came into view. It was named "Bountiful" and the sign beneath the name used these words:

From where the river flow matters not,
Nor where it empties to.
Come and engage nature,
The bountiful moment.

They headed onto a gravel driveway that ascended steeply to the main lodge. There, on the grounds, were eight cabins surrounded by pine trees and an open space that contained basketball courts, horseshoe pits, and a net that could double for badminton or volleyball. Off to the side was an in-ground pool whose water was now drained. Joe looked about and imagined his family here in years past. *It could have been fun,* he thought.

Nicole drove the car up close to the house, stopped, and shut off the engine in what seemed like undefined space to Joe. They got out and sweet, crisp air filled his lungs, erasing his thoughts about what his family had missed out on.

"Looks like no one's about," Nicole said, while surveying the grounds. They walked through the front door of the main lodge, which opened into a series of rooms that felt like an updated farmhouse, set up more for vacationers than farm hands.

After entering the kitchen, Nicole inspected a couple of pieces of paper on one of the counters—bills mostly. Joe looked around the room, appreciating its efficient design. A large butcher block table in the middle could be used for preparing food, and all around the exterior was a variety of appliances. Pots and pans hung from pegs on a wall.

"I suspect my mom's gone into town. I bet I know where my dad is too. Follow me."

They walked out the back door into an area with supplies that a family-owned business of this kind required but were better kept hidden from plain sight. Appliances, used for parts, and half-finished projects for the garden were strewn about. On the other side of the yard, Nicole and Joe entered onto a path that meandered through the woods.

They continued a few minutes without saying much to each other. The sound of the birds gave them plenty to consider. Their song boosted Joe's enthusiasm for the coming day's activities.

Their pace slowed as they came in sight of a stream flowing powerfully from the winter melt. The bird songs were drowned out by the rushing waters. Joe had never been in the country at this time of year, only the winter on occasion for skiing and a couple of times in the summer for hikes. But never when the ground and streams were opening up.

Nicole motioned up ahead, pointing with her finger. Joe could see a man in the middle of the stream. The two stood there watching him for several minutes. *He must be fly fishing,* Joe thought with a mixture of admiration and envy—he had always wanted to try. Back and forth the line spiraled in the air before resting in the water. Over and over this motion was repeated, a graceful dance.

They began moving again towards Nicole's father, but differently because the spirit of the place took hold of them. Lost was Joe's nervousness with Nicole and the disastrous meeting with Senator Bain the night before. Replacing it was a desire to explore what this country retreat, this day, had to offer.

Her dad detected their movement and looked up. A grin spread across his face and he waved with his free hand. Nicole waved back with a big smile, and Joe watched her whole face brighten and soften.

Nicole's dad made his way to shore, and they were there to greet him.

"This is Joe," Nicole said, letting her introduction hang awkwardly in the air as it dawned on her that she didn't even know his last name. To fill the awkward silence, she continued, "He helped me out of a jam with some jerks last night at the bar. He's up from Harrisburg, so I thought I would show him around the campground."

"Well then, I'm glad to make your acquaintance. My name's Gabe." He reached out his hand and Joe shook it. Gabe's hand was bigger, more calloused, but Joe met his pressure with equal force and neither were disappointed.

"Thank you for taking her side. But she is formidable, I can tell you. I wouldn't want to get on her bad side." His face cracked into a grin halfway through his comment, as father and daughter both laughed.

"I was happy to do it." Chivalrous acts were not something Joe frequently engaged in, but he liked being thought of as someone who did.

"Won't be long before she's up working at the lodge, shooing off the lonely fishermen staying with us." More laughter followed, though Joe wasn't sure how to react to this bit of news.

Joe watched the deep glimmer in Gabe's eye, his love for his daughter shining through. Gabe's white hair and beard flowed in soft curls. *I wonder how many times he's played Santa,* Joe thought. Gabe's eyes were softened now, but Joe sensed they would not always be this way. Gabe was older than Joe's parents. Joe guessed he was 65, a good ten years older than his own dad.

"Come take a look at what I caught!" Gabe called while walking over to a grimy bucket sitting on the nearby bank. "They were really jumping today. Best I've seen in a while. Maybe you two brought me some luck—I should be out there turning the fields, but I just couldn't break away, not when they're cooperating like this. Wonder how understanding your mother is going to be." Gabe pulled his collar away from his neck with his index finger, grimacing in mock anxiety.

He pulled away an old shirt covering the bucket and unveiled four fish, each around 16 inches long: big, meaty trout.

Gabe took off his gaiters and draped them over his shoulder. His hands were full with tackle box, fishing rod, and fish bucket, but he didn't let it impede his movements.

"If you like, I can come by later with the fish and tell Mom I picked them up at the market," Nicole joked. "You could get started on the fields. She'll be never the wiser."

They walked up the path to the house at a leisurely pace. The ground and grass were damp with the morning dew. It was that time of year when the haze of morning air fell on all the surfaces of the earth, bringing forth abundant forms of life.

"I appreciate the offer, dear, but that would rob me of the opportunity to prove to her what a great and powerful provider I am," said Gabe, guffawing this time, having puffed out his chest and lowered his voice to a deep bass tone.

"And rob her of the chance to complain about how you're behind in your work in the fields."

"That, too." Gabe responded with more laughter, relishing the thought of this mock verbal tussle he would have with his wife. "I have to admit it."

Gabe and Nicole walked along, edging closer to one another, having just put on one of their favorite acts—a conspiratorial alliance against the "domineering" mother/wife who, they knew, wasn't domineering at all. Joe trailed behind, content. He didn't feel left out—if anything, he felt lucky to be able to witness the exchange.

"They'll make a fine dinner," Gabe said. "Enough for the two of you, too, if you want to stick around." He raised an eyebrow at Nicole, knowing Joe was looking.

Joe was glad for the opportunity to re-enter the conversation, "Not sure when I'll be heading back. But either way, I'd be happy to carry that bucket the rest of the way. And I won't make up any of my own stories about where the fish came from."

Gabe, tacitly accepting the offer, extended the bucket to Joe, who was surprised by its weight. They walked a short way without speaking, until Gabe started to talk about the work that needed to be done in the days and weeks ahead. After they reached the lodge, they made coffee and sat around the kitchen table.

"We got about two months to get things ready before the rush hits," Gabe said, addressing Joe. "We have these eight cabins and a couple rooms here in the main building we rent out. We cook breakfast and dinner for some of the guests. Keeps things hopping. We like it mostly. Lots of the same people year after year. Sorta like family.

"Nicole's brother moved away, but we're thankful she stayed close by to give us a hand." Gabe looked at her, gratitude shining through his expression. "She was always a worker, and somehow it hasn't driven her away—yet. Expected that would be the case. She started off in that art college down in Philly; it seemed that was where her life was headed, but then after five semesters, she decided she'd had enough and has been back home ever since. I'd be lying if I said that wasn't one of the most pleasant turns of events ever to happen to us."

Nicole sipped her coffee and accepted the compliments without feeling the need to respond. Instead, she said that she figured she had about a month to go before quitting the waitressing job and then would come back to the lodge to work full-time. She turned the conversation back to Joe, saying, "As soon as you finish your coffee, I'll give you a tour of the grounds. Maybe we'll even get to see my dad in the fields, if he doesn't find another way to distract himself."

All three smiled at this and drained the last of their cups.

Joe and Nicole walked towards a cabin that had not been reopened since the end of hunting season. The temperature inside felt colder than outside and made Joe feel as if he'd been transported much farther north than where they actually were. The entire visit was like this, descending deeper and deeper into an unfamiliar world, but one that was both fresh and alive.

"The cabins will be opened soon and cleaned top to bottom. Any damage will be repaired too. My dad can do a little bit of everything, which is what you need to be able to do if you own a business like this."

They went back outside, and Nicole showed him the plot of land that would be farmed. She commented that her dad had still not gotten started and wondered what he'd wandered into instead. Joe could tell from her tone this sort of detour was not a rare occurrence.

The tour ended at the barn with an explanation of its different uses. Joe was astonished by what he saw and all she told him. He felt as if he was in an office building or factory instead of an oversized garage, which was how he was used to imagining barns. He had no idea of their complexity and would never view them the same way again.

"Amazing," he said to Nicole, struggling to take in all he had seen and put his feelings into words. "So many parts to running this place. Way more than you'd think. The work must never end."

"That's true. And back when there was other work in the area, like at the furniture factory in town, everyone would pick up shifts just to have some steady money coming in."

"And what do people do now for steady work?"

They were standing on the dirt-packed floor, beside a tractor and a grass threshing machine. The hay and grass from last fall lay decaying in clumps around them, emitting an odor both sweet and sour that saturated their sense of smell.

"Isn't that something you should know about, Mr. Politician-in-Training?" There was an edge to the comment he hadn't expected, although he could tell she had made an effort to keep it light.

"I know the hospital is a big employer, and farming, of course," Joe said with his at-work tone, while deliberately not mentioning the box stores that he knew Nicole would frown upon.

"What if you're not a farmer or doctor?" Nicole said. "What are your options then? It's not like there's a lot to offer around here. I love the place. Don't get me wrong. But almost every way of making a living has been swept away." If Joe wanted to know the problems area residents were up against, she was going to tell him. "And don't, whatever you do, start singing to me the praises of fracking! All those companies want to do is come in here and tear up your land." She stopped herself from continuing, fearing Joe would feel personally attacked if she dove deeper into this topic. Already she worried she had expressed too much of her frustration.

"Look, I don't know all of what Senator Bain is attempting to do to improve the economy. I'll get back to you with an answer on that. But I can tell you the meeting last night was related to this, and the senator nearly got his brains knocked out trying to do some good for the people around here."

Nicole looked at Joe, who seemed upset by this exchange. He was her guest and not the enemy, and she would do what she could to undo whatever harm she had caused. "Alright, truce," she offered. "How about we grab some lunch and then, if you still have time, we can go for a hike?" Then she added, giving him a wry smile to show she had no hard feelings towards him, "That is, if I haven't scared you off with my tirade."

"Lunch sounds amazing right now," Joe said, glad to not have to field any more of Nicole's questions that he didn't have good answers for.

They returned to Nicole's car and after a last look around, headed back on the road. Instead of going towards Williamsport, Nicole found her way onto a different highway and traveled along it until she reached what seemed like an ordinary truck stop. They got out of the car in front of a large rectangular brick building with a weathered off-white sign reading "Food, Gas, Candies, Cigarettes" in hand-lettered, fading red script. The only other things close by were a couple of gas pumps.

"All the world's a box store," Nicole said, smirking. She knew she had said aloud what Joe had been thinking.

"Not what I was expecting from you," Joe said. "Figured we'd end up in some coffee shop—you know, something quaint, something country."

"What you're talking about doesn't hardly exist anymore. Towns up here have been hollowed out from the inside."

Joe gave one more look at the building. It was large and featureless; it had to be more than 100 feet wide across the front and not a window anywhere in sight. *This building is an abomination,* he thought quietly to himself. *It seems dropped down in the middle of a beautiful setting.* He noticed then that the parking lot was near capacity, filled mostly with rusted-out pickups and old American sedans.

They walked through the main entrance and Joe was surprised by what he saw. Beneath the rows of artificial fluorescent rods was a hub of activity. They were told it would be a 20-minute wait, and Joe took this time to look around, try to make sense of all that was happening around them. Tables in the middle of the large dining hall seated whole families, and in some instances groups of families, out for a Saturday luncheon. Kids wandered from their seats but didn't stray far. The two men in charge—the owners, Nicole later told him—seemed to be everywhere, helping wherever help was needed. They talked in a familiar way with most of the patrons, and sometimes pulled up a chair and sat with a party, catching up for a few minutes. Everyone knew someone sitting at an adjoining table.

It was as if Nicole could read Joe's thoughts as they waited to be seated. "You don't need things all quaint and prettied up if what you got runs deeper," she said.

Joe now suspected the lack of windows in the building was strategic, allowing the occupants to slip back to a preferred time and place. It was like a big house party, a Bruegel painting even, and all so unlikely.

Joe figured about half the occupants were Amish. He'd really only encountered the Amish the few times he drove alongside them in their horse-drawn buggies, passing them in his car. Now they sat in the neighboring tables, seemingly unaware of his presence even as he studied them. They were more dressed up than most of the other patrons; the girls were more buttoned-down, but the boys wore pastel-colored shirts and most had shaggy hair. They had that androgynous look of Ralph Lauren models.

After they took their seats, Joe said, "I didn't know I could be less than three hours from where I live and feel like I was in another country, another *time.*" His face expressed his bewilderment.

"Nice to stretch yourself, see the world differently, especially when it's in your own back yard," Nicole responded.

Joe passed a menu, which rested behind the napkin dispenser, to Nicole, and took one for himself. They were old, the paper yellowed with age. The prices also seemed from another era.

Joe's food preferences were traditional so he found plenty to satisfy him as long as he stayed away from the pickled and peppered sections of the menu.

"Looks like you'll be a cheap date," Joe said, chuckling as he closed the menu.

"You don't have to pay for me," Nicole responded. "I wasn't expecting you to."

"Actually, I'd like to. One way for me to show my appreciation. This is all very cool. Even in this short amount of time, you've given me the chance to see things I may not have had the opportunity to experience otherwise. And I would be worse off for it."

He raised his water glass and extended it in an offering to Nicole. She raised hers and clinked them together, setting off an unexpectedly clear tone that managed to break through all the noise around them. Their gaze lingered on each other, carrying muted notes of interest and desire.

They both ordered hamburger platters, which were delivered quickly despite the size of the crowd. The burgers were large but were overshadowed by the overflowing sides of coleslaw and French fries.

Joe's eyes widened. "I'll be surprised if I make it through all this."

"Do your best," said Nicole, who had already doused her burger with ketchup and was biting into it with gusto.

"So, you spent a couple of years in Philly," Joe said, directing his attention back to Nicole.

"Yeah, after high school I wanted to see more than these woods, this community."

Nicole didn't seem like someone who wouldn't finish something she started. She acted as if she'd figured out what was important and lived accordingly.

"So what happened?"

"What happened is after two years of art classes that I liked okay, I got my first internship. I was assigned to one of the better marketing agencies in town. I got through three months of that and then decided it wasn't for me. Working in that office felt like a slow form of dying. Everything about it was unhealthy. Trying to care about products that were ridiculous, unnecessary, and wasteful. The office politics. Not ever getting outdoors. One day I just packed my bags and headed back here."

"Yep, that's a pretty good description of work. I've just never felt so bad about it to get up and walk away. Really had no better place to walk to," Joe admitted.

"I felt like a failure at first, but I soon realized I was genuinely happy up here. And that's how I continue to feel now that I'm back."

Their focus returned to the piles of food before them. When Joe broke the silence, he gave voice to a thought that had been forming since entering the building. "If you don't mind me saying so, you seem different than the people around here."

Nicole stopped eating mid-bite and looked at him quizzically. "What do you mean?" she said.

"I don't know," he said, he did know but didn't have the words to describe it. "How many of these people would have ventured off to art school in Philadelphia?" he asked, but was only partially satisfied with this observation. "You just seem like you could do anything you wanted to, and be comfortable being who you are in any situation. And that person is very cool."

Nicole looked surprised, but not displeased, at the compliment.

"Really, I don't deserve such high praise. And you may change your mind if you get to know me better," she said, raising an eyebrow playfully. "And besides, you're pretty cool yourself."

"I hope I get the chance," Joe said with subdued optimism. And then continuing in a self-deprecating tone, "Not sure where all that came from. I wish someone had pulled out the hook and dragged me off stage before delivering that little speech."

"No, really, that's fine. In fact, it was nice of you to offer your impressions of me. But look around." Nicole smiled and gestured to those surrounding them. "There's lots of different types of people. And we're more accepting than you might suspect. I'm not the only one living here who might surprise you."

Nicole motioned to the waitress for refills of their iced tea and said,

"Better eat up. We've got a couple more stops to make. Then I'll put you back on the road to our beloved state capital and the Second Street bar run, inaccurately known as Restaurant Row."

"I don't hang out there much," Joe said in an attempt to deflect Nicole's critical gaze.

Nicole laughed and Joe followed suit, not because of what was said, but because her laughter was infectious.

"It's not so bad, really. I rent a row house in town with a couple of guys. It's affordable and has some style."

"Ah, you must be talking about the four streets that have been gentrified," Nicole said, displaying a degree of insight Joe had not suspected. "Walk beyond them and you're in neighborhoods so run down it'll soon be too late to reclaim them. Of course, white people with money have little reason to venture into them now."

"Can't argue with that, but you need to start somewhere. Maybe all that money from the bars will help turn things around for the rest of the residents."

She looked at him as if not quite comprehending but, of course, she did. Her perplexed look was to let him know she was not so gullible. Instead of responding, she got up to go to the bathroom, and when she returned, the check had been delivered and Joe's credit card sat on top of it.

After paying, Joe started towards the entrance, but Nicole said, "No, this way. I want to show you something before we leave."

She led him through a doorway which led to a series of twisting hallways and stairs that got him turned around and left him slightly disoriented. A thought in the back of his mind—that the building seemed larger from the outside than the space in the restaurant—came to the foreground. He heard noises along the passageway on the other side of the wall that seemed out of place, like knocking or trampling, but he couldn't identify them.

They entered a room that was irregularly shaped, with curves and angles jutting out of walls where you wouldn't expect them. People stood at different levels behind planks of wood. It was not clear if they reached the different levels by steps or if the floor was continuously sloped. The area of interest was at the lowest level. It was a ten foot-by ten foot opening and the floor appeared to be compacted earth. Joe would not have guessed he was so close to ground level. The setting reminded him of the barn he'd visited that day, but also of ancient courts of law where the accused were harassed by commoners crowded around in the upper chambers.

In the midst of these reflections, a commotion began on what seemed to be the stage area. Doors were locked and unlocked by men who looked like farmers, which is what most everyone here looked like. They walked with confident strides from one part of the stage to another. A man behind one locked gate started talking to the assembled group, microphone in hand.

The babble became more indecipherable as it took on the sing-song cadence of an auctioneer. Then one of the gates flew open and ten piglets charged into the pen. A large man, maybe fifteen times bigger than all of the piglets combined, tried to corral their movement with a stick, without much success. Joe smiled and wanted to let out a laugh, but when he looked around, he realized this was serious business for the men peering down at the farm animals. The kids were alternately looking at the animals and running in the corridors, which, fortunately, were wide enough for both activities.

The bidding went higher quickly. Small movements of the head or hand indicated increased bids. Joe remained still, but was sure his presence barely registered on the assembled group. His city looks disqualified him from consideration, but he felt no hostility and continued to observe. He sensed something good going on here, some well-worn tradition, and was grateful to be let in on it, awestruck at the unspoken ritual of it all.

The man again moved into the center of the stage, this time to corral the piglets, most of which seemed willing to comply with his steady prodding. One of the piglets tried to break free and got poked in the side, sending him tumbling in the direction of his mates, squealing all the while. Joe flinched, thinking it unnecessarily rough, but could tell he was the only one reacting this way.

Joe's eyes met Nicole's, who had been watching him without him realizing it.

"They're not pets. They're bacon," she said, with a note of kindness in her voice. She placed her hand on his. "But I know what you're feeling." She removed her hand from his and put it in her jacket pocket, leaving both to consider this brief contact.

In the meantime, there must have been a sale made, but Joe had no idea to whom or for how much. Men who were grouped together discussed the outcome amongst themselves. The piglets raced along in a surprisingly straight line back behind the gate, which had been opened for them, and were not seen again.

They watched the sale of other farm animals: a rooster that would not be cowed, and calves that needed to be sold one or two at a time because of the space they took on the stage. Then there was a pause, like an intermission between acts in a play.

Nicole said, "I wanted to let your food settle before heading up the road for a hike, if you're up for it."

"Lead the way. There's no reason to stop trusting you now," he said, surprised he was able to describe exactly what he was feeling. They walked along the hallway, dodging children, avoiding low ceilings, and getting turned around until they were standing in front of a door different than the one from which they had entered the building.

Nicole went out first and Joe followed. They were in the back of the building, and before them sat seven horse-drawn buggies the Amish had used for transportation.

"Of course," Joe said, chuckling but intrigued by this way of life and how seamlessly it was integrated into society here.

They stood, admiring machines that were as much a spectacle as a Ferrari on the street. Then they walked around to the front of the building, which Joe now saw in an entirely different way than he had when they arrived.

Back in the car, they drove along the winding side roads that defined this area. He looked across at Nicole shifting through the gears, getting from the car whatever power it had to offer as she remained expertly in control.

They drove twenty minutes to a Loyalsock State Forest entrance and parked in a lot containing only a few cars. For the relative warmth in the air that greeted them, they both felt grateful.

"There aren't too many things like this that you can count on to lift your spirits," Nicole said as they began their trek. Joe considered responding but remained silent. He was having a great day, but wasn't sure this forest would have the same power over him that she had described for herself.

They ascended a trail and hit a marshy area, causing them to sink into the muddy surface.

"I should have warned you about the mud. Not sure those sneakers will ever look the same. I guess you had no reason to pack any hiking gear for this trip."

"You're right about that," Joe said, not telling her this was the most appropriate footwear he owned for this type of terrain. "I needed some new ones anyway." He laughed.

From the openness of the bare deciduous trees, they passed into a stand of evergreens. As their feet stepped upon beds of pine needles, they felt wrapped inside a green oasis.

"This is about the closest thing to old growth forest you can find around here these days."

This was a new term for Joe but one that made sense to him immediately.

The air grew still, and as they moved into the depths of the wilderness, its mystery penetrated him. "I feel like a kid up here," Joe admitted sheepishly.

"That's the way you should feel," said Nicole, smiling. "These grand trees are great levelers. You asked why I hated office work. This is a big part of the reason. And a big part of the reason I came running back is because I was afraid I would forget how important these forests were. These woods were pretty much clear-cut a hundred years ago. It's hard to imagine this place barren like that. But maybe it's just as hard to think about what it was like before then, when there wasn't such an appetite for wood. Would the spirit be even grander, picking you up and leaving you even more enchanted, more connected?"

These comments unsettled Joe, and when he figured out why, he shared his feeling. "Funny, as soon as you mentioned the world outside of these trees, I didn't feel like that kid anymore."

"Maybe what you need to do then is forget about that world for a little while, give that office worker a break. You can't always be pulling the levers, greasing the skids."

There were elements of truth in what she said, he decided, but that was who he was, and he usually felt good about it. He caught a buzz from his work environment, and he was doing at least a little good at the same time.

"The senator showed me a side of himself last night I've never seen,"

Joe said, thoughts of work detouring him in this direction. "He's always in control and people around him generally fall in line."

"You mentioned things didn't exactly go his way."

"At some point, he shut down, realizing he wasn't going to win them over, and allowed the meeting to crash and burn."

"Sounds like a free-for-all."

"It wasn't fun … not for me anyway."

Joe provided a brief overview of Senator Bain's proposal to consolidate government in the region and make it more efficient, and the response with which it was met.

"Sounds like the first worthwhile thing I've heard out of a politician's mouth in a long time," Nicole said. "No wonder they hated it."

"I'm surprised we weren't thrown in the local jail."

"How dare you try to shake up the existing order?!" she said and wagged her index finger at him like a grade school teacher would to an unruly student.

"And all he said afterwards was that he understood them. The time wasn't right for making a big change of this kind. I guess things need to get worse before people will take a risk, force a change."

"Or come to some different understanding of what is going on around them," Nicole said, extending her line of reasoning. "Or maybe they finally accept the fact that they don't have the power to make important decisions about their own lives."

"But will enough people ever really consider these questions if they're not pushed to do so?" Joe asked.

Nicole let the question hang in the air; Joe left it, too, deciding that is where it belonged, for now at least. They were both happy to return their focus to the trail, the cadence of their steps, and the fresh air as they continued their hike upwards. Their surroundings acted as a salve to the region's problems they were discussing.

They walked in relative quiet for about a half-hour, enjoying the sounds, smells, and sights they experienced on the trail. They stopped occasionally, giving Nicole a chance to point out a view, or to dispense some information.

"Best time to see various song birds is around Mother's Day. So be sure to take your mom out for a walk to look at the birds."

Nicole was not afraid to dig her hands into the still cold ground. Indeed, she relished doing so, bringing into display an early flowering plant or to show that a deer or other small animal had walked through not long before. Joe enjoyed watching her get excited with her discovery. She truly cherished everything out here.

Then the path ascended one last time and left them in an open, flattened plain that was the summit of the mountain.

It was not the highest peak of all the surrounding mountain ridges, but very nearly. The mountains extended for a long distance, beyond sight. These were not lazy old foothills either, but mountains with peaks and severe facing.

Joe spun himself in a full circle, taking it all in, fully feeling the joy of the moment. He turned to Nicole and extended his hands to her. She understood the gesture, gently took hold of each hand, and drew him closer to her. They held their gaze, and continued to smile but in a more subdued way until they kissed, and then all they felt were their hands and lips.

CHAPTER 5

Back at work, Joe helped organize a conference at the Wildwood Center of the Harrisburg Area Community College and was rewarded with an invitation to attend. It was always a good sign when an event was scheduled here instead of a conference room in the State House. Nice pleasant getaway amidst subdued surroundings, plus wood paneling everywhere and comfortable seating. It was a great place to be if you had to sit for hours at a time listening to people make less than enthralling presentations.

Joe was there to assist with logistics, and when there were break-out sessions, he'd shadow Senator Bain. The conference ran from 9:00 AM –12:00 PM. The title of the event, plastered throughout the convention hall, was "The Bright Future of Oil and Gas in Pennsylvania."

In this hall, there were more Armani suits than Joe had seen in some time. Donuts and coffee were available, but most in attendance chose only the plastic bottles containing what was advertised as spring water. But there was a difference here, a reversal of roles he was not used to. He closely observed one knot of interaction and then another, each following a similar pattern. The business people held court, projecting superiority as if that was the most natural thing in the world. Most surprising to Joe was seeing the senior members of government content to play the role of servile underling.

Joe had no illusions as to the caste to which he was relegated,. He sidled up next to two of his fellow untouchables, Ron Prescott and Sue Myers, both of whom were indulging in gooey sticky buns and Starbucks coffee.

"Mary Lou's got a bug up her ass about this fracking business," Ron said. "I've never seen her so upset. Even old friends of hers say her outbursts are way out of character. Kind of nice to see the old gal's still got it in her. As long as she doesn't turn whatever it is on me."

Ron was referring to Mary Lou Branch, the Lieutenant Governor of Pennsylvania. She'd been a fixture in the state's political machine for forty years, working her way up from ward lackey one rung at a time. Because Jim Cemcast's political base was Pittsburgh, he needed someone with name recognition in the northeastern part of the state to run with him. The fact that she would soon be closing out her career was also a plus in his mind. Though a man of low self-esteem and low confidence, he never worried during the campaign about being upstaged by her. Mostly, she could be called upon to get out the vote in all those small coal counties in the northeastern part of the state, areas he needed if he was to win statewide.

And they did win that election. But from the time they stepped into office, there was a general unease about Mary Lou. She was 72, not too young for others to wonder about the onset of dementia, a rumor that was most widely disseminated. Joe was surprised to find she was worked up about anything and wondered what was behind it.

Twenty-five comfortable, lightweight chairs were placed around the main conference room. Three screens were set up in front of them with a podium made of solid mahogany set off to the side. The presenter stepped towards the podium, the cue for the crowd to settle into their seats. The hushed welcome, the tense, unspoken desire that all would go well, was in turn, the cue for the presentation to begin.

"I am grateful to have been chosen to speak to this esteemed group today," a well-dressed man began. "More than that, I am thrilled to be here because of the opportunities that await you, and that we, as emissaries of the oil and gas industries, are here to share with you."

With that, he pointed a small wand in the direction of the screens, and they instantaneously lit up. On the left screen was a listing of the agenda for the day. The right had still-pictures of happy, good-looking farm families in displays of bucolic bliss. The center screen, which was twice the size of the others, showed aerial photography of unending areas of mountains and forests.

After a minute of being soothed and distracted by these images, all three panes became still, and the speaker addressed the main theme of the day.

"Energy, ladies and gentlemen, is something we cannot get enough of. You and your constituents are sitting on vast untapped reserves of natural gas. We've known this for some time, but only recently have technological advances given us the means to extract these resources. Hydraulic fracking is a game changer. It can bring great wealth to residents of this state, not just in the form of royalty checks, but also in jobs and potential revenue to the state government. There is no better way to grow the state's economy and perform a service to our country than to embrace this opportunity."

The speaker, Pierce Darling, allowed the intro to sink in. "Before I give you some insight into how we have transformed ailing communities through economic growth, I would like to play a short video that describes the fracking process that has been perfected in the last decade."

The lights dimmed as Pierce waved the wand in the direction of the screens. An animated, five-minute video streamed onto the middle screen. First shown was the drilling of a well, portrayed first as an undisturbed straight line down, then penetrating successive layers of rock. Along the way, the water table was traversed. It all looked so easy and effortless. The technological wizardry climaxed with the drill making a 90-degree turn from its original descent, so it could reach and penetrate the rock where the natural gas was trapped.

The drill could travel up to two miles downward and then another two miles linearly, bursting through the shale where the gas had been for hundreds of thousands of years. The video went on to show that the drill's metal casing was placed through the hole made by the drill, magically curving along the bend that resulted in the ninety degree turn. Once the casing was in place, a cement slurry was forced down through the pipe, emerging out the other end. The continued pressure caused it to travel back in the direction of the earth's surface on the external surface of the pipe. Along the way, it coated the pipe and filled every crevice made during the drilling process. The final preparation was sending explosives down the pipe and setting them strategically along the area where the gas was trapped. When the explosions occurred, fine cracks formed in the rock, and the gas started to flow upward.

Any doubt about this man's ability to captivate an audience was dispelled by this video. It created a Disney-like vision of the fracking process and the future it would bring. All those seated were far removed from real want, real need, and, they couldn't imagine a future not driven by a steady supply of fossil fuel. They would not describe this as an addiction but could not ignore the nagging discomfort this recognition left them. Their response to the video was almost rabid; it dulled the discomfort and reaffirmed their confidence. It allowed them to think that their lifestyle was not so wasteful and selfish.

"This is your future. This is what we offer you," Pierce said. "But I would be remiss if I did not address the risks we will face together if we can realize a true partnership. We have one last video for you, which will show how people working for our companies respond to events in the field."

With a few more twists and turns of the wand, lights dimmed as a rumbling sound spread across the room like the whirring of a helicopter. The sound grew intense, but it was a second noise, a bass note, beating like a human heart that everyone felt joined to. The aerial view again pointed skyward, but to a darkened sky, and to a disturbed natural power. The camera angle veered back to earth and searched the landscape while the rate of the beating heart increased. Fire was spotted in the distance, becoming the focus of attention, the camera zooming closer and closer until the source became clear. A gas rig had just struck the mother lode!

As the camera came closer, men in formation could be seen rushing towards the rig to control the flow, and the sense of danger from the burn-off was palpable. For several moments, the outcome was uncertain, but the men addressed the situation with precision, knowledge, skill, and courage. The well was capped, the danger, averted. The crew was clearly in control. Whether or not this was staged was immaterial, because for everyone in attendance the sound and the actions of the people in the video were real and immediate.

The light came back partially, and the sound transformed to a gushing.

"That is the sound of money, ladies and gentlemen. It is the sound of economic growth and energy security. Security from governments hostile to our way of life, and security from economic want. Regardless of the naysayers, the world would be a brutish place without a steady energy flow and, with your help, we can provide it to our citizens for a very long time to come."

Pierce walked out from behind the podium and folded his hands in front of him before speaking again in his most dolorous tones. "Will there be risks? Yes, of course. Never in the history of mankind was there progress without them. But I will leave you with the words of one of our great presidents, one with a long history as an environmentalist." With a wave of the wand, this quote lit the central pane and he read it out loud in its entirety.

"It is not the critic who counts; not the man who points out how the strong man stumbles, or where the doer of deeds could have done them better. The credit belongs to the man who is actually in the arena, whose face is marred by dust and sweat and blood; who strives valiantly; who errs, who comes short again and again, because there is no effort without error and shortcoming; but who does actually strive to do the deeds; who knows great enthusiasms, the great devotions; who spends himself in a worthy cause; who at the best knows in the end the triumph of high achievement, and who at the worst, if he fails, at least fails while daring greatly, so that his place shall never be with those cold and timid souls who neither know victory nor defeat."

—Theodore Roosevelt

The audience was now his to do with as he wished. The lights came back on, and the panes flanking the middle panel provided fragments of information that he elaborated on in the next part of his speech. They trumpeted his two main themes—"jobs, jobs, jobs" first and foremost, and then service to community and country. After forty-five minutes of this, most of the attendees would have welcomed, even cheered the opportunity to have a drilling rig in their front yard if given the chance.

The *coup de grace* came at the end, when a couple was asked to come up and stand next to the podium. They were Barbara and Jake Daniels, middle aged and as different from the speaker as could be. While everyone else wore gray and black suits, they were casually dressed. The man had on a brown corduroy sports jacket with patches on the elbows, and the woman wore a simple cotton dress, one she would likely wear to church on Sunday. Both had full heads of hair, and their facial expressions were intelligent and unpretentious. A good guess was that they were descendants of northern European farmers, and that this genetic composition had not been diluted much over the generations. What a handsome couple!

While there was no way to upstage Pierce Darling and his grand oratory and sweeping visuals, the audience needed to hear from someone they could trust, and Barbara and Jake delivered with the same level of mastery. The

Wilkinses were introduced as owners of a family-run cattle ranch in Paradise, Wyoming, home to one of the country's most productive shale gas drilling operations. "They asked me to come here and tell you about the rig they installed on my property," Jake said. "When they first talked to me about this, I suggested you all come out to the ranch for a chat and have a look, but they didn't think everyone would fit into our living room."

The audience responded with good-natured laughter, his words quickly transforming the conference room into a homey space.

"A few years ago, things were tough and getting tougher. The price of beef was down, and we were getting squeezed by the commodity markets. Me and Barbara saw how we could improve our situation, but that would have meant borrowing more money.

"Even if we decided we could afford to take on that debt, there was no guarantee we could find a bank willing to take a chance on us. Wouldn't have blamed them either. Mostly, we were keeping our machinery together with baling wire and duct tape. We kept struggling, but we were headed in the wrong direction.

"Then we were approached by members of Mr. Abrams' company." Jake motioned to a man in the front row of the audience. "They came and talked about setting up a drilling site on our property. Apparently, we were sitting on a deposit of natural gas and they'd found a way to get to it. I was ready to sign on the dotted line almost as soon as they made the offer, but the brains of the family, Barbara, convinced me to first make sure everything was on the up-and-up. You know how cautious women can be." Jake chuckled with a wry smile, and trained a loving and dutiful gaze on his wife. He then swapped places with Barbara, keeping a hand on the small of her back as he directed her toward the podium.

Jake's six-foot-two frame had dominated the podium while he spoke, with his hands clasped to both sides of it. Barbara projected a similarly captivating figure. Her skin, toughened by the fierce prairie winds, lent the appearance of someone formidable and independent.

"We heard the stories about fracking and how it was dangerous and could affect the quality of your water. As much as we needed the money, I wasn't about to do anything that would put my family or community in danger. So I researched it exhaustively. And, ladies and gentlemen, I'm here to tell you it is 100% safe. They have worked out all the engineering knots so that the gas trapped under the earth can be extracted without showing up in anyone's well. Once we understood that, and we were assured that any problems would be corrected promptly, we signed. That was three years ago, and now I'll let Jake tell you about life since then."

Jake strode back to the microphone and launched right into the topic he had been waiting for. "That's right, we signed and immediately got a check for $112,000. We've been receiving royalty checks ever since the well began producing, and that was almost right away. Ladies and gentleman, you can buy a lot of baling wire and duct tape with that kind of money."

He paused to allow the laughter to play out. "Seriously, this money was a life saver. We were able to pay our bills, fix machinery the right way, and make some upgrades to our operation. We're not leaving. We'll keep doing what we love doing, and now we can do it the right way. If you're ever driving through Paradise, be sure to stop in—because that is exactly what it is now with the help of Paragon Oil and Gas." Jake stepped away from the podium and accepted the hearty applause.

Pierce reasserted himself at the podium and displayed a victor's smile. "Before I let you go to your break-out sessions, I want to provide you with a few more thoughts to consider. No offense to Barbara and Jake, but I think we can extract far more gas in Pennsylvania than we're getting out of Wyoming. So far, the Pennsylvania state government has been very friendly to the gas industry, and we are thankful for that. Many core industries have left this state, and it's difficult to replace the lost jobs and family income. This is the game changer you've been looking for."

Two more slides were displayed. One projected the thousands of jobs and millions in municipal and state revenue that could be realized. The other was a map of Pennsylvania with potential drilling sites.

"The jobs from drilling are only the tip of the iceberg. These jobs will create other, ancillary businesses. Areas that have been depressed for years will rebound, and become dynamic regions of commerce again. As you can see from the map, there is almost no end to it. Our research tells us that the Marcellus region can support the drilling of as many as 100,000 well pads.

All of these will need to be managed, and to be networked together. There is no end to the potential.

"Ladies and gentlemen, more than anything, the harvesting of fossil fuels is what has allowed the west to assume its dominant cultural and economic position over the last 500 years. And once again, it is what will lead the United States out of the economic doldrums it finds itself in..

"This is surely an exciting time to be alive. The world is watching the shale experiment occurring in Pennsylvania right now, and we need to show them how revolutionary it could be. You are in the forefront of history, the decisions you make now are important. We hope you will continue to provide superior leadership and allow this innovation to proceed for the good of your citizens, the country, and civilization as we know it."

The presentation ended, and Joe found himself following Senator Bain into the breakout session for executives, where invitees included Governor Jim Cemcast, Lt. Governor Mary Lou Branch, and the heads of various state agencies, including the Department of Environmental Protection and the Pennsylvania Department of Conservation and Natural Resources. The representatives from the energy companies were all senior VPs from the three companies hosting the event: Universal Energy, Paragon Oil and Gas, and Phoenix Natural Gas.

The presenter and moderator, Sally Kandu, was from Universal Energy. A map lit up a screen with 100,000 drilling sites represented on it, the future envisioned for Pennsylvania resembling a pin-cushion. The image morphed into a 3-D format showing underground pipelines connecting all the wells; most of the underground metal was located in the large rural sectors of the state, which, Sally said, would be transformed for the better.

Other slides showed tens of millions of dollars being pumped into municipalities and universities in Pennsylvania, and rehashed the potential job bonanza—all kinds of jobs that would magically appear. Those listening did not mind that there was nothing new being conveyed; repetition was acceptable when the message was so agreeable.

Then came slides about safety.

Slides about how "clean" gas was.

Sally was practically giddy by the time she was done, and then opened the session up for questions and comments, the first of which came from the Governor.

"You know we are very interested in what you are proposing here. We need a way to jump start this economy, and we've always been a business-friendly administration. What do you need from us?"

Each of the three VPs sitting across from Cemcast would have loved to respond to this softest of softball queries, but the two gas officials flanking United Energy's VP, Mike Manikon, deferred to him for an answer. UE was valued at tens of billions of dollars more than the other two combined, which explained the pecking order.

"Thank you for asking this," Manikon said ingratiatingly. The Governor's demeanor brightened. " It is the most important question for us all to deal with here. If you want us to invest in Pennsylvania the way we want to, we need a certain. . . commitment, a certain understanding from the state government. The naysayers will be out there, as I'm sure you know, Governor, but we can't let them deter us from what *we* know needs to be done, what *we* know will be best for the citizens of this state. . . . So we need some assurance that you will work with us to mitigate the road blocks some will try to put in our way."

"Well, we have a state to run, Mike," the Governor said, "and the laws of our state to abide by. There are limits to what we can do for you."

"We certainly understand that and recognize that the law needs to be upheld, " said Manikon, "but the attitude coming from the leaders in this room will determine the level of success we will have in opening up the Marcellus region to its fullest potential."

"Please, gentlemen, let's stop beating around the bush, shall we?" Mary Lou Branch said, employing the corrosive tone she had perfected during the last year. She looked haggard, her eyes expressing the need for a good night's sleep. The source of her agitation was a day spent back in Scranton shortly after the election.

Mary Lou was enjoying her morning coffee and browsing the morning paper. Her eyes stopped on a story about a local woman, Sadie Wilkins, who had gone missing. She was one of the earliest anti-fracking activists, and fracking was bigger in this part of the state than anywhere else in Pennsylvania at the time. Her approach to activism was unique. All day, nearly every day, Wilkins, video camera in hand, sought out fracking activity and its effects in every variation she could find. Her video showed fire and gas spewing from uncapped well heads, and trucks carrying gas and water to and from sites, careening dangerously all over the road, day and night. She conducted scores of interviews of homeowners on whose land fracking was taking place, where spotlights blazed into people's homes for months at a time as adjoining properties were being fracked, landscapes abutting farmland and housing stripped of all beauty, wells gone bad, pockets of unexplained sickness, and continuous truck traffic on roads intended for infrequent traffic on scenic byways.

Wilkins said she wouldn't stop until she had exposed all the fracking injustices she could find. It got to the point where this environmental gadfly was sued by the gas companies. In a legal case evocative of *Citizens United*, they persuaded a court to slap an injunction on her. She was now forbidden to step on their properties.

That became quite a problem for Wilkins. The gas companies owned almost everything in the county in which Ms. Wilkins lived. She was effectively banned from her home and community. She asked legal authorities how this was possible, but could do so only by phone, because the property surrounding the court was off limits to Sadie. Slowly, her calls stopped being answered. Her vigils became more intermittent, sightings of her and her ubiquitous camera less and less frequent as well. No one noticed at first, but then she was gone and all but forgotten. Now this reporter was trying to find her; she did not have many places to look, she reasoned. But as yet, she hadn't found her.

After reading this story, the thought of Ms. Wilkins hung around Mary Lou like a malevolent spirit. For days and weeks, when she should have been reveling in the greatest success of her political career, she was unable to show any joy or satisfaction, which was not like her at all.

Then it happened. From out of the fog, a hologram coalesced, the spirit of Sadie Wilkins given form. All she did was scream a continuous tirade of the injustice meted out to her and the cause she championed. After a week of being haunted by this ghost, the videos that had gotten Sadie into trouble began playing above the hologram. This proved too much for Mary Lou. She could not deny or compartmentalize the images. This mild mannered, respected elder of the political community began making unseemly comments in mixed company where comments of that sort rarely filtered through. The Governor and his entourage were trying to figure out how to put a gag on her, keep her from situations where she could be an annoyance, but she learned of this meeting and was determined to attend.

"We all know what is being asked for. Requests can either rise to the top of the pile or fall to the bottom. How many layers of bureaucratic review are put in place before complaints are acted upon? How much corroborating evidence is required? Who gets to see the data the government collects, and how transparent is it? Indeed, what data is compiled and by whom? We all know the drill."

Mary Lou blinked, and her body sent out a little shudder. Sadie was there in the foreground as she often was, but never before like this. Out from the back of her head, a sprinkling of light sprayed as if the Aurora Borealis had been unleashed from that spot. Sadie was quiet, too, and smiling. Something unheard of.

The other members of the group couldn't decide if they were more uncomfortable watching Mary Lou trance out or being scolded by her. She gave them another dose to help them decide.

"I've been doing a little research and found that your combined companies are planning to allocate 10 million dollars to Pennsylvania universities for gas exploration research and —"

Jason Witherspoon, one of the corporate titans, interjected before Mary Lou could complete her thought. "Yes, ma'am, that's one of the things we're most proud of. We continue to look into ways to improve the drilling process. We see this as a way to invest in the local economies and the overall economy of the state."

"That's all well and good," Mary Lou said, jumping back in before Jason had a chance to stress what good neighbors his company wanted to be, "but there are some who would not look at this investment the way you are spinning it. They would wonder how safe the current process is if all this money needs to be spent to make it safer."

Etiquette had been broken by Mary Lou's comments. Having kept her thoughts pent up for so long, she now seemed to enjoy flinging them in the faces of the leaders of this industry. "We've had your fracking in the eastern part of the state for a few years now, but we haven't seen all the growth you've been talking about, all the jobs, all the improvements to infrastructure."

She was about to roll into more of the Sadie-inspired wisdom when the Governor stood up. He was a taciturn man by nature. Nothing riled him. In fact, he could seem almost Zen-like in his demeanor. But his tone, which contained a silky somnolence, was that of an apologist for big-business, and this mixture creeped everyone out. No one got close to him or trusted him. This ability to create non-relationships gave him staying power and could explain his perseverance, longevity, and slow rise to power.

While he listened to Mary Lou, he wondered how he could have blundered so badly in his choice of a running mate. Nothing in her past explained what she had become.

"Mary Lou, we will take this offline." His demeanor contained the same rigidity as his words. "These spokespeople are our guests and deserve to be treated with a degree of graciousness. They have come to offer us a way forward for our state, and we intend to provide them every opportunity to grow their business. In fact, we will make sure that nothing stands in the way of their having full access to government resources. We will partner with them in every way possible to ensure they successfully reach the goals they have put on display for us today."

By the end of these comments, the words were spewing out of his mouth. His face was beet red, his neck bulged beneath his collar. He perspired grotesquely. The Governor's gaze turned from Mary Lou and found Bill Danzig, head of the DEP. Nods were exchanged between them, and Cemcast looked back at Manikon and said, "Yes sir. I know exactly what you mean, and I can assure you we will manage the situations you refer to. The barriers you are concerned with will be dealt with. If that is not possible, they will be dismantled." The last line was said with force, almost to an alarming degree.

Mary Lou was silenced, but she smiled inwardly. She knew that her comments would be swept aside, seen as unwanted, impolite feedback. But she had exposed the Governor. The image she and everyone at this meeting would take away, was one of the Governor's ruthlessness, instead of his normal milk-toast demeanor. She had sensed the harsh quality in him moment by moment in her private interactions with him, but he rarely put it on display, and never to this extent.

CHAPTER 6

Joe needed a weekend away, and Ted Callum was who he wanted to join him. Ted, a longtime childhood friend, was like an older brother to Joe. They grew up in Bucks County, Pennsylvania right down the street from one another. Ted was four years older than Joe, but they remained friendly to a surprising degree, even through Ted's high school years. Joe would query Ted on a variety of topics such as girls, current events, who the best teachers were… but mostly girls. Ted's counsel was always level-headed, and Joe came to expect that everyone who was four years older than him had things figured out way more than he and his peers. A few years later, he realized how flawed this conclusion was.

When Ted went off to college, Joe lost a close confidante. The physical distance between them was too great a barrier, and during the second semester, they lost complete track of one another. Ted got a job with the Pennsylvania Environmental Protection Agency after receiving a degree in geology, and he worked in the field for several years, testing air and water quality around the state. After he got married, he decided to take a job in PEPA's main office in Harrisburg, because it meant being on the road less and a higher chance of career advancement.

Joe and Ted became friendly again when they discovered each other living in the Harrisburg area, but they rarely found time to spend together other than to eat lunch at the capitol.

So, the idea of renting a cabin at Bountiful for a weekend gave them an opportunity to re-connect and spend an extended period of time together again. In addition to the fishing, Joe was planning to see Nicole. They had communicated online during the couple of months since Senator Bain's disastrous meeting. She worked at the lodge full time now and told him she would try to get away from work for a while so they could do something together.

Ron Prescott was an avid fisherman, and Joe asked him to come along, too. They barely got in the car heading north when old patterns reasserted themselves between Joe and Ted, reinvigorating the bonds of their youth. Joe, who was the link between Ron and Ted, looked for an opening, a way for Ron to enter into this camaraderie.

"So is Mary Lou still on the warpath? I thought she was going to send that meeting off the rails," Joe asked Ron. This was the first chance Joe and Ron had to talk about the meeting with the energy executives.

"She goes on a tear pretty often about it," Ron said. "Talks in riddles sometimes. Compares drilling to rabbit holes. The closest thing we can figure is she thinks the technology is flawed. Defiling our abundant natural wealth is another of her frequent comments. She looks half-crazed sometimes. I wonder how much of this the Governor will put up with. Then again, I'm not sure what he can do about it."

Ted joined in unexpectedly, "I've been in meetings with her too. It was the first time I've seen a lieutenant Governor show an interest in the details of what we're doing. She was asking technical questions about the whole fracking operation. Some of them none of us could answer, which did not sit well with Director Danzig. The day after the first of these meetings, Danzig had all the senior techs attending fracking seminars. I'd like to get the Lt. Governor in these classes asking some of her questions and demanding corroborating evidence for the claims being made, because it was made real clear to us we were there to learn how to deal with the critics, not to be skeptical or to engage in scientific questioning ourselves.

"The guys running these seminars are the same jerks that have been holed up in conference rooms in the back of our wing since about the time Cemcast took office. Steady stream of young, arrogant bastards who look you in the eyes and smile but you know don't respect you. And of course, they all work for the energy companies we should be keeping an eye on."

"Maybe Mary Lou's onto something. Maybe she's not the crazy, senile old lady she's been made out to be," Ron said.

"I don't think she's at all senile," Ted said. "The techs in the DEP are happy she's speaking up. She is the only ally we've got, even if she's acting a little eccentric. The crazy ones are sitting in those conference rooms. What I wouldn't do to be a fly on the wall during their strategy sessions."

Ted paused to think about the deteriorating atmosphere at work during the last year. "She muttered about those rabbit holes to us too, but I got the feeling it meant something different than what you thought, Ron. It sounded more ominous than merely describing technical failures like breaches in well linings. She was referring to state policies that either don't exist or aren't anchored in ethical thinking. I think she's afraid she's letting down the people she's represented for so many years. Then there's the lack of good science to back up the claims of how safe the process is, and how effectively the waste is managed."

Ted continued, back to his normal, buoyant tone now, "But we did our best to assure her that we were doing the research and putting the regs in place that were needed to ensure the drilling was done safely."

"Did she buy it?" Joe wanted to know.

"Not even a little," Ted laughed. "It just gave her something else to hit us over the head with."

"Sounds to me like you should spend more time studying those lessons you got from those consultants, memorize their sound bites," Ron laughed.

This set them all off laughing, as each considered the warped interactions they'd had with the consultants and lobbyists swarming state government.

———

The next morning, Joe was the first out of bed. He drank as much as the other two the night before and sat on the porch feeling sorry for himself, jealous of his friends still draped over their lumpy mattresses.

He figured out how to light the stove on a table by the cabin. It felt like an eternity waiting for the water to boil. During that time, the birds chirped all around him, but it didn't bring pleasure. Instead, all he sensed was their fidgety energy, a noise that couldn't be turned off. It frazzled his nerves, and he wondered if coming up here was a big mistake. What, really, was here for him?

Joe decided to take a walk to quiet his mind. He followed the path he took on his last visit, and it was not long before the rushing water eclipsed every other sound.

He found the stream and gazed upon the water tumbling over and around the rocks scattered in the stream bed. The mystery of the flowing water drew him. Its force and movement implied a declaration of shape and substance, while simultaneously demonstrating a lack of those things. The water flowed differently than on his last visit. Back then, the thaw had arrived two months earlier, and the river was boisterous, moving with power straight and true over any obstacle it encountered. Now, the flow was weaker, its path more discerning. The water was content to meander and conveyed a more contemplative quality. Both now and before were beautiful expressions of the stream for Joe, and he would not have this deeper appreciation for one without the other.

The trail led up-river and he followed it. Around a bend, he saw a fisherman, hip deep in the water in the middle of the stream. As he suspected, it was Gabe. They did not make eye contact, and Joe did not believe Gabe was aware of his presence. He stood silently and watched. The arm, hand, and rod were moving as one. The gentle but forceful flow of the casting movement evidenced a dancer's grace and precision. The loosening of the line by some manipulation he did not yet understand caused the line to glide upon the air, reminding him of a butterfly's triangulating, rapid meet-up with its desired destination.

Joe watched, transfixed for about ten minutes. Before, when he had seen Gabe, his attention was diverted by Nicole's presence, but it was now easier to focus on the fishing line and the path it took. With each time casting, Joe tried to learn a little bit more about the mechanics of what he observed. Few things engaged him like this, and he had a strong desire to learn more about it, to stand midstream and be the one directing the fishing line fifteen to twenty yards upstream. As he was about to leave and return to his mates, the fisherman looked up and smiled at Joe.

It was time to go back to the cabin and rouse Ron and Ted so they could do their own fishing. But they would not be joining Gabe in the river. Instead, they rented a small fishing boat with an outboard motor at Hills Creek State Park. Joe had brought his newly purchased fly fishing gear and hoped to spend some time later that weekend mimicking Gabe.

They got a late start, but once they got moving, they showed an efficiency Joe had not expected: throwing together the makings for lunch, securing bait, and buying ice for their ice chest where they would store their catch. Ron was the most experienced fisherman among them and Joe and Ted were happy to follow his directives.

Their rented boat was small, but the three of them fit in it comfortably, wedging the ice chest and the rest of their gear in with them. The engine sounded like a lawnmower and Ron steered the boat with the rudder.

Nestling into a sheltered portion of the lake, they fished for a little more than an hour, with some teasing nibbles on the lines, but nothing more to show for their efforts. To pass the time and to prevent getting discouraged, Ron told story after story about fishing trips he'd gone on with his father and friends, each more fantastical than the last.

In an instant, Joe's line pulled away with tremendous force. His hands barely held onto the rod, which bent wildly down to the water's edge. Everyone on the boat immediately sensed a force on the other side like nothing they'd expected. Joe recovered himself enough to start reeling in the line, but the tug on the other side was more than he thought he could control.

Twenty minutes of him pulling in one direction and the fish in the other left him soaked through with a mixture of sweat, river water, and uncertainty. Ron offered to work the line for a while, but Joe declined the offer, wanting to finish what he'd started. The fish lessened its resistance after twenty more minutes of tugging and reeling and he felt closer to his goal.

It came up alongside the boat, and Joe and his friends were awed by its size and shape. It was more than three feet long; the body was muscular and powerful looking. Joe saw rows of sharp, bony plates that ran the length of its body. He hoisted it out of the water, and Ted put a fish net around it, guiding it onto the floor of their small boat. It lay at their feet and terrified them. This was the big one they had no thoughts of catching, but had nonetheless.

It was not a pretty fish and gave the illusion that it had too many sides. The hook still lay embedded in its mouth and Joe chose not to dislodge it. They found out later it had no teeth and would have paid money to have known this while the fish lay astride them. The atmosphere was surreal and caused Ted and Ron to holler and carry on, but Joe was left with a deeper experience. The fish carried a near prehistoric quality. It was more than he was banking on and, now that it was his, he felt a new sense of responsibility.

The ice chest they brought for the fish could not contain their catch. Instead they emptied the ice into a large plastic bag. Joe's fish was raised by the hook and dangled in the air. The thrashing had left its body. They lowered it into the bag and placed it between Joe and Ted. Their fishing for the day was over, all three of them spent from the effort and drama of Joe's catch. They turned and headed back towards where they'd shoved off. A few minutes into their return journey, Ted shouted to his mates, "It's a god damned sturgeon."

He held up his iPhone. The surface reflected the sun back into the sky; the picture of this prehistoric beast attempted to give some perspective to their experience.

They got back to shore and would have shown off their prize, but the launch was deserted. Instead, each of the young men got their picture taken separately, holding the fish from the line still firmly attached by the hook, hoisting it high in the air, the trees and lake providing an idyllic backdrop.

Back at the lodge, there was more carrying on, as they regaled anyone who would listen to their tale of adventure. Gabe walked by and stopped to see what the excitement was about. The bag was open and the sturgeon lay on what remained of the bed of ice.

"I'll be damned," Gabe said. "There's been rumors of sturgeon in these lakes but none that I'd ever seen. And this guy's been here a little while. Look at his shape—bigger, wider in the middle than you would expect. This is the oldest species of fish you will ever lay eyes on."

Gabe turned and looked at Joe, peering deeper into him, trying to extract a sense of this young man. Their random points of interaction were now aligning, and he wondered if there was a reason this gift had been bestowed upon Joe. Joe looked back, unafraid to meet the man's gaze, even welcoming it. The day's experience left him feeling bewildered, with a heaviness that was something to be reckoned with. He had given little thought to what they were doing up here. It was a weekend away to do some fishing, drive around, spend a little time with Nicole, and find excuses to drink too much.

But then his rod almost snapped in two and from that moment a new reality took hold. The struggle to get the fish into the boat had exhausted him.

He had sat quietly beside it, half afraid it would rise up and take a chunk out him or flip itself out of the boat. When that concern seemed unfounded, he felt himself pulled in another direction. While Ted and Ron chatted about the bits of information Ted pulled back from his Google searches, Joe felt taken over by an elemental force, as if he were being dragged into the water's depths from which the fish had been pulled.

"I wouldn't have believed it if I didn't see it," Gabe said, turning to the fish that had come hurtling up out of another era and now lay in front of him. "I was thinking of offering you a few tips on the fly fishing you were watching but maybe I should be the one taking the lessons."

Joe let out what sounded more like a snort than a laugh. "The only skills I possess are those of rank beginner. Beginner's luck is what was responsible for me catching this fish, and I would be happy to learn whatever you care to teach me. I really enjoyed watching you cast this morning. You make it look easy. The line reminded me of a butterfly dancing in the wind."

"Butterflies are pretty erratic in their movement," Gabe responded with mock displeasure, and then changed his expression to a smile. "But I get your meaning. . . . What you planning to do with that fish?" Gabe asked. "It's a god-awful looking thing but would still make a great trophy to hang somewhere."

The idea of hanging this pre-historic fish in his apartment made Joe smile. *It has no place there*, he thought, but right now he wished it did. "Not sure I want this guy looking back at me," Joe said, deflecting the suggestion. "I hear they're good eatin', though. I guess we could get a fire started on the grill and cook it up. You and your wife are welcome to join us. I don't think any of us know the right way to filet this monster, so if you have any ideas, we'd welcome them."

"I guess I could do that," Gabe responded. "I'll give myself a few hours off. Have to admit, never thought I would see a sturgeon taken out of the lake that feeds our stream. Don't generally speak in these terms, but this is a blessing, and I want to thank you for the offer."

Gabe, with his gray beard and longish hair, suddenly looked more like a backwoodsman than Santa Claus. Joe realized that all the things he was enjoying—seeing tangible work being done, having something to offer these people, not feeling like such an alien in this setting—were things he once would have scoffed at. Of course, he would welcome Gabe into the preparation of the meal, which had suddenly taken on the feel of a ceremony.

Gabe went to his house and returned with a cutting board and fileting tools. Ron, Ted and some other guests set to work collecting wood, making a fire and setting a table for the meal. Gabe and Joe brought the fish into the cabin's little kitchen, where it took up the whole counter space. Gabe went to work with focused determination. Placing the fish on its back, then becoming momentarily lost in some esoteric calculations, he snipped here and made minor incisions there. Then he took his primary fileting knife, made an incision at the base of the fish, and proceeded to cut almost its entire length. He pulled back the flesh and was stunned by what he saw.

"Do you see this?" Gabe said, pointing his fish blade at a sack stretching halfway along the incision. The sack was blackened and ruby colored and they stared, mystified by their discovery.

"Never thought I would see this," Gabe said again. "This was the delicacy that did these devils in. Back in the '20s and '30s, the rich bastards couldn't get enough of these golden little eggs. Pretty much wiped out the whole species so they could have their caviar and impress their rich friends.

"These fish were in all our lakes a couple of hundred years ago; they were teeming with them. And yours, despite its size, is relatively small. They can grow to 7 feet and 200 pounds, and females can live to 150 years. Can you imagine what it was like to be able to catch fish like this? Or how much food it provided the local population? All that's long gone, of course, because of greed. Because people didn't know how to manage their relationship to the things they loved and desired.

"I'm going to put all that aside, though, and not let it ruin something I'll likely never get to see again the rest of my life." But he was unable to silence these thoughts and continued, "Don't you wish you could just go back in time and stop something like this from happening? But once it's gone . . . there's no turning back." Gabe let his last comment hang in the air.

Joe now saw another aspect of Gabe that he had not anticipated; contempt had risen full and raw in his voice and face. But Gabe quickly moved beyond his anger and, instead, immersed himself in the gift bestowed upon them.

Gabe shook his head and then removed the sack of caviar and placed it carefully in a large ceramic bowl. He cut through the sack containing the eggs and gently freed the pasty substance from the casing. The contents filled the bottom third of the bowl, and Gabe sifted his fingers through it. He withdrew a small portion, and began expertly separating the eggs from the membrane holding them together. He placed them in a strainer and ran them under cold water from the faucet. *Is he a woodsman or an aristocrat?* Joe asked himself, again awed by Gabe's array of skills and knowledge.

"You're sure you've never done this?" Joe said, chuckling and nodding his head at Gabe's seemingly practiced motions.

The caviar was now like sparkling pearls heaped together, reflecting light like jewels off their ruby-colored surfaces. Gabe deftly grabbed a small sample from the bowl, placed it in his mouth, and savored the delicacy. He then held out the bowl to Joe, who attempted to mimic Gabe's effortless gesture. He fumbled, dropping the slippery eggs several times before actually bringing them to his mouth.

Joe had never experienced anything to compare with this sensation. The eggs exploded with flavor that was fresh, tangy, and salty. Each bursting egg was its own little epiphany.

They savored the experience in quiet for a couple of minutes. "So, you've lived up here your whole life and never seen one of these?" Joe asked.

"Actually, grew up in Philly during the '50s and '60s, in the Fishtown neighborhood. Only fishing I did back then was off a pier in the Delaware. Caught some decent fish, too. But we were city kids. Spent our time on the streets playing stick ball, half ball, games like that. Stayed out of trouble the best we could."

Gabe seemed more talkative than usual, not as reluctant to reveal his past as he usually might be.

Gabe had the fish laid open and studied its exposed interior, becoming absorbed with deciding the best way to remove the bony skeleton and prepare it for the grill.

"You're a long way from the city," Joe said, wanting Gabe to reveal more from his past and also build a relationship with Nicole's father.

Gabe momentarily paused from his dissection, looking lost in thought.

"Lots of changes since back then. Might just be the nostalgia of an old man, but lots of times I think we didn't know how good we had it. We had our problems, but we dealt with them ourselves. Not sure what caused us to lose what we had there. The counter-culture, the war, the lure of the suburbs? Whatever it was, there's not much left of what was there except for memories."

Whether it was the historic fish or Joe's gentle prodding that brought Gabe back to his youth, Joe wasn't sure. But something had raised a curtain on a side of Gabe that he had never expected to see, at least not so soon after meeting the man.

"Don't get me wrong; I've got no regrets—it's been a helluva ride. But you get caught up in what's important at a particular time, and there were plenty of important things going on in the '60s. Then you find yourself settled down someplace different and you've moved beyond those events. Everyone who was *with* you when you were young and going through those changes are settled down as well, only they've settled down so differently from yourself that you barely recognize them."

After another pause, Gabe concluded, "Back then, believing in the right things was easy and obvious. But today I couldn't tell you what's right. Don't know if I'm a socialist or libertarian or some shade between the two. Used to know. Used to be damn sure about these things. Was as far left as left could be. But that didn't work out. Not for me or just about anyone else I knew. Not a popular thing to say, but I'd bet a lot of them would agree with me on that."

Which is why Gabe had ended up here with Sophia. In the mid-'70s, they watched one dream after another get ground down, co-opted, or saccharinized. Their interest in anything pop vanished about the time John Travolta made the scene with his pompadour hair style and retro dance steps. They did not wait around to give *them* a chance to make them question themselves or wonder if the new direction had any kind of merit, which they were certain it did not. There was no turning back, and moving forward was something they would need to manage on their own.

Gabe was skilled at a number of trades—in fact, any that he set his mind to and, because of that, rarely had trouble finding work in and around the small towns dotting the north central tier of the state. Local colleges and the few remaining manufacturing sites kept him as busy as he wanted to be, which was plenty busy.

In 1991, this lodge had come on the market, and Gabe made his move. The cabins were the big draw. But the stream backing up to the property was the thing that had stolen his heart. Though it was a well-guarded secret, he already knew it provided some of the best fly fishing in this part of the country. Within close proximity, there were enough tourist attractions for families, and the same could be said of the hearty food and drink for hunters coming off long days. This allowed his business to be good for much of the year. Farming kept them busy, too, and most years, they even made a profit from that. He wasn't getting rich, but he was surviving, and looked forward to getting up every day and taking care of what needed to be done.

Gabe went back to work on the fish. Its long history was contained within its flesh and bones, and nature spoke to him of abundance at this moment. Its wide flank and the fleshy filets it rendered pushed back against the dark thought he couldn't escape.

The fish should not be here, Gabe thought. *It's probably on an endangered species list and would have been better released back into the water.* But that idea never registered with the young fisherman, and there was no reason to bring this up now. For it would tarnish the feast. The killing and preparing of animals as food, even with good intentions and little suffering, could be divisive among good people.

The same with people arguing against windmills because of the harm they cause to bird populations. *It's no wonder we lack the skill to forge solutions to important problems. Does it require a hammer from some autocratic leader or oppressive religious text to align people to act together?* But Gabe pushed these thoughts aside and focused himself on meal preparations. He felt the need for a celebration.

The next morning crawled for Joe. He wondered if it was possible to have a fish hangover. He remembered videos of grizzly bears made docile by the feeding frenzy during salmon runs and suspected he felt the same somnambulant quality that they experienced.

The celebration had gone on long into the night. Campers from other cabins strayed in and out, and there was enough fish to share with all of them. Joe, Ron, and Ted had planned to start drinking down at the bars early, but found the current gathering more desirable than anything they would have found elsewhere.

For much of the evening, Joe and Nicole sat around the fire, absorbed in their own conversation as they continued to get to know each other, and Joe gaining a deeper connection with these surroundings. They found their sense of humors compatible, and felt a charge as their gaze met and lingered. They planned a hike the next day, and Joe now attempted to rouse himself in preparation for this outing. The contentment of the night before still hung in the air and aided his recovery. The idea that he was stepping into a new phase of his life played at the fringes of his consciousness.

They hadn't discussed where they'd go, but he decided he'd like nothing better than to walk the same trail they'd walked when he'd been up here before. He wanted to see that area in every season with Nicole. When she arrived at his cabin, Joe told her of his preference. She shrugged and displayed ambivalence, which disappointed him. He'd hoped she would understand. Finally she responded, "Here, I plotted a different path for us, knowing how you city folk need to be stimulated with something new all the time." She let out an abrupt, nervous laugh.

"It all feels new to me up here," he said. "Everything about it." He looked intently at her as he spoke. It was because of her he felt this way, and for now this was as close as he would come to expressing it.

"We just hope we can keep it available for those who want to call it home," Nicole said, in an evasive way. But when she spoke again, her tone was much lighter, "Wherever you want to go is OK with me. I'm just glad you were able to escape from the clutches of bureaucracy for a whole weekend. And look how far you've come! All hail the great fisherman."

Joe realized his hangover was not the only carryover from the night before.

As she shifted the VW through its gears to negotiate the curving roadway, Nicole was silent, clearly focused on the driving. Joe felt no need to carry on a conversation. Instead, he peered out the window, amazed at the transformation that had occurred in the two months since his last visit. Winter's cloak was no more than an indistinct memory; life's emergence spread out in a myriad of forms. They parked in the same lot they had on their previous trip and, although they embarked onto the same path, it was like being in a different world, with so much lush greenery surrounding them.

They continued through the patch of old-growth trees that even the sun's rays had trouble penetrating, and their moods matched the solemnity of the place. When they broke free from the stand of trees and approached the summit, their mood changed dramatically in ways that were difficult to define.

Then it struck him—there was too much space in front of them, with no trees to block their immediate view. The land up ahead was being cleared—that much was for sure. But there was also a dust particulate everywhere that hadn't been there before. Then they saw a road, and that hadn't been there either, or at least Joe did not remember it. He asked Nicole if the road was new and she confirmed it was.

They saw the bulldozers and other construction equipment, monstrosities that immediately looked out of place in the otherwise pristine landscape. The worksite was idle, presumably because it was Sunday. Several full-sized cement trucks were parked along the periphery of the site.

"My God, what's going on here?" Joe asked.

"You don't know?"

From her tone, Joe knew full well that she was speaking to him again as a member of the state government. "No, I don't. Like I said, I don't get that involved in the policy end of things." He sensed just how stupid that sounded now.

"How convenient," she responded, rolling her eyes. "They're drilling. These are the first fracking pads to go in state forests that I know of."

He knew a little about the technology involved, so he could make out the drilling device, the waste pond under construction, and the storage units.

"But why here?" Joe asked.

"Because they can."

"You're right about that," Joe confirmed. "Unfortunately, that's usually all it takes."

"We're lucky we came today," Nicole said. "In fact, I only come on Sundays. At least some days are still sacred. Way too noisy during the week. Not just the work on the pad either. There's truck traffic all the time. Kicking up dust and dirt. Ruining the existing roads so I guess they need to build new ones."

Joe searched for something that would make sense of all this, but his disgust would not abate. The enchantment he'd experienced since arriving at the lodge had been shattered in the blink of an eye. He shuddered as he considered the degradation being caused, and bowed his head. He felt Nicole's hand on his shoulder through his coat and he placed his hand on hers. This comforting touch was not the type he'd envisioned would be happening this weekend, but he found that was what he needed in this moment. He would never have felt this way a few months before. He would have balanced what he saw with all the information dispensed by the lobbyists at the State House. But it was different now. It was personal. *Political issues should never become personal,* he often told himself. *That would make me ineffective in my job.*

But the worm had entered his consciousness, and it was too late to cast it out.

CHAPTER 7

Gabe sat at his kitchen table. It was lunch time and he was going through the mail. The only one in the house, he puzzled over a letter that had just arrived. He read it again and again. At first it was incomprehensible, but then, little by little, he cracked the legal jargon code and came to understand something more horrible than most anything he could imagine.

The lawyer writing the letter contended that Gabe and Sophia owned the land where Bountiful stood but not the mineral rights below the ground. The preposterousness of this took some time to settle in. It triggered a grade school memory about the Indians selling Manhattan for $24 worth of trinkets and the smugness he felt even then at the poor bargain the Indians made. Later in high school he learned that Native Americans knew nothing about *owning* land, so why not let the white man think he owned it? They would continue to roam and hunt as they always did, and live as they always lived. Gabe had wondered if it was possible to not understand the idea of owning property, or if this had been made up to explain the bad deal the Indians made for themselves.

But now he was being told something that seemed every bit as ludicrous to him as what the Native Americans must have imagined they were being told. The notion that you could own the top layer of land but not what lay beneath it gave him a sense of vertigo.

The "property" below the surface had been retained by the former owner, Thad Thomas, said the letter. He'd believed Thad was a good man and that they'd settled on a fair price for the land that Thad could no longer care for. Gabe would see him from time to time and their meetings were always cordial, an opportunity to trade stories about the place. But Thad died recently and the title to the mineral rights had been deeded to his two children, neither of whom he'd ever met. There was natural gas under this land. Everyone knew it. It worried Gabe for some time, made him wonder what effect it would have on this place he'd come to love—both his own property and the surrounding community. This letter provided a look into a future that was bleaker than he had envisioned.

The letter went on at length explaining that a gas company was in dialogue with the owners of the substrata, who were interested in granting a license to drill on the property. According to the letter, the substrata owners would be in contact to determine the best way to proceed with minimum impact to Gabe and Sophia's livelihood. Each sentence just increased his surreal reaction to the message being presented. *How thin a layer of earth do we own? Does someone else also own the sky above this infinitesimally thin layer that was apparently all that's ours? Do these substrata owners own the dug-out part of the pool, or the plumbing? How could any of this be true?* The letter concluded with a request that Gabe contact the law firm and ask to speak with the lawyer whose signature was at the bottom of the letter, Conrad Smith.

The first letter arrived the end of June 2012. Three more followed over the next two weeks. Gabe read them all but refused to respond. He and Sophia sat down and talked about what to do. They were of one mind that there were no good options, and for now they would ignore these entreaties. It was not a good plan, they knew, but they could not think of a better one. In addition, they would try to find a lawyer they could trust to verify the legality and bleak future conveyed by these communications.

Then another letter came, and it became clear that this nightmare was moving into a new phase.

———————

Gabe walked out his front door. It had been two weeks since the last letter arrived—a two-week period of immersion into law, local politics, and the effects of fracking on his community. What he'd learned was that the law's logic regarding property ownership worked against him, and that he was far from the only one caught in its web. Hatfield and McCoy-type feuding was erupting all around him. People either wanted to cash in quick or be freed from their new gas drilling reality, which had come at them from nowhere and could become all-consuming.

The closest of these conflicts involved two adjoining hunting camps whose members had once been each other's friends, had worked together to protect the land, and had cleared only what needed to be removed and no more, ever mindful of and responsive to the need to maintain and encourage the wildlife—bear, deer, turkey, and rabbit, to name but a few. All of it was important, and even the most drunked-up numbskull who came up on the occasional weekend knew and understood this or was kicked out of the camp—even if no replacement could be found and dues would go unpaid.

What had caused the peace to unravel? The influence of money—big money—the likes of which had never been seen by the people around here. The word *millions* was uttered in sentences directed at these poor souls, which was like having the world's most beautiful woman tell each and every one of them that they were her one and only. Some of these guys never had a chance. The things previously held dear to them were now gone, simply and utterly gone, leaving no memory.

One camp, Camp Liberty, was lured by the first offer. But the other camp, NiceAndEasy, held out, not so blinded by the large purse. They worried about fracking's effects on drinking water, the well pad itself, and of course, on the wildlife. While the internal battle raged, the opportunistic Camp Liberty signed contracts, and within months was pumping out gas. This in itself left bad feelings with NiceAndEasy, which saw itself taking the moral high road, a place that caused fierce debates. Camp NiceAndEasy decided to negotiate with a gas company, but when the offer came in, it was at a much lower rate than Camp Liberty's contract. The amount, they were told, was "market-driven," and they would have gotten a better offer if they had gotten in the game more quickly.

A totally different dynamic took shape between the two camps. Camp NiceAndEasy accused Camp Liberty of pilfering their gas supply; this was horizontal fracking, mind you. Camp Liberty developed a smugness reserved for the well to do and accused their neighbors of sour grapes. They showed interest in investing their newfound wealth, and market reports were strewn around the camp where before there had been hunting and fishing guides. Topics of conversation between members changed accordingly. They planned additions to the camp, even talked of upgrades like Jacuzzis and swimming pools. They regarded their former companions as poor relatives. Rancor existed between the members of Camp NiceAndEasy, but it was overshadowed by their disdain for those in the neighboring camp. They felt betrayed by their neighbors, who they once saw as like-minded hunters and friends. Shots could still be heard ringing out, but now there was more of a concern about stray bullets than there'd ever been before.

This was big history—the kind that most people don't look for and don't affect. And if they dare to try, they do so at their peril. Each succeeding wave of energy extraction follows a similar narrative flow. No one can staunch it, at least for long. A leading scientist in favor of fracking referred to the counties in the Marcellus Shale region as sacrifice zones, much like the boys from these poor areas were seen when their options disappeared and the military beckoned. Each extraction cycle was its own wild west that would be forgotten, trivialized, and framed within a larger American narrative of entitlement; the right to use nature and human frailty to attain some greater good.

But it was also *small* personal history—Gabe's history, colliding headlong with this well-greased machine. He continued to be uncooperative with the lawyers and was expecting unwelcome visitors from the Resources Unlimited Gas Company this morning. He'd driven his truck to the edge of his property and parked it in such a way that no vehicle could pass from one side to the other. There were guests staying in the cabins, and he made up a story that he was working on the road and that they should let him know when they wanted to leave or call him when returning. He sensed some understandable discomfort from them and wondered if his business would suffer as a result. But he was determined to not allow those who would force their will on his land to proceed any closer than the entrance.

However, he could not stop them from calling, and he answered that call. Few words were spoken as he descended the front steps of his porch. His steps were measured and unhurried and masked the fury inside him. When he got to the edge of his property, he met the gaze of those on the other side of his truck. The police were there with the company inspectors. He knew the police from around town, and never had any problem with them, but he'd never seen the company employees.

"Good morning, Gabe," said the officer he knew best.

"Can't say I agree," Gabe responded gruffly, surveying those opposing him more closely. Two police, three company men. Each was uncomfortable with his role in this standoff, but they told themselves they were just doing their job, following the law as it was written. "You know why we're here," the same officer continued. "These men are here to survey your land. You know they have the legal right to do it."

Gabe did not respond, but continued to look at those aligned against him. He had already thought through his limited options, so he did not waste his time on this. He was content to stare at the faces looking at him, searching out any recognition that what they were attempting to do was perverse, regardless of how the law read.

"We don't want any trouble here, Mr. Marshall," said the man who seemed to be the group's foreman.

"No, of course not," Gabe responded with a short, sardonic chuckle. "Just want to come onto my family's land, poison it, and ruin my business at the same time."

"There won't be any of that, Mr. Marshall. Been doing this a long time, and we know how to do it safely."

Gabe had had this conversation often enough and did not have the stomach for it now, so he cut to the chase.

"Martin," he said, directing his attention back to the officer, "I have no intention of letting you or these men on this land for the purpose of fracking it. It's not going to happen as long as I'm alive."

They were prepared for some pushback but were surprised by the strength of his comment. Martin and his partner took on a significantly different attitude. They were prepared to meet Gabe's ferociousness head on.

"C'mon, Gabe, you're not leaving us much choice here," Martin said with resignation.

There seemed to be nothing left to say, and they stood like this for some time wondering what the next move would be. Before this turned ugly, the foreman spoke again.

"Like I said, we don't want any trouble. Listen, Mr. Marshall, I've been given some leeway here. We have some time to let things simmer down, see if we can work something out."

Gabe had no burning desire for a showdown. He begrudgingly nodded his head, and the men returned to their cars and drove away. He knew it would not be long before another attack on what he knew was right and good would be launched.

CHAPTER 8

G abe sat inside one of the well-appointed brownstones on State Street in Harrisburg. A-block-and-a-half west, the Susquehanna River flowed. The same distance to the east, the state capitol towered above all of its surroundings with its grand staircase and domed roof glowing in the morning sunlight of late summer. Gabe had been contacted again by the law firm and threatened with legal action and a court appearance if he failed to show up at this meeting. Sophia would have joined him if he had wanted her there, but she had no stomach for it, and Gabe told her he could handle things alone.

Gabe had cleaned himself up in anticipation of the meeting. He trimmed his hair and got rid of the beard, having decided this was not a good look when marching into the lion's maw.

The room was impressive and oversized. Elaborately framed portraits of pasty old men, respectable men no doubt, adorned the walls. The lawyer, Conrad Smith, sat behind a richly hued mahogany desk that extended many feet in length and width—more than necessary, really—yet somehow did not dwarf him.

"What your gas company wants to do to my land should be illegal," Gabe said. "What you want to do will put me out of business."

"It shouldn't need to come to that," the lawyer said. "We are willing to work with you on the placement of the well."

"I run a hunting and fishing lodge in the spring and fall, and families visit in the summer. I also farm a piece of the land. Organic food, mind you. Where in the hell do you think would be a good place to construct a gas drilling site on a property like mine?"

"We need to do what we can. This is not your decision and not mine. And to clarify something you just said, Resources Unlimited, which will own and operate this well, is not my employer. I am a middle-man. I simply make things happen but have no skin in the game, no loyalties to any party."

"And no responsibilities, either."

"Yes, if you like. You can say that too."

This first skirmish resulted in a momentary pause, a brief inward and outward searching. Both learned something of the other and this allowed them to recalibrate the direction in which they would try to move the conversation.

"This is my land. I should be able to do with it what I know is best," Gabe said.

Conrad rose from his chair and walked to where a large, portable cork board was positioned. Gabe noticed a quickness to his step, which was at once confident and surprisingly casual.

A topographical map of Pennsylvania was pinned to the cork board. The Marcellus region, covering much of the northern half of the state, was split into rectangular shapes. Scattered around the region were colored tacks pressed through the map and into the cork, some at compressed rates, others far flung.

"This is a pretty accurate view of the current drilling locations," he said, pointing at a large concentration of drilling icons. "They're changing all the time, but we can see from this representation that your property is smack dab in the middle of where the action is right now. For better and for worse, the gas industry chose to focus on your region, presumably because it feels its gas deposits are the most abundant.

"Your case is the most onerous type because you own only the surface property. You won't gain financially from this and quite frankly could be a loser if we don't manage this properly. Which, really, is why I wanted to meet with you. We get a lot of complaints, sure, but believe me, they all don't receive the attention we are giving you. I am not heartless and, contrary to what the media says, the gas industry is trying to be fair and responsible while at the same time making a profit, which, the last I looked, is still the premise upon which our country operates."

"You don't know how this is affecting life up my way," Gabe shot back. "I have to admit, I didn't really look into it until I found myself in its crosshairs. The traffic, noise, the roads disintegrating because of the constant truck traffic. Stories of wells gone bad. Towns overrun with the rough crowd this industry brings in. I could go on."

Conrad listened to these complaints, the same ones he had heard many times before, and responded with his version of the truth.

"You're right, there have been mistakes. But most of these are being worked on by the industry and the state government as we speak. Most, if not all, of those stories of tainted wells are just stories. Maybe some substrata material gets loosened up to cloud the water, but that can be managed with filtration, which the companies doing the drilling will pay for if you can prove they caused this to happen. And there are water taps that can ignite when turned on. Before and after the drilling, we had that. But methane is naturally forming and only has a half-life of thirty years, so it is much less a threat to the atmosphere than carbon and other gases.

"As for the threat of gas leaching up through the fracked rock and contaminating aquifers, consider that it takes four million gallons of fluid, under more than ten thousand pounds of pressure, to drill and frack each well. If it was so easy for gas to leach up through the shale, that force would not be necessary. In other words, the lack of porosity that keeps the gas trapped down there today will keep the fluid down there, as well as the gas that we don't bring up through the wells.

"As far as the problems with your infrastructure deteriorating, the state has started collecting an impact fee. The proceeds will be used for just what you're talking about. It's taking some time, but we'll get it right. And then there are the jobs coming to the people of the area. They're not all going to outsiders.

"The other thing you should keep in mind is how this is helping our country become energy independent. You think I'm a company shill? That's alright. But I believe in what I am doing because it will benefit not just our economy, but also our country and the people who live in it."

Gabe felt a constriction in his chest and tried to inhale, but he could not catch his breath. He had come into this meeting certain of the rightness of his claims, fully confident of his ability to give voice to the injustices done to him. But he was unpracticed and, as he tried to express the feelings and ideas that were his core beliefs, he could not disentangle the words.

"That all sounds very nice," Gabe finally got out. "Wrap it in a bow, and many people will see a bright future in it. But it is not serving the people in my community now, and there is no reason to believe it will in the future."

Even these words, though spoken truthfully, did not get to what Gabe yearned to express. He was aware of an insistent banging in his head, and felt as if its origin could be found in some distant memory, a much earlier period in his life.

Conrad, however, was in his element; he was sure of his cause and the truth of his message, which, unlike Gabe, he could deliver without having to think about it. He pulled from behind the corkboard another map that was attached to the top of the frame and draped it over the map they had just been studying.

"This is a future map of drilling in Pennsylvania. Each of the rectangles you see represents five hundred wells, and there are two hundred of them. You know what that gets you? One hundred thousand wells! That's Governor Cemcast's vision by the time all is said and done.

"Gabe, I'm telling you, no matter what you do, the community you know now, including the good and bad of it, won't be there in a few years. Or, it will be there, but you won't recognize it with your current set of eyes. The boom is happening, and it won't be stopped. Not by you or anyone else. And I feel sorry for those who don't hop on board and take advantage of the benefits it offers. Many of those who try to fight it will have a tough time, but those who embrace the change will reap reward upon reward.

"You've been in the north country long enough. You've seen that the little industry located there has left. No offense to your business, but how many people can you employ, and how many people can make a living doing what you're doing? And you know the state and the Feds are not coming to your rescue. So here is an opportunity to grow, really grow, and an offer of good jobs for the residents. It's not perfect, but what is? And who's offering you a better deal?"

Conrad was now taking on a different role. He had the demeanor of a wise parishioner trying to return one who'd lost his way to the fold.

The light went out inside Gabe. He lost touch with the better truth he fought to live by, and all that was left was Conrad's market-driven perspective. Even the sense of yearning he'd just felt was extinguished. Instead, he felt the smallness of his own experience.

"You have no idea what it feels like to see the woods torn up by this industry," Gabe said, still struggling to make his point and expose a deeper truth. "The good you say it is doing is not reality. I see it every day. Is it worth even one well destroyed, or one child who comes down with a disease he or she would not have had?"

"We don't live in a world without risk. We can't if we want progress," Conrad responded. "You do believe in progress, don't you?"

Gabe considered the question. "I don't believe in a notion of progress that has such a negative impact on my life, that views me as collateral damage. You'll have to find yourself a different poster child."

This last comment resonated. Fracking's all-out media blitz was even filling the air waves in rural Pennsylvania. Sixty-second, corporate-funded ads showed people who'd made lots of money from drilling: farmers whose farms were in foreclosure and could now pay their debts; retired school teachers setting up scholarships to help needy kids advance in their studies; good-looking, healthy, salt-of-the-earth type people surrounded by some of the most beautiful natural surroundings you could imagine. People who had made this country strong, made it all the wonderful things it was. What was there not to admire?

"We'll do just that. And there are plenty of people to choose from," Conrad responded, almost scolding.

Gabe shuddered a little. Driving around his county, he could see just as many signs in front yards in favor of fracking as against it. Jobs were necessary to revive his region; he could not argue with that. Whether the gas companies would deliver on these jobs was secondary to the promise of them, and they were promising them plenty.

"Listen, I understand this is difficult for you," Conrad began, this time in a conciliatory tone. "But to be honest, there's not much you can do about it. The wells are going up in your county, and one will be going up on your property. I do, however, have one more piece of news to discuss with you."

Conrad had returned to his desk and began rifling through the papers lying on top of it, as if he had not known until now that he would need this one document.

"The owners of the mineral rights on your property are not terrible people. They understand they will be impacting you and your livelihood. As a result, they are offering you one-third of the initial payout from Resources Unlimited and the same percentage for any royalties from the actual gas extraction. An even split with the two principal owners of the mineral rights. This is not something they have to do, but it's what they want to do."

Gabe was again surprised by the tone of the conversation and the direction it was now taking. He was unprepared for any kindness from these people."And what do they want from me?"

"Nothing really—nothing other than for you to stop harassing them and let them get on with their business."

Gabe felt a wave of exhaustion roll over him, coupled with something else, something unfamiliar. He felt old and weakened, incapable of arguing his point any longer. He didn't even have the energy to summon his deep feelings of violation. The focus of his argument had been reduced to something personal. How, he wondered, could his concerns stand up against progress and freedom?

Conrad had returned to rearranging the papers on top of his desk. He wasn't being pushy but his body language suggested the conversation should be coming to a close. Gabe sensed this and felt the same, for few options remained to be considered. He rose to his feet shakily and, his voice faltering, offered his final comment. "Thank you for your time, Mr. Smith. I will consider your offer and will get back to you in the next couple of days."

Mr. Smith stood, made his way to the other side of the desk, and extended his hand. Gabe offered his with little of the vigor that had existed in their initial handshake, and felt a tremor throughout his body when their hands touched. He cast his eyes away as he offered a final goodbye, and ambled through the doorway.

CHAPTER 9

From the moment Gabe signed the papers, he regretted it. Not that he could have done anything about the drilling, but the agreement made him an accomplice. There was no good place to put the well, but because the cabins were their main source of income, and they needed to try to retain that business, this meant placing it on the far side of the property where crops now grew.

He and Sophia talked over their options for a week. They had twenty acres and farmed about ten of them. They allotted five acres for the fracking operation and cut their farming activities in half. This was more than what was required for the well, but they hoped it would buffer them from what was coming. They signed a contract during the first week of September. The harvesting of the crops was almost complete; most of the cabins were empty. This was normally the time when the work slowed, but they were not granted a rest this year.

Within a couple of weeks of signing the contract, the fracking machinery had become a constant presence. The workers began their activities on the far corner of the property. This five-acre parcel that had nurtured them was now a cancer they would need to expel from their thoughts.

Gabe had returned within an hour from a visit to the County Extension office. In years past, he would stop by and speak to the two master garden-ers, Jake and Marie, with whom he'd become friendly. Together, they had spent hours learning about organic farming practices. Mostly, though, their conversation came around to their favorite topic: What disease or vermin was causing the most harm to crops in the current year? Considering the passion emanating from these discussions, it seemed certain they would be disap-pointed if a problem-free growing season ever occurred, however unlikely this was.

Gabe approached them with different intentions today, interested in quickly growing trees that grew in a densely-packed formation. As quickly as possible, he would plant them along the border of the land they set aside to block out the fracking machinery.

The usual sense of camaraderie was absent from this particular meeting, and none of the usual niceties preceded his inquiry. When they realized he was inquiring because of a fracking site going in, Jake responded the way he did with others who'd made the same move.

"Sounds like you hit the jackpot," Jake said with as much emotion as you would ever hear from him, which was never much. "This mean you turn into a gentleman farmer? What's next? You going to have us researching hydroponics?"

"Like hell I did. If I could keep those bastards off my land, I would."

Mary was blown back by the heat in Gabe's comment, but Jake took it as a personal attack and met it head on.

"You come in here telling us about a windfall any of us would jump at and then get nasty when we congratulate you? Who the hell do you think you are?"

"You don't know what you're talking about." Gabe was equally uninterested in finding common ground or explaining how he'd gotten to this point. "Anyone who's in favor of fracking is an idiot. All you need to do is look around at how it's changing everyone's life up here and taking everything that makes this place worth taking care of."

"Neither you or your people are originally from up this way," Jake said, "so don't go telling me what's worth preserving and what's not." Jake could trace his family back four generations, and most of them had made a life in the surrounding communities.

Gabe had lived here for thirty years and could still somehow be made to feel like an outsider. Most times he'd took a comment like that in stride, but not today.

"I've run a business for 20 years and lived here 10 years before that, and you still try to make me feel like I don't belong. Well, you can go to hell, and you can take your small-minded bullshit with you."

Gabe stormed out of the building while hurling a final comment that he would never set foot in the office again. On the way home, after he calmed down, he reflected on how deadly the well had already become. The first casualty was his long relationship with Jake.

He now stood in the late morning sunshine with Sophia beside him. He was determined to keep from her what had happened with Jake, but she knew him so well that she sensed something was bothering him. Soon, he was recounting what now sounded ridiculous.

"You've been friends a long time," Sophia said after hearing the story, "and you don't have many of those. When the emotions settle down, you should go in and patch things up."

"That doesn't seem likely. You weren't there to hear how crazy it got. Not sure they'd even let me through the front door."

They stood on the border separating the farm and cabin areas, looking out across the field to where the excavation was occurring.

"We made our decision, and now we have to find a way to live with it," Sophia said with a sigh.

"What decision?" Gabe asked. "What choice did we have, really?"

"It's not the first time we've dealt with disappointment," Sophia countered, "and it won't be the last."

She took his hand and gave it a firm squeeze. He didn't think his mood could brighten, but Sophia always managed to put a smile on his face, even if it was a small, halfhearted one.

Sophia would survive this intrusion no matter what direction it led them. She loved the life they'd made for themselves, but she loved it easily. Gabe was different. She'd seen him before they moved here and started this business. He wasn't unhappy with their former life, but something burst free when they moved to Bountiful. Dreams were realized, and contentment was found. No matter how difficult the work, or how much, they always found a way to meet the challenge. He especially. His energy exploded into any problem confronting them; she dealt with it quietly and steadily. But he couldn't power through this problem. It was bigger than him, and she saw how helpless that made him feel.

"Maybe this is a good time for you to cut back on the farming," Sophia said. She said this with a slight chuckle, because this had become a family joke. During the last few winters, he would threaten to farm a smaller piece of the land, and every spring it would extend to the far corners of the property with new crops, and Gabe's new ideas for keeping them healthy.

He knew she was trying to help him put the best face on the situation, and he loved her for it. Over the years, he'd more and more come over to her way of thinking. He looked at her now. Her hair, once long and chestnut colored, was cut short in an almost boyish style, and now a silver that lit up in the unfiltered sunshine. Her skin, wrinkled and loosened, showed the effects of age, but her eyes sparkled as they always had, even more than in earlier years. He had never thought that human aging could look so beautiful.

"Maybe it could be the right time for doing a little less farming," he said, "but not under these circumstances. Nothing good can come from being forced to do something this intrusive, something so fundamentally against who we are."

"That's up to you," Sophia responded. "If you need to see it that way, it will be much harder for you. Only you can decide if you'll let yourself find a way to make peace with it."

They walked along a little farther, to where the crops were. They stepped through the low stalks of summer vegetables that had been picked-through weeks before; straggling heaps of husks were all that remained. When their steps touched the damp ground, it gave a little, accepting their foot-falls, almost as if they were walking through a bog.

"Do you remember those first years of farming?" Sophia asked.

"Made that wall with the rock I pulled up," Gabe said, pointing to the stone wall abutting the roadway.

"You were unstoppable. A force of nature," Sophia said, marveling at memories that hadn't surfaced for a long time.

"Had to be. The size of the task would have stopped me cold if I'd thought too hard about it." Now, his thoughts traveled back to the past. He grabbed her hand when she stumbled slightly, and held on even after she'd regained her balance.

"I remember our first trips up north, before we lived here," Gabe said. "Had to visit the parks with names like 'World's End' and 'The Pennsylvania Grand Canyon'. The thing I remember best were the farms we passed along the way. Beautiful, rich soil extending as far as you could see. Amish, mostly."

"That's when you decided you had to have a place up here."

"Yes, ma'am. For better and worse, that pretty much sealed the deal, but I never heard much complaining from you."

"Never had much need to. Except, you could get pretty ornery while you were waging war out here." Whatever problems his behavior had caused were now smoothed over by the passage of time, and all she felt was the beautiful passion that had guided him.

"Every day I tried not to think of the irony of owning this craggy heap when what brought us here were the loamy fields we gazed on."

"But we stuck with it and got things to grow here," she said.

"Little by little."

She turned and pressed her head into his chest and squeezed him close to her, feeling and giving comfort and warmth. His cheek pressed against the top of her head. The smell of her was intoxicating, and he became aware of other aromas—these from the earth, expressing change, the passing of summer. There was no better experience than the one they shared, and they held each other in this embrace for several minutes, both wishing it was an eternity instead.

When finally their arms fell and they separated, Sophia looked up at Gabe and was surprised to see his eyes reddened, tears forming on their outer edges.

"And you expect me to just accept what's been forced on us? Pocket a few dollars, tip my hat, and watch them demolish all we've worked for? It's not just the land. It's us. Our stories, our sweat, our lives are bound up in it. When they cut into it, they cut into us."

He hated to retreat from their embrace, from the wonder and joy of the shared memory that it held, but he was powerless to do otherwise.

———

Joe had been coming up to Bountiful regularly, whenever he could afford to and didn't have something else planned. Gabe was surprised when he kept reappearing. It was obvious that his main draw was Nicole, and Joe's interest did not displease Gabe. He figured Joe was also out to catch another big fish. He'd seen this before in fishermen and hunters who had accomplished something extraordinary and tried to recapture that excitement, that rush, which he knew would not reoccur, at least not in the same way. He watched when Joe returned from a morning or afternoon of fishing on the river with little or nothing to show for it. He was glad to see only the normal amount of disappointment. It elevated him in Gabe's estimation.

When he came with friends, Joe always stayed in a cabin, but when he came alone, he would stay in one of the rooms in the main house. Joe was more surprised than anyone that he wanted to spend so much time in this country setting. Within days of leaving, he always found himself planning his next trip.

His times with Nicole were the highlights. They would go out to dinner or hear music at a local bar, music of a type he wouldn't get back home— Rootsy, rockabilly bands that included fiddles and screaming guitar work. People went loose on the dance floor, and there was lots of hard drinking. Neither Nicole nor Joe drank that much, but the intoxicating atmosphere fit well with their budding romance, which both welcomed.

Joe took an interest in all Nicole's family did to keep the lodge running. On his most recent trip, he had asked Gabe if there was anything that needed to be done around the farm that he could help with. Gabe had just cut two cords of wood from a large tree that had fallen on the property, and told Joe it needed to be stacked with the other wood they used to heat the lodge. It took Joe a couple of hours to finish this task. Later, every time he passed the row of wood, he measured the section he stacked against the rest and was pleased by how well it aligned. This time, when he asked, Gabe said he could use some help planting trees he'd recently purchased.

Gabe decided to create a border with arborvitae trees, those ungraceful sentinels used to demarcate property in suburbs and farming communities alike. He wanted the border to be about 150 feet long, so he bought 50 trees. They were three to four feet tall and would grow a foot a year. Not nearly fast enough, but Gabe saw no better option.

Joe was happy to help. He had never planted a tree, or anything else for that matter, and dug into the dirt with purpose. He gave no particular thought to the relative ease with which his spade cut through the dirt. They dug the hole, mixed a little peat into the dirt they'd removed, scored the root ball, put the tree in the ground, and covered it back up. He got a little rush from each tree they planted.

It was tedious, but Joe felt satisfied with their progress. He tried to draw Gabe into conversation a few times but failed, his sentences petering out into awkward silence. Nicole told him they were forced into allowing the well to be installed but avoided describing the amount of anger and pain it had caused her family. She told Joe they'd make some money, and he assumed the financial compensation made it easier to live with.

As they worked, Gabe hardly seemed aware of Joe's presence. He took no pleasure in creating this barrier, grimacing each time they started digging a new hole. The day they stopped drilling and dismantled the rig was the day he would rip these trees out and make his land whole again. But he knew that day would never come. Even if the drilling stopped, the land would be scarred.

"Got a pretty good start," Joe said after the eighth tree was planted. As he had seen Gabe do, he used his foot to level the space between the root ball and the dirt. Gabe looked up at Joe, this time shaken from his own dismal thoughts. To Gabe, the spindly trees looked like spikey invaders or pawns on a chess board, primitive creatures that would be the first to be sacrificed.

Gabe tried to resume the tone of speech he usually used with Joe, one characterized by humor and confidence, but the words would not come. All he felt was a tremendous weight. In earlier times, he had often returned to an image of himself that revitalized him. In it, he rolled a large boulder up a mountain, inch by inch, but he could sense progress nonetheless. This was now replaced by a vision of himself pushing the boulder with all his might, but finding mere stasis was the best he could manage. Even this standoff was exceedingly tenuous. Finally, he was able to break through the strain and confusion to respond to Joe.

"I'll be satisfied when they are twenty feet tall, and we can't see what's on the other side of them."

Joe could sense Gabe's distress, but still had no idea of the depths from which it came. "It might not be that bad," Joe said, trying to sound encouraging. "When they're all done, they'll clean up the construction site, and you can get on with your life again."

"Not likely. You see the mess they're making. Ripping the farm to shreds. Once they put that pad in, it will never be removed, at least not in my lifetime."

"Yeah, but when they're done, they'll have things set up over there, and you'll be able to live pretty much normally over here."

Gabe looked at his young friend, who he understood was trying to cheer him up, "I know you probably have plans for later," Gabe said, "but if you have some time, I've got something to show you."

A few hours later, night was settling in. The drop in temperature could be measured almost minute by minute. Joe felt the world drawing in and felt the need to do so too. Instead, he was seated beside Gabe in a rusty old pickup. He knew, now, who had taught Nicole to drive. Gabe applied a focus to the road that left little room for other activity. That was alright with Joe, who loved the period of dusk at this time of year. The mystery of the evening exerted itself, hidden just beyond the shapes passing through the headlights.

After about ten minutes, Gabe pulled the truck to the side of the road, tucked it into a little break in the woods, and got out. The river running through the lodge fed a man-made lake that they could see through gaps in the trees. "This is the town's main water supply," Gabe explained.

A gate on the road signaled the area's closure at dusk, but it was unlocked and easy to pass through. As they walked along the roadway, feeling a bit like silent intruders, they passed a series of tanker trucks straddling the road, sitting idle. They were nondescript, military-looking vehicles, and were the first indication that things were in an altered state, that their walk was taking them into a darker realm.

"They've got it all here. The perfect storm, as they say these days," Gabe said, feeling his stomach tie in knots. It was a feeling he experienced with a frequency he had never known before. It was borne from hopelessness and resulted in a deep sense of fatigue. Part of it, he knew, was age, but only a part. It was here that the weight was greatest for him, the place where he had first looked at evil directly and felt how unequal he was to it.

"Have you noticed these trucks passing in front of the lodge?" Gabe asked Joe.

"I have, but never gave them a second thought," Joe replied sheepishly, realizing his naiveté.

They continued walking on the road, away from the lake and the restive quality emanating from it, and continued their conversation.

"Well, if you were here every day, like I am, you wouldn't be able to ignore them," Gabe said, and turning away from Joe, cast his eyes downward. "Every day these trucks fill up here, taking this area's best source of clean water away to the fracking sites sprouting up all over this region. They actually said in a town meeting that if the lake went dry, they would pipe water in from another county. Can you believe it? It was the stupidest thing I ever heard."

"Back in Harrisburg," Joe said, "what I hear most about are the jobs being created, the economic boom it's bringing to this area."

"You better believe that some people are making a bundle, but the jobs, the good paying jobs, have gone mostly to outsiders who have the experience. They're not part of the community, and they'll move on when something better comes their way. And most of the jobs actually going to locals are dangerous as hell."

They came around a bend in the road and arrived at what Gabe had brought Joe to see. Another lake appeared in front of them. Not really a lake but a carved-out basin, maybe half the size of a football field. Even with only the last bit of sunlight, they could tell there was something different about the liquid here. Joe gazed at it and realized it was totally still, lifeless, and grim. His other senses tried to repel the environment. His nose itched as he deciphered a pungent, iodine-like smell. His eyes watered from an irritant he could not otherwise detect.

Gabe pointed at another series of trucks to the side of this pond, exactly like the ones he had just passed.

After letting Joe take in his surroundings, Gabe offered an explanation.

"They fill up at the lake and bring the fresh water to the fracking sites. When the fracking fluid comes back up, it gets loaded back in these tankers, and they bring it here and dump it right where you're looking.

"It's hard to think or talk about. They won't tell you all that's in the fracking fluid. And I can't remember or pronounce the names of the chemicals we do know about. Add to that what they might bring up from two miles below the earth. What carcinogenic stew might they be dredging? Tailings are the radioactive outcroppings of rock that gets ground up by the drill. How could they not get mixed into the fracking fluid and end up above ground? And here it is, not 200 yards from the town's main water supply, where if we're lucky, it will evaporate into a toxic slurry that won't migrate anywhere. But these pits are only lined in plastic, and any breach could be a disaster."

Joe's breath caught in his throat as they stood looking in silence. He reflected on all he'd been told and felt sickened by it. Gabe was well beyond this, to a place where no words could be applied. It was a vision of a landscape populated by zombies. The lifeless creatures performed this circuit ceaselessly and without thought, transmuting this purest life sustaining substance into a killer that would continue to gain dominance. It was this beast the zombies cherished, something they didn't have the power to reflect on or separate from themselves. At first it was when he gazed beyond his property, but now even that had been invaded and overthrown and he was powerless to keep them away. It was beneath his skin now where he felt them crawling—the parasitic marauders. He knew there could be no happy ending to this invasion.

CHAPTER 10

J oe spent the first couple of days back from his most recent trip researching the issues Gabe had raised. He drafted some agenda items to discuss with Senator Bain and asked the senator if they could have a short meeting. Bain said he had also wanted to speak with Joe, calling it serendipitous, and scheduled the meeting for the beginning of the following week.

Joe and Jeff Bain got along remarkably well, having established a solid working relationship years earlier. In Jeff, Joe saw a mentor, someone who tried to be fair and to do what he could for his constituents. Jeff recognized Joe's inherent talents. Despite his relative youth, Joe was a fixer—someone who made things happen. That was a rare skill, and a necessary one in the political sphere in which they operated.

"Thank you, Senator, for finding the time to meet with me," Joe said.

"You must have done something really awful to be starting off a meeting with me that way," Bain responded with a chuckle. "Either that, or I'm in a heap of trouble I don't know about yet."

"Neither one, I'm happy to report."

"Well, that's good to hear," Jeff said, wiping imaginary sweat off his brow. "If that's not it, then what's on your mind?"

"I'm not sure if you know, but I stayed in touch with a waitress that I met at the Loyalsock Inn last spring."

It was a little unsettling to bring up the events of that weekend, but Joe could find no way around it.

"Well, I'm glad to hear there was at least one positive outcome to that meeting," Bain said, laughing. All of the worry and angst he had previously expressed about the meeting seemed to have disappeared.

"Yes sir, you could say that. Since then, I've also learned what some of the people are up against up there, and I'd like to tell you about it if you wouldn't mind."

"I'm always interested in hearing reports from the field," Bain said, adopting a serious expression.

In the intervening week, the disturbing aspects of the walk by the lake had become muted for Joe. The heightened emotion he felt there was replaced by his days in the office—days he did not find unpleasant. He tried to re-experience the evil, the dread that haunted Gabe, but mostly he recalled a darkening fall evening, mysterious like many others. He wasn't sure anymore what had gotten Gabe so freaked out, and began wondering if it was even really his battle to fight.

Joe did his best to explain how Gabe had lost the right to decide what his land was used for, how the law differentiated ownership between the surface and the mineral right below the land. He explained how the gas company came after Gabe, forcing his hand, changing his life, and potentially taking away part of his livelihood.

The senator listened carefully to Joe; any trace of the lighthearted joking before the conversation was replaced by a steely quiet and serious-ness in Bain's demeanor. Joe was heartened by this, thinking the story had struck a chord with Bain, and this drove Joe to speak more boldly about the negative effects fracking was having on a significant portion of the senator's constituents.

When Joe was done, the senator responded, "I'm sorry your friends have been inconvenienced, and I wish I could do something for them, I truly do, but the law is the law, and the hard truth is that it won't always be fair."

After a brief, uncomfortable silence, the senator asked, "How long you been working at the state, Joe?"

"Around four years," Joe said.

"Right, just about what I figured. Most of it in my office I'd say. Isn't that so?"

"Yes sir, that's right."

"Then you've seen enough to know how this place operates. There's a reason they compare the legislative process to making sausage. You'll never get everything you want, and you'll definitely get some things you don't. If you're not prepared to accept that, you should find another line of work."

Joe grew uncomfortable as he realized how he'd miscalculated the senator's take on his report. He recalibrated as best he could, struggling to regain his footing without seeming like he was backpedaling.

The senator continued, "We see it all the time. Activists and concerned citizens walk through the door into our office and tell us their version of the truth, as if it's the only version out there. But it's our job to look at the greater good for the people we serve. Natural gas from the Marcellus Shale formation has the potential to transform my district for the better. We see the jobs starting to come into the region, lots of them are good paying, too. This has the potential to start a renaissance here, the shot in the arm we needed because coal and industry have moved out over the last fifty years. I'm going to do what I can to not let that wealth slip away. And we'll use it to move this region into the twenty-first century by funding industries that will remain long after the fracking boom fades, although from the estimates I'm looking at, that won't happen any time soon."

Joe felt himself pulled by the strength of these words. As a willing underling, he jotted notes, listened intently, and pushed aside what he now perceived as his earlier missteps. His silence prompted the senator to continue letting his thoughts unwind.

"There will be mistakes, and some people will not be happy with this change. But we need to embrace change that's good for the majority and find a way to bring the others along. In fact, I'll let you in on a secret. I'm co-sponsoring a bill, to be made public shortly, that will help expand the footprint of the gas industry in Pennsylvania. I'll need all hands on deck because we will be facing some stiff opposition."

They fell silent. Joe knew his career wasn't in jeopardy, but his loyalty was being tested. The response he was about to make would determine if that would continue to be the case.

"Yes, sir," Joe responded with an upbeat cadence to his speech, "I'm glad you shared this with me and took the time to explain what the future holds. You can count on me to help move this legislation along in any way I can."

The senator let out a sigh, visibly relieved by this, and cast aside Joe's earlier comments. In a leap he had not expected to take, he described a vision that was only beginning to come into focus.

"You know this has a lot of potential for anyone willing to grab hold of it. Someone in government needs to provide leadership for how this industry operates. Governor Cemcast is a good enough man, but he's letting the industry run amok, not extracting what he can for the citizens of this state."

Several moments passed. The senator's brow furrowed, until the thoughts that demanded to be expressed burst forth.

"It's been a long time since there was a Governor from the mid-state. The power brokers in Philly and Pittsburgh usually take turns choosing who that honor will be bestowed upon. But what if there's a shift in wealth and power to the central region? If that happens, it's not hard to see the door to the Governor's mansion opening up to someone from our area willing to seize the opportunity."

Jeff allowed a few moments to pass, letting the meaning of his words sink in before proceeding.

"And that person would need a team to help maneuver through the process, people who know how to organize and get things done. People with the skills you have shown me during your time working in this office."

The halls of power suddenly came into sharp focus for Joe, sharper than they ever had before. There were stories of meteoric rise for a select few staffers in the state apparatus. They mostly shared the same skill set, one that Joe had tried to hone since he recognized what it was. There was always something else in these stories, a certain bit of luck, being in the right place at the right time, being favored by those in power . . . probably a mixture of all of these.

They both tilted their heads slightly to the side as if hoping that would bring those images into still sharper focus, but they both knew that only action would bring this desired reality within their grasp.

CHAPTER 11

When he planted the new row of trees, Gabe spoke briefly to the men working on the site. There were just a few of them and he tried to not take his feelings out on them. They were just doing a job, he reasoned. A couple of days later, the same workers approached him, this time for a specific reason.

"Hi, Gabe," one of them said. "I wonder if you have a few minutes to speak with us." He was the eldest, a little north of forty-five, Gabe figured. His speech was relaxed, and he was comfortable looking Gabe directly in the eye.

Gabe was on the porch of one of the cabins, replacing the sill of a door frame that had been damaged during the summer. He walked down the steps and assessed the men. They were not unlike him. Skilled workers, not from around here, probably, but just men trying to make a living. Probably taking care of families living in some far off place.

"I suppose. What can I do for you fellas?" he responded.

"We're up from Oklahoma, as you might have guessed from our accents," the man said. "From the southern part of the state. You might not realize it, but home looks a lot like the country here."

"No, didn't realize that," Gabe said. "Never been down that way but always pictured a lot of open space, prairie land."

They laughed, for different reasons, but it was a shared laugh nonetheless.

The man took this as an opportunity to move the conversation to what he and his co-workers wanted to discuss.

"Well, we've been living in hotel rooms mostly and have been admiring your cabins since we started working here. Got us to wondering if you'd be interested in renting them to us. If they're available, I wouldn't be surprised if we filled them all. We figure to be here for a good long while. And we're willing to pay top dollar."

Gabe was blown away by this offer. His response was immediate and expressed the visceral shock coursing through him.

"I'm sorry, but that's not going to happen. I have nothing against you men personally, but you're not welcome here. What you're doing to my land should be criminal. The same can be said for the change you're bringing to my community. The sooner you leave and take your mess with you, the better."

"I'm sorry to hear you feel that way, Mr. Marshall. We'll be on our way then." And unlike the lawyers and politicians, they did indeed leave, fully understanding why someone would feel this way.

This exchange sent Gabe into a further tailspin, and one he wasn't ready for. He was beaten, and now he counted additional adversaries lined up against him. They were just working men like himself whose company he would probably enjoy otherwise.

That night, he took a bottle of Jack Daniel's from the cabinet. He had to dust it off and wondered again if it had gone bad. It hadn't, and the way he felt tonight, it wouldn't have much more opportunity to.

The next day saw the start of a massive acceleration of activity at the fracking site, with the so-called "critical path" items given the highest priority. It was a marvel to watch all the working pieces come together in apparent unison. Gabe watched and was reminded of Robert Duvall's comment about loving the smell of napalm in the morning.

The first surprise for Gabe was watching the land itself reshaped by the ground-moving equipment. All the widely different farmland was densely packed, then leveled, and as far as Gabe was concerned, deadened.

In succeeding days, the bottle of whiskey was replaced by another and yet another. Gabe didn't always wait for evening, either, to send the fire down his throat. He was in it for the long haul, perched in front of his living room window, taking in the show from morning to dusk. Sophia did everything she could think of to rouse him: set chores before him, reasoned with him, and finally became a hell-raising bitch she figured he'd have to get away from. But nothing worked. He barely engaged her. Instead, he was determined to witness every detail of the destruction of his land, the upheaval of his life.

At night, he combed the site. After the land had been resurfaced, the heavy machinery moved in. It was like a military encampment. He inspected the rows of trucks, most of which were used for moving water in its various states. He peered into a trailer which he determined was the central command and saw that it was outfitted with a bank of computers and other technological devices. What disturbed him most were the rows of compressors mounted on trucks. They were interlinked with pipes and hoses like the heads of a hydra. *Cut off one head and two grow back.* This was the heart of the operation: where the water, sand, and chemicals were pressurized and sent deep within the earth.

Gabe stood in the midst of the angry swirl of connectors and felt their full malevolence wash over him in a powerful wave. He imagined the sea serpent ensnaring him, snapping his bones and squeezing the life out of him. His thoughts turned to when the nodes on the network were fired up and put to their intended use, and he imagined the fury they could bring, the thrusting motion, the violation they were capable of producing.

The next day, the drilling began in earnest and continued for a week. Whatever it was he had expected from the fracking process, the reality was far worse. Like most major traumas, there was no way to prepare, and the effects of it would leave him a changed person.

The investment in machinery and manpower was at its peak, and efficient use of them was the fracking team's main concern. They worked around the clock. The water trucks lined up, blowing their diesel and noise into the air—air that was already frenzied by the diesel-consuming compressors and the mechanical gnawing of the drill.

By the time the drilling was done, somewhere in the neighborhood of five million gallons of fresh water would be contaminated to drill this well, and they would be delivered one truckful at a time. Spotlights, hung high from posts at various angles, lit up the work site and the surrounding area throughout the night. It was like giving birth to something malignant.

Gabe was there to greet it every morning as the sun rose. Each night brought a new layer of dust and dirt that carried across his fields and covered his home and cabins. He'd worked hard to get organic accreditation for his land, and suspected the material raining down on it now rendered that invalid. The days were horrible for Gabe, but the nights were worse. His nights were sleepless; the noise, light, and stress made it impossible to forget what was happening just outside. He had learned to manage a good life for himself, but that is always a tenuous enterprise, and believing otherwise casts doubt upon one's idea of a good life. So Gabe, having lost the necessary balance, plunged and plunged.

On the seventh day, which should have been a day of rest, he began hearing the sound of explosives break through the usual din. He wondered if these detonations were intended to break up the rock at the lowest depth and free the gas. If so, they were reaching the end of the process. Gabe's attention became more focused as the concussions continued to occur in a random sequence.

One explosion was followed by something unexpected. From where he stood in his living room, a geyser could be seen. He watched it spew twenty, thirty feet in the air. There was a great commotion from the workers, but the gushing continued unimpeded.

Gabe stepped outside and proceeded towards the drilling, stepping through the new layers of material where his crops grew, giving it the gray appearance of a moonscape.

The hive of malevolence was now in disarray, which was heartening to Gabe. Then he realized the reason for this, and he stopped and watched midway into his fields. A breach in the system had occurred with the last explosion. The fluid belched up from unknown depths with tremendous force. It showered the drilling site with an angryspray, soaking men, machinery, and vehicles.

The land was fighting back, Gabe reasoned. The devastation it wreaked was warranted and just, and he reveled in its vengeance. As the fracking fluid rained down on the site, he realized that it would not be contained there. It was seeping now, slowly at first, but then quickening, onto the land he intended to continue farming. The fluid proceeded beyond the arborvitae, which were no defense against this encroachment. The ooze spread over his entire farmland, coming up to Gabe and forking around him as it continued on, as if he weren't even there. He felt negated, as if he had become one of the evil ones, too. The fracking fluid was the court room's punishment, issued from the bowels of the earth.

He noticed the sky first. It was wrong—pink and moving. The plane of vision in front of him was split and then was completely gone. Then other areas of his visual field moved, and then they, too, disappeared. His body tingled, and a bolt of lightning starting in his chest ran through his body, felling him instantly. He lay on his back, not feeling the muck. The sky was normal again, and he gazed at it. It was whole and real.

It was a good fifteen minutes before one of the workers looked over and noticed the farmer lying on his back in the field. He put aside what he was doing and ran over to Gabe, but it was too late. The heart attack was thorough; Gabe was dead.

CHAPTER 12

oe attended Gabe's viewing and funeral. Both were held in a funeral home about 10 miles south of the lodge. When Joe found the building, he was surprised at how different it was from where Gabe had lived. This was suburbia. The funeral home was flanked by office buildings and a strip mall. Its owner tried to set it apart by installing a black metal fence around the property, but nothing could raise it above its shabby surroundings and the dissonance they conveyed.

A crowd of about fifty people was milling around the lobby before the service began. Joe spotted Nicole and Sophia receiving condolences from those who had ventured out on this steel gray morning. On the way up from Harrisburg, he thought about what he would say, the praise he would heap upon Gabe, and what experiences he would recount that they had shared during the eight short months they'd known each other. But the longer he stood in line, the more futile his preparations and the more disorganized his thoughts became. The only emotion he was aware of was an oppressive loneliness. The two people he cared for were deep in their own experience, assuming leading roles in a ritual where he played only a minor part.

"I'm so sorry this happened," he said to Sophia, knowing it wasn't enough, but he was at a loss for all other words. He then let his eyes pass over to Nicole and the young man to her right.

Sophia looked exhausted but managed to respond. "Gabe was a good man. You know that, Joe. He would be happy to know that you took the time to pay your respects."

Joe wished to speak of the sturgeon, fly fishing, the tasks they'd performed together, and most of all, the talks they had while walking along the river path or through the vegetable fields. Before Joe was able to convey any of this, though, Nicole, who'd been observing the interaction, made an introduction.

"Joe, this is my brother, Joshua. Joshua, this is Joe. He's been coming to the lodge over the summer and helping Dad out with some chores during his stays."

Joe tried to interpret all the signals that were occurring simultaneously. The first thing to register was the fact that Nicole had omitted any mention of their relationship. He also realized at that moment that Nicole had hardly talked to him about her brother. Joe extended his hand to Joshua and sensed immediately why he did not go by Josh. Severe in his bearing, and probably around thirty, he had a pencil-thin, neatly-groomed beard. As Joshua extended his hand, Joe could see a deeply unsettled expression on his face, a many-layered expression representing a puzzle he wished he could unravel.

Joe remained mute. He felt it prudent not to express any of his thoughts or comments about Gabe, whom he considered a father figure. Here before him was Gabe's actual son, and Joe suspected Joshua was struggling with his own, deep emotions. He had no desire to make the grieving process any more difficult for Joshua.

The air grew tense as each searched for the best way to proceed with the conversation. Joe glanced over his shoulder at those standing behind him. Joe quickly retreated, saying he would move along so others could have their turn.

He stood by himself, aware only of the hollowness inside him and a tremendous sense of lost opportunity.

He saw someone he knew from the nights in the bars, Judd, the guitar player for the band "Hard Ridin'." His guess: a former boyfriend of Nicole. They weren't particularly friendly, but Joe needed someone to talk to.

Judd's eyes were normally glassy. His brown leather cowboy hat was missing, but his hair was in its customary braid and hung to the middle of his back. Joe felt unnaturally relieved to be joined with others, but the look in Judd's eyes showed none of the same expression reflected back to him.

"Listen, Joe, we know who you work for and what you do." Joe looked at the three others in the circle, all of whom were staring at him with the same intense glare. "It takes a hell of a nerve showing up here. As far as we're concerned, you're part of the killing machine responsible for Mr. Marshall's death. I won't cause a scene; that family's been through enough. But you should know you're not welcome here."

Judd turned away, closing in on the circle that no longer contained Joe.

The atmosphere in the room was one of grief, certainly, but there was anger there too, militancy, caused by the way Gabe had died, and that took Joe entirely by surprise. This was tribal, and he was seen as a member of the tribe responsible for the death of one of its members. He wondered how concerned he should be for his own safety.

Joe took a seat and cast his eyes downward. He'd considered staying at a hotel afterwards if there was reason to, wondering if Nicole would want him to be there for her. But there were levels of complexity in play that went beyond his comprehension and negated his ability to help with the needed healing.

The last time he saw her that day was on his way out of the funeral home. The cars formed a procession leading to the cemetery but Joe, instead, headed south, returning towards home, uncertain if, and when, he would return and what would be there for him if he did.

CHAPTER 13

It was the middle of winter, a couple of months after Gabe's death. The cabins were shuttered, the lodge empty except for Sophia and Nicole. The drilling team, which had ceased all activities until after the funeral, was working again. The company that owned and operated the drilling rig also started removing the top layer of land tainted by the fracking fluid, but had to stop when winter dug in and said they would complete the cleanup when the land thawed in spring. Watching them working every day, as if nothing was different, caused Nicole's contemplative mood to tack in unexpected directions. She decided she had to make them see the blood on their hands.

Joe came back up for a visit. After the funeral, Joe and Nicole had kept in touch, online and by phone, but this was the first time they were together. They met for lunch at a diner adjacent to the hotel where Joe was staying. It was 2:00 PM on a wintry Saturday afternoon, after the lunch crowd had moved on, so they had the place pretty much to themselves.

They gazed out the window onto a barren street that reflected the anonymity of their thoughts; anything else would have been glaring, boisterous. Joe noted the difference in Nicole. Instead of her usual flowing, layered garments, she wore black jeans and a long-sleeve black shirt. As before, she wore no make-up. In past visits, this had given her skin a natural looking quality, but today it lent her features a gaunt, unhealthy appearance.

After failed attempts at small talk, Joe ventured onto the topic both of them were thinking about. "Your father was a great man," Joe said. He recognized how thoroughly inadequate this comment would come across in the face of such continuing loss. "He died in the fields that he loved. I suppose that's something."

Nicole recognized the kindness behind the words, but they did not in any way lift the cloud under which she was living.

"I never told you the whole story about my leaving college," she said.

"Truth is, I couldn't wait to get out of here after high school. Dead, nothing-to-do town and rural county. Many of the kids I went to school with were sticking around and on their way to getting strung-out on meth. My mom and dad worked all the time and had little to show for it, always fretting over bank loans to keep them afloat while renovating old cabins or building new ones.

"So I ran away to college. Became a graphic design major. If all I wanted to do was make art, I could have stayed home or rented a loft and done that. I worked my ass off the first couple of years. Learned all about marketing and selling. I was determined to have some skills that would allow me to make some money, and not have to struggle as much as they did, or live with so much uncertainty.

"Then I got real excited. Because I was in the top tier of my class, I was able to land an internship with a major marketing firm in Philly. From the first day, I realized I still knew nothing about how business was done. I felt so far behind everyone else. I was prepared to use my skills to persuade people to buy the product I was promoting.

"But what I experienced was totally different. The new game was to *get people to sell your product for you.* All of your interactions were rigged. The game changer was that everyone wanted to be associated with major products and major labels, which included ... celebrities. So, you manipulated the game. You sent out a news clip at 6:00 PM eastern time, watch it gather steam on the west coast, then get another clip queued up and ready to go at 6:00 PM west coast time. You wanted to build waves of responses, pulse by pulse, and then manipulate them . . . but at the same time, always make sure you stayed behind the curtain.

"The real currency then were 'likes' and 'retweets.' This is how you showed the world how popular your products were. Kids wanted to be part of the buzz that you were manipulating, and would do just about anything to be noticed as a top commentator for a label, which they could then spin into their own self-promotion. Or, you held out hope that the really committed tweet-machines would get a tweet from one of the stars, spinning out there in the rarified air of celebrity.

"I could go on, but I knew from the first day I had walked into hell—I couldn't take part in this game, this lifestyle; it's not who I am, and it's not how my parents raised me. After three months, I was exhausted and physically sick. So I walked away from that internship, and from college itself, with a feeling of disgust and a mountain of student loans. Sometimes I wonder if this world has become even more insidious in the three years since then."

Nicole paused, taking a deep breath and briefly closing her eyes to regather her strength. "But I didn't mind so much, because when I came home, I appreciated all I had here. All the hard work made sense because it kept away the evil that was the basis of most everything I saw out there in the 'real world.' But I couldn't keep it away. They came after us. They found us and destroyed us. Killed my dad as sure as if they put a gun to his head and pulled the trigger."

When she started opening up and talking about herself, Joe hoped that it would be good for her, but it was clear the opposite was true. She looked out the window with a fierce, empty glare.

"Get me out of here," she demanded.

They had already ordered their food, but it hadn't arrived yet. Without questioning her, Joe got up, put enough money on the table to cover the meal, and followed Nicole out into the cold. She knew where he was staying and walked in that direction. They arrived at his room, and he led them in. Inside, they looked at each other, her dark brown eyes piercing and vulnerable. They had never before progressed to this deep state of physical intimacy, but Nicole now dove headlong in that direction.

She pulled and tore at Joe's clothing and he followed suit. Tears streaked her face, but she was oblivious to them, so intent on finding some source of release from the anger and frustration. He touched the tears and felt their sadness, but was also electrified by the desperate fury of her passion. Their naked bodies made their way to the bed as each part performed a push-pull motion against the other, like breath itself. Each touch, each entanglement for Nicole was a way to assuage the pain, to beat back the loneliness.

When they were done, Joe pulled the covers over them, and they lay in silence a long time, huddled into each other. For this brief period, the animal need for clarity and peace seeped into them. But the chill soon returned. The harsh light waited, and desolate winter still lay beyond the drawn curtain. Nicole reached for a cigarette and began to smoke it, something Joe had never seen her do.

He placed his hand on hers while she sat up in bed, and he remained reclined, but she found an excuse to move it away.

Sensing her distancing herself from him, he asked, "Did I do something wrong?"

"No, no, nothing like that. It was just what I hoped for..." She opened her mouth to continue speaking, but no words came out, and she withdrew without offering additional explanation.

The room, so recently charged and darkly alluring, was again a featureless motel room. It had nothing to offer besides a TV, a bucket for ice, and prickly, peeling stucco walls.

"You want to go for a walk?" Joe asked. Trying for a little humor, he added, "I could stand the cold long enough for a quick walk in the woods."

"I don't think so, Joe. In fact, I think I should go back to the lodge."

Nicole mashed out her cigarette in the ashtray on the nightstand, stepped away from the bed, and gathered her clothing from where it was strewn about the room.

This was not at all what Joe had longed for over the past couple of months. The idea of being alone again so soon after their passionate lovemaking disturbed him. He was open and vulnerable, and his thoughts raced to comprehend what was happening and to figure out a way to create a better outcome.

"I wish you could stay, or at least I could be with you," he said.

She continued to dress, quickening her pace.

"I don't think so."

"How about tonight? Can we have dinner together?"

She was fully dressed now, and he stood next to her without any clothes.

"No, not tonight. Not for the foreseeable future." Joe saw in Nicole the same frozen emotion he'd seen as she looked outside the diner's window, that of a wounded animal, shutting down all but core emotions.

"Look, Joe. Things up here are changing, and you don't want to be a part of it. The less you know, the better."

He had no idea what she was talking about, but it sent a chill through his body.

"Can I be the judge of that?" he asked, trying but failing to sound assertive.

"No, I'm sorry. You can't."

She was standing by the door, car keys in hand, Joe still beside her.

She turned to him and in parting said, "My dad liked you a lot. He wasn't sure he wanted to, but he did. Ditto for my mom. We all did. . . . but sometimes things don't work out. If what just happened makes it harder for you, I'm sorry. Maybe someday we can see each other again, but right now it wouldn't be a good idea, not for either of us."

She turned to him and placed her keys back in her pocket. She held his head with both her hands and drew him towards her. Their lips touched softly, tentatively, for a too-brief moment. He tried to prolong the kiss, but she pulled away abruptly and turned to leave the room. He was left alone, naked and in shock.

After the summer rush ended, Nicole had rented a small studio apartment in Williamsport, PA. She had liked it there and enjoyed being on her own, but after her father's death, she stayed at the lodge most nights. Her mom needed her, and she needed to be there, close to where he had lived and where she could still sense the warmth of his spirit, the vibrancy of their relationship.

The first week was manageable. There was so much to do. Friends stopping in to pay their respects required her and her mom to tidy up the place. Gabe had been 64 years old and was fit and active. They were told this over and over again, the words filling Sophia and Nicole with sorrow instead of comfort.

After the first few sets of guests, Nicole sensed her role changing from being comforted to providing comfort. Sharing this devastating experience with kind neighbors and friends became commonplace for Nicole, who accepted the prepared meals brought to them with a nod and a vacant smile.

It was during this early stretch that she walked onto the front porch and saw her father sitting on his favorite chair. He slowly turned his head towards her until their gazes met. He had a faint smile, but there was something missing in his expression, as if he were lost and still finding his way. As he turned back away, his figure slowly disappeared. This was the first of many such encounters between them. Nicole had no sense these images were real, or that her father was still alive. Rather, his presence asserted itself where he should have been, where he *had* been up until a short while before.

She retreated into imaginary dialogue with these apparitions, and they lent a quality of normalcy not otherwise available. He teased her about the fastidious way she folded laundry, a habit she'd picked up from her mom. He also teased her about what he imagined were the trove of men seeking her company. And they discussed the work needing to be done around the lodge. These mundane conversations—these externalized creations of her mind—continually played out in her thoughts.

She depended on these visions, and knew the lodge was the place where she could feel her dad's presence. So she didn't leave, even when she could have. Three weeks after Gabe's death, without warning, his likeness ceased to present itself, forcing Nicole to experience his leaving a second time. The visitors also stopped coming, so she and her mom sat together when tasks were not occupying them. They sat like this one evening in the living room, the wood fire spreading warmth to both of them.

"What are you planning to do now, Mom?" Nicole asked, addressing this issue with her for the first time. Nicole had avoided the subject, not wanting to let in the new reality that bore down on them, because their story had been a good one. It was one of the few she knew to be good, and the thought that it must change now brought waves of grief.

"Haven't given it much thought," Sophia said. She had never been exactly dependent on Gabe. It was a symbiotic relationship, and his loss was now causing her to noticeably decline in real-time. Nicole sensed a dream-time quality in Sophia similar to what she experienced with her father's recently departed ghost.

"Before your father died," said Sophia, "when all the fracking business was coming to a head, he talked to a couple realtors about the property. They told him its value was only a fraction of what it had been worth before the drilling site was erected, that is if we could find a buyer, which was doubtful."

This came as no surprise to Nicole.

"And, of course, we don't own the mineral rights. Any future buyer wouldn't want to deal with whatever they're planning to do next."

"Well, we could keep the business going," Nicole said.

"Not sure how that will happen either. Your dad was having trouble keeping up with all that needed doing every year. Paying someone to do that maintenance would cost too much. Maybe the lodge can stay open, but I don't know about the outer cabins. We have some time to think about this. At least we've got some money coming in from the well. Enough to keep us going, for now." Nicole could see her mother struggling to remain strong, to be there for her, but the effort of planning a whole new life seemed too overwhelming for either of them to face right now.

Sophia's attempt at finding a silver lining was entirely unsettling to both of them. They were suddenly on welfare, or felt like it, and the check, they thought, was being written by the devil.

Neither had a way to spin the situation differently, although that is what they both tried separately, desperately, to do, over and over, but they always returned to the same start and end points.

Nicole did not want to accept this revenue, but realized they had no other choice. She summoned up what strength and courage was available to her and said, "Then we'll keep the lodge going and figure out what we have to do to make the cabins functional."

They left it at that, contemplating their plodding, unknown future.

CHAPTER 14

On an anti-fracking news outlet, one of a few sites she now viewed regularly, Nicole saw that Gas America had filed for more drilling permits inside Loyalsock State Forest, and that this development had caused a renewed uptick in activity from local and regional activist organizations. Accompanying the article was a notice for a meeting to discuss ways to oppose the company's request. It was organized by a local group, Gas Aware, and would be held at a church in Williamsport.

Nicole entered through the rear of the church as instructed. She walked into the common room and saw a circle of chairs off to one side. A handful of people were seated, and a few more stood around chatting. Nicole moved slowly around the perimeter of the room, looking at notices and programs being offered at the church. She stayed longest in front of the children's art. Words like *compassion, love,* and *faith* were woven in and out of the bright, primitive artwork. It made her yearn for a time when such simplicity and naiveté was still possible. But this was not her real interest. She was studying the others attending the meeting, picking up what bits of conversation she could.

The man organizing the meeting, Artie Landon, asked everyone to be seated so they could get started. He looked around and counted ten people. He thanked everyone for coming out and then said, "I see a couple of new faces, so maybe we should start by introducing ourselves. If you'd like to say what brought you here or what related activities you're involved in, feel free to take a minute to do so."

Some people described their roles in other organizations. Most, like Nicole, merely stated their names and a vague desire to do what they could to stop further gas extraction from the state forest. She did not even consider describing the actual reason for her attendance tonight. When she introduced herself, she was greeted warmly.

"Cases like this are why we need to fight back!" Artie boomed, banging a fist on the small wooden podium he stood behind. "We need to organize a rally against Gas America's plans to expand drilling in the Loyalsock." The sound of his voice and the impact of his fist reverberated through the church. "We need to reach out across the state to other environmental groups, and together we'll make a statement that we won't stand for additional degradation of our public spaces, especially one of such pristine beauty."

"Do we know anything about Gas America's plans?" came a voice from the circle. "Have they made their proposal public, or provided blueprints at a public hearing where community feedback was given? Have they conducted *any* environmental impact studies at all?"

"None that I'm aware of," Artie responded to all of the above. "Is there anyone else who can answer these questions?"

When no one spoke up, Artie continued speaking.

"I guess we shouldn't be surprised at their lack of transparency. What I do know is that when they expand a drilling operation, they set down two or three additional well sites close enough to one another to be networked. The whole operation becomes much more extensive when this happens. They'll probably end up building a compression station along with an onsite water waste disposal pond."

A man named Mark Stone spoke up. "Once we have the specifics of what we are planning to do, I can get the word out to the organizations we communicate with in the western part of the state."

"Great, then" Artie said. "Let's discuss those issues now. First question is: When and where do we do this?"

A woman identifying herself as Linda Bishop said: "One of the biggest decisions is whether we do this on a weekend or during the week. You'll get a better turnout on the weekend, but if you want to catch gas workers or government officials at work, it probably needs to be during the week."

"I don't think that's a problem this time," said someone else in the circle, "because those boys at the gas company are working Saturdays too, and I think that's who our target is right now, not a government agency. We already know the government doesn't care about our well-being. We need to focus on the people who are actually doing this!"

"I'd agree with that," Linda said. "OK, we'll do it on a Saturday then."

"We want to get this done as soon as possible, so we can stop them before they get started. March 12th is the Saturday after next. Can we be ready by then?" Artie asked.

Those with smart phones and calendars pulled them out to check their availability.

Mark voiced his concerns. "No way. As much as I'd like to move quickly, we'd never be able to mobilize everyone by then. I say we wait until the 26th. It will give us more time to make our contacts and send out press releases."

"This issue is getting a lot of attention right now," Artie said. "The longer we wait, the longer the gas companies have to put their spin on this and dig their claws in. The Governor is pushing this hard. We need to respond with force as soon as we can."

Another member spoke up, "What about the 19th? That gives us a little more time, and I agree, the quicker we act, the better. Does that work for everyone?"

Most of the assembly nodded in agreement, although Mark still looked skeptical.

"I think we have two options for where to stage the demonstration." Artie said, moving onto the next topic. "We can go out to the current site where the drilling is happening, or we can do a short march somewhere in Williamsport."

"It would be great to be by the wellhead in Loyalsock, but the police won't let us anywhere near where the drilling is happening," Linda said. "Just standing in the woods wouldn't be too effective, and if we did it there, we'd probably lose any chance of getting press coverage."

Now that others had weighed in, Artie offered his own opinion. He ran his meetings democratically, but everyone recognized he had the most experience organizing rallies. "Gas America has an office in the old City Hall in Williamsport. We could meet at the new city hall and march over to the old one, and then have our speakers make their presentation to the crowd on the plaza in front of the building."

No one voiced opposition to this idea. Indeed, there was general agreement this was a good approach. A ripple of excitement spread through the group as each member sensed the demonstration taking form.

They discussed the agenda next. It was agreed they would try to get a state senator or two to speak to the crowd. All of the local politicians backed the drilling companies, but across the state, a few were offering resistance. They would also get some local speakers who'd been negatively impacted by the drilling companies, with wells gone bad or falling victim to unexplained sickness. The comment was made that more and more people were seeing the harm being caused and were willing to speak up about it.

"We'll need to make some signs."

There was a general sigh in response to this task, which was onerous to most in the room.

"I studied graphic design for a couple of years in college," Nicole said, speaking up for the first time since introducing herself. Some in the circle measured her more respectfully than they had before, raising their eyebrows in surprise. "I should be able to pull together designs for a few signs."

The circle shifted at that moment, and she felt she established a stronger link than had been there before. Plans were made for anyone wanting to work on the signs to meet in the barn at Bountiful. A few of the members offered to buy paint, brushes, cardboard and anything else people thought would be useful. They would use the next two Saturdays to create signs and posters.

Nicole left feeling as if she belonged in this group. She was happy to have something constructive to focus on, and hoped she could channel her anger and grief into fracking opposition instead of bottling it up.

Over the next week, Nicole made sketches for signs. She dove headfirst into the activity, which provided her the first powerful expression of herself since her father's passing.

When the sign painters arrived, she recognized about half of them from the meeting at the church. There were seven participants, all women except for Artie, and all about her mom's age. In fact, Sophia had shown an interest in helping and was counted among the seven.

They were fortunate to have a warm day for this time of year, and a kerosene heater blasted additional warmth into the semi-enclosed space in the barn where they were setting up.

"Isn't that a gas well on your land?" Marge, one of the unfamiliar faces, asked, with a sharp gasp. Short and wiry, with big bulging eyes, she was the first to state what was on all the guests' minds. Nicole had not thought about the drilling rig when offering to do the signs, but immediately after she left the meeting at the church, it hit her, and it made her break into a fit of nervous, slightly hysterical laughter. When she recovered, she grew serious and decided she would not be ashamed of it, and while she would be honest about what happened, she would not tie her father's death to the rig.

"Yes it is," Nicole said. "We found out the hard way that you can own the land on the property without owning the mineral rights. We couldn't stop it from going in."

"That's the absolute craziest thing I ever heard." Marge was in high falsetto now, but Nicole could still discern the bass rumble.

"Just about," Nicole said, looking at her mom as they both understood intuitively what they would discuss and what was off limits.

"I'll be damned," Marge continued. "I'm surprised they didn't have to cart you off to jail for trying to stop them from trespassing on your property like that. They would have had to if it was me." Nicole tried her hardest not to take what Marge said as a slight against her father and his eventual acceptance of the well's presence—she knew the woman meant no harm.

"Sometimes, it just gets too hard to stand up to these companies on your own. That's why we need to band together and fight this," Nicole said, hearing the anger rise up in her own voice.

Marge looked ready to go to the mat then and there. If she were given the assignment to tear the CEO of Gas America a new asshole, she would have set off to do so. Her vehemence could have been interpreted any number of ways, but Nicole and Sophia took it with unexpected ease and found it vaguely amusing, even touching, that the woman was so worked up about their family's story.

Marge's feistiness was sincere, and it cut through the distance, the unfamiliarity, and the anxiety everyone in the assembled group felt to some degree. So they were grateful for Marge's outburst and were determined to build upon it, both because they were in this together, and because they needed to find a way to become comfortable in this setting.

"Hi, I'm Cindy," said a woman whose attire was steeped, unapologetically, in '60's style, except the buttons she wore raged against fracking instead of war. Cindy offered her hand first to the daughter and then the mother of the house. "Too bad you weren't warned about Marge's temper. But to be honest, there isn't much that can slow it down once it gets started."

"Not much? I'll say!" Artie chimed in, more as a way to make his acquaintance while he laid out the tarps upon which they would work. "In fact, I've never encountered a force strong enough to do just that. Not sure I'd want to either,"

Cindy's attention turned to the sketches Nicole had made. She was impressed—dazzled in fact. There was a poster with the phrase "Fracking kills communities" with a backdrop of a devastated landscape. Another contained a portion of the Pennsylvania constitution: *The people have a right to clean air, pure water, and to the preservation of the natural, scenic, historic, and esthetic values of the environment.* A basic, forest green background with brightly colored flora and fauna ringing the edges served as a backdrop to this poster, so that the words could take center stage. "Fight politicians using their own documents against them!" Nicole seemed to be saying.

Cindy then studied a model of a fracking rig made of furring strips. Notes jotted down beside it listed its specifications. It would be eight feet tall, made of 1 x 4's, and supported by a couple of cross pieces of wood. A pole attached to the top by a hinge would allow it to be free standing. Faux diagonal crosswise supports were made from heavy plastic. It was painted white, and on top of it, in a variety of colors, were the names of the major gas companies looking to make a killing from the Marcellus Shale.

"You've been busy," Cindy said. "More importantly, you're going to keep us busy." She laughed while saying this. "But that's a good thing. Too many of these sessions end up with nothing to show for them. We definitely won't have that problem today."

"We don't need to use these designs," Nicole said with a cautious tone. "They're just some things I've been thinking about, so I decided to give them form."

"Just some things?!" Cindy said. "We'll use them alright, if I have anything to say about it. They're perfect."

Nicole was grateful; her role in the group was quickly becoming cemented.

It wasn't long before the barn was buzzing with activity. Three work teams formed easily. Sophia and Cindy bonded quickly and started work on the derrick. Marge teamed up with Jessica, who had a saintly quality about her that would be tested. The other two women, Peg and Linda, began fashioning a workspace for themselves. Nicole oversaw the three pairs working on her designs, and sketched the more difficult segments, giving direction on color schemes, proportion, and materials. After helping to set things up, Artie made himself a little desk area, using his phone as a hotspot and starting working on press releases and making contact with other activist groups across the state.

It had been four months since Gabe's death, and this was by far the most social Sophia had been since then. She and Cindy were both happy to be teamed with another woman who knew how to work with a power saw and the other tools needed to assemble the structure with which they were tasked.

"How long you been living here?" Cindy asked.

"Feels like my whole life," Sophia said, a dreamlike tone suggesting the charmed quality of her time spent here. "It's been about thirty years since we moved up to this area. It was a few years before I got pregnant with Nicole. Those were challenging times, but we got through them. Been on this property twenty years. Farmed it and rented the cottages. It was a good life for my family. But my husband died a few months ago, and we're trying to put the pieces back together."

Marge let out a scream that first rattled around in her throat before bursting across the soundscape. When the sign was moved, she'd accidentally splattered some paint across her design. Wisps of black paint had made their way onto her face, giving her a feline look.

Nicole, who'd been hovering near her mom as she described her life to Cindy, rushed over to Marge and Jessica to triage the damage, which was not catastrophic. She was surprised to hear her mother speaking so freely. It was something she herself was still incapable of doing. She tried to be happy for her mom, but betrayal and irritation were what she really felt.

Artie had brought a radio that now blared the song "Woodstock" in the background to which he sang along in a pleasant tenor, "Goin' down to Yasgur's farm," and continued to sing a couple of verses of the event's classic retelling.

"I was there. Anyone else make it to Woodstock?" Marge posed the question to the group after the song ended.

"I was," Cindy responded. "It was transformative. I wonder how many lives were changed by it."

"All of them in our age group, for better and for worse," Linda said. "As much as we, here, may have loved it, it was polarizing. The fault lines still exist."

"Just think of the music," said Peg, diverting the conversation from where Linda's comment could have sent it, an approach she was used to taking in discussions with her friend. "Jimi Hendrix, The Who, the Band, Janis Joplin, and Crosby, Stills, Nash & Young, just to name the ones I can think of off the top of my head."

"Still the best music around, from my point of view," Artie said with a depth of feeling.

Marge asked him if he had made it to the big show.

Artie laughed and responded, "I should say not. I was a first year seminarian in '69. In those days, it would not have done for a future member of the clergy to be in the midst of such fun-loving worship. No siree. That would have sent entirely the wrong message."

"Artie, you never told us you were a man of the cloth. Never saw the collar or robes on you," Marge said with a wink, teasing, but with the curiosity they all shared.

"And you never will. Stayed there until the end of that year and then parted ways. Woodstock, the war, and a bunch of other things happened, and that path just didn't make sense to me anymore. Just wasn't meant to be, I guess."

A short period of silence followed, allowing each to reflect on Artie's story and consider their own life changes.

Jessica was the next to speak. She asked her question with genuine interest: "What about you, Nicole? Does this music still resonate with you?"

The truth was that it did, but she resisted admitting it, and responded with the lukewarm "Some of it, sure, I guess" while trying her best to seem flippant and disinterested.

Nicole watched and listened as the conversation continued, touching upon familiar topics, even for her, surrounding this seismic event. This could have been a group of women sitting around a sewing or knitting circle, and this made her laugh unkindly to herself. The meeting had turned into nothing like what she expected or wanted. Her disappointment ignited a yearning that burned from the inside out, and she felt the need to shelter this experience from those around her. Woodstock, and the failed experiment it represented, held no comfort for her, but she marveled at the rest of them, these older people and their shared zeitgeist. The warmth still emanating from that experience blanketed them indiscriminately.

Nicole removed herself further. She found she could sustain this separation, that the disappointment could be turned into something beautiful if she cloaked herself in her sadness. Her attention turned back to the poster on which she worked. The image was a simple faucet, but it gushed with flames instead of water. She went beyond the penciled-in template, and the free-form flames exuded a malevolence she'd not intended with the original design. But now it felt so good, so right. The conversation occurring around her was a swarm of incomprehensible sound, and she was glad to be absorbed creatively. Her only conscious thought concerned another faucet on the other side of the sign. A mixture of fracking fluids spewed forth from it rather than water, turning a landscape into a withered, toxic graveyard.

This was the legacy of Woodstock, Nicole thought. *Not the fine talk, the pretty music.* And right now, she faulted the ladies and Artie for sharing their fond, muddled remembrances of a failed, and in many ways embarrassing, revolution.

"But it wasn't just the music I remember," Sophia said, with a far-off look in her eyes. "What I remember is the newness, the freshness. Even the bad weather each morning awakened the spirit."

The talk plunged Sophia deeply into her feelings of loss, and she struggled to not be overcome by them.

Marge, who hadn't been heard from in a couple of minutes, provided her own commentary, "The free drugs were what set the mood. Or was it the free sex? Sorry, the whole thing's gone a little fuzzy."

"Those things helped, maybe," Linda said. "But they were not the animating force. At least I hope they weren't."

Marge continued to focus on her sign, especially her lettering of the word "communities," but her comment had derailed the conversation, which never again found its footing.

CHAPTER 15

The former Governor was a schmoozer who made you, no matter how low your status in life, feel so welcome that you could imagine the two of you sharing a beer and a ballgame, or chatting about anything at all or nothing in particular. The current Governor, if you could get him to talk, seemed to commune with blank spaces, which had the effect of obliterating anyone within auditory range—a change that cascaded down to the department heads and from them to the operating staff.

The change in Governors had less impact on Joe and those working on the political side of the state bureaucracy. Life continued for him much the same as before, except he had started paying closer attention to policy decisions and the process leading to them. That led Joe to schedule lunch with Ted at the cafeteria—something they used to do regularly but had allowed to lapse the past several months.

Thinking about the changing of the guard at the top, Joe reminded himself he needed to be pragmatic to be successful. Ted, on the other hand, prided himself on doing his work for something he believed in strongly. As Joe got closer to his cafeteria, he felt a little buzz, and realized how much he missed seeing Ted.

They got their food and sat. Joe looked over at Ted's plate; a foodie he was not. Ted could be counted on to pick the least appealing food combinations on the menu, though today wasn't too bad: peanut butter sandwich and a couple of deviled eggs. Still, it made Joe laugh.

After they got settled, Ted asked Joe if he was still seeing Nicole. The only things Joe had told him recently were the bare facts surrounding Nicole's father's death. He told him now how he went up one time after the funeral, that he and Nicole were then getting along, but that all of a sudden, she left, and they'd had little contact afterwards.

This piece of news made Ted more upset than Joe had expected. His changed demeanor made him look older and more troubled than Joe had ever seen him.

"Nothing seems to work out anymore," said Ted somberly.

For Joe, Ted was the antidote to the suits walking around them. He had longish dark hair and a barrel chest. His shirt contained a discordant swarm of colors, brought together in a plaid geometric pattern. The ability to filter out the world around him and live the way he wanted to was Ted's most endearing characteristic.

"I can understand needing some space after her father's death, but she made it seem more permanent than that," Joe said. "Maybe I remind her of state government and the problems it caused her family, but I also got the idea she was headed off in some direction that she didn't want me to know about."

Ted shivered, his neck twisting to the side. A tic? A spasm? He started to say something but seemed to change his mind, his mouth gaping for a moment before closing again. They resumed eating, engaging in nothing but casual conversation the rest of the meal.

"How about we take a walk outside?" Ted suggested.

"Sounds good. Feels like spring has finally arrived today."

They walked out the back of the capitol. Joe's spirits lifted when he saw water spouting from nearby fountains and people sitting around them, but Ted was unmoved. They maneuvered to the street and Ted opened up about what he would not discuss inside the building.

"Nicole had good reason to be suspicious of you," Ted said in a low voice. "Good reason to be suspicious of all of us, really."

This was not something Joe wanted to consider, but occasionally he'd had the same thought. It was one reason he did not pursue her intensely after she abandoned him at the motel.

"In the eight years I've been with the DEP, I've been able to do my job, more or less, the right way, but that's all changing. I don't believe much of anything coming out of the agency anymore."

Ted did not talk of the other dramas confronting him. He and his wife had never connected on a deep level; they married for convenience and, for him, sex. The suffocation his marriage caused him now extended to his job—the job he had once loved and was even proud of. Using science to protect people had morphed into the science of obfuscation, science at the behest of big corporations and big government.

What little control Ted had over his world seemed to end with the birth of his daughter, Evelyn. Unfairly and subconsciously, she had been created as the fix to a marriage lacking intimacy. Soon after her birth, her lack of interaction with the world around her became obvious. More doctors and more rounds of testing became the cycle of his life in the six months after her birth, and they were no closer to determining the root cause of Evelyn's problem.

They walked down a block of row homes, a favorite of theirs. Brownstones from the early 20th century, attractive and well maintained for the most part. They picked their steps along the uneven cobblestone walkway in silence for half-a-block, and then Joe tried to figure out what was bugging Ted.

"What's got you all bummed out?" Joe said.

"You wouldn't understand," Ted said, quickening his step unconsciously.

"What's that supposed to mean? Since when have we not been able to talk about what's going on?"

Ted was a few inches shorter than him, but somehow Joe felt as if he Ted was looking down on him.

"No offense, Joe, but I'll bet what's got me like this wouldn't really shock you. You see this every day, probably worse. You work on the political side of things. The legislation you guys make is all about compromise, bending your beliefs and ethics. I've never understood how that game was played. Never wanted to find out either.

"So I walked into work about a week ago and reviewed the quarterly water quality reports I'd been working on for a few days. They didn't look right to me. I logged into the system, ran my analysis, and the numbers squared with the report, but they were not what I expected. I spent the next couple of hours working the numbers, and then I found an anomaly. The results from every third sample had been made to look significantly better than those surrounding them, a statistical impossibility. There is a column on the table in the database to say when the data was last updated from the online system and that date was accurate, but the data was not. I'm sure of this."

They walked along a while longer. Joe did not have the technical background Ted had, but could tell something wasn't right. At that moment, Ted made a decision he hadn't been sure he was going to make.

"Someone's fucking with the data. This stuff is proprietary. People could go to jail if they got caught. Almost nobody has the authority to update this data directly. As far as I know, only a couple of database administrators are allowed. And like I said, changes made in the online system would cause the last-update column to change. The bosses could probably get access, but I doubt they'd know how to fudge these numbers. They're awfully cozy with the consultants, though. Hardly ever talk to staff anymore. Those consultants are stooges for the gas industry. I'd bet it's them, but I can't prove it, and there's no one at work I trust to tell this to. I'm being made to make sausage, and I don't like it; I can't stand knowing this is going on and not doing anything about it."

Ted was right. Try as he might, Joe could not summon the moral outrage his friend expressed. He'd not heard of examples of data-fixing, but it didn't surprise him. Was it worse than the deal-making of elected officials and business leaders, or the way important information was diverted from public view? Maybe a little bit. But by sticking his neck out, could Ted change anything? That was almost certainly not the case. The gas industry was far too powerful in Pennsylvania politics. Too much control had been ceded to it, and it could run over most anything put in its way.

"Can you talk to any of your supervisors?"

"No, they're all involved in making the gas company look like we're witnessing the second coming," Ted said, laughing with disgust.

"You could go to the media. But be sure you want to do this. They could probably trace it back to you whether or not you give them your name."

"I just—I feel like I've got to do something."

"The main thing you've got to do is look out for your wife and kid. If you go to the press now, the likely outcome is a media flap and promises of change and you get fired. That won't actually change anything—you know that. Everything will go back to how it's always been, and your career with the state will be ruined."

"I knew you'd see things that way, Joe, and I know you're right, to some extent. You know how I feel about this job. I haven't told you, but Beth and I aren't getting along. We were hoping the baby would change things between us, but Evelyn isn't getting any better. She's been to all kinds of specialists, but they still haven't been able to diagnose her." Ted covered his face with his hands for a moment and then rubbed his temples.

"This job was the one thing I looked forward to. The time and place when I could set everything else aside and do what I was meant to do."

They again walked along in silence, pondering their options. They had walked their customary two blocks away from the capitol, and were now circling back. Soon they would be back at their desks. A plan was needed, and they both searched their minds for one.

"Listen," Joe started, "if this is an isolated issue, no harm no foul. Maybe there was some overriding need to make their numbers this quarter. I'm not excusing it, but if it is not repeated, and it's not a pattern, maybe you can find a way to overlook it and get back to doing your job without feeling like you're working for the devil. Instead of broadcasting this, keep tabs on it. Document everything you see that doesn't look right. Keep me informed. We'll figure out what to do if you find out there's widespread abuse. Until then, we keep this to ourselves and hope it's an isolated incident."

Ted considered this for a full block. The state house loomed in front of them. "I guess that makes sense," Ted said. "I'm going to feel like a spy, but for now, I don't see a better option."

They continued their walk to the capitol and then separated. Ted continued a few blocks farther to the Rachel Carson building while Joe stepped through the main doorway, into the rotunda, and onto its circular stairway, where muffled echoes of shoes resounded against marble steps and hushed conversations.

CHAPTER 16

Nicole was feeling a tad dizzy as she watched her mom dart around the kitchen. Also a bit lazy. Nicole herself had stumbled down from her bedroom to slump down in a kitchen chair and drink coffee. She watched her mom make breakfast for the two of them and realized she was also baking a batch of cookies.

"What's up with the cookies?" Nicole asked.

"Nothing really. Thought I would bring them along and share them as far as they would go."

"We're not going on a picnic, Mom," Nicole said in a chastising tone. Cindy had given Sophia an oversized shirt with an anti-fracking message on it, which is what she now wore over a light sweater. Nicole couldn't decide how she felt about this, except she regarded the shirt as showy and youthful.

"Maybe not, but everyone likes homemade oatmeal cookies."

There was an undeniable logic to this observation, and the aroma from the baking cookies provided an exclamation point.

Nicole wanted to express how inappropriate all this seemed to her, but held back from doing so. Even as a teenager, she got along well with her parents, and Nicole realized the feelings she had now would have been more appropriate ten years ago. Sophia was attempting to move on with her life in some way. It seemed likely she and Cindy would become more than casual friends, and she would stay in touch with the other women who'd taken part in making the signs. Nicole knew this should make her happy, but she couldn't help finding something distasteful in the changes taking place in her mother.

As they finished their breakfast, there was a knock on the front door. It was Artie, who'd come up with his van to transport the props and signs to the demonstration site. Nicole greeted him and walked him out to the barn. Ebullient by nature, he seemed distracted and on edge.

"You OK?" she asked.

"Been better," Artie said. "At this point, I don't know if there will be 20 or 200 people at the rally today. I sent notices out to organizations which support us but didn't get much of a response. Same with media outlets. Got some speakers coming, but I always worry at this point whether they'll be talking to each other more than to anyone else."

"You'd think people would be willing to commit to something that affects them so directly," Nicole said angrily.

"It would be nice." Looking at Nicole allowed some of the stress to lift from him. He took a deep, cleansing breath before continuing. "But people have a lot on their plates. They bring what they can bring."

Artie was retired and filled his days with community-related activities. Even in earlier days, when he held a normal job, it was as a community organizer. It's what kept him going, and in touch with his own humanity, and he'd learned long ago there was no benefit in railing against people's apathy or stupidity. If he focused on that, he'd get annoyed, and that annoyance would turn him into someone he preferred not to be.

Nicole found no comfort in Artie's words, nor was she persuaded by them. When he sensed the conversation on this topic had ended, he simply turned his attention to their next task. "How about we pull the derrick into the van before it gets any more crowded in there?" They walked over to the main prop Sophia and Cindy had built, which measured eight feet in height, and slid it lengthwise into the van.

"Every demonstration's different," Artie told Nicole. "You hope it will be a time to bring people together, but the movement's in a tough phase. So many people are on the sidelines. You see the articles in the *Williamsport Gazette* every month listing all the new properties that have been leased. Gas companies got things sewn up pretty much. And people with signed leases are just waiting for the wells to be put in. Like a lottery, more than anything else . . . waiting for those big royalty checks to start rolling in every month. They don't let the extra traffic, or the threat of water contamination, or the general degradation of the landscape bother them. So we come together and remind each other what we're fighting for and that we're not doing it alone."

When they were done, Nicole and Sophia gathered their belongings and hopped into Sophia's old Subaru. Artie followed behind in his van. Nicole always liked this first part of the trip south to Williamsport. The road twisted, and the river was off to the right, and because she was not driving, she had more opportunity to study it. It was rarely obscured from view, and she could usually perceive long stretches of it. The water along the surface shimmered and flowed with purpose. She wished she were close enough to hear its chattering conversation.

"I wonder what Dad would think of us getting involved with this demonstration." The river had allowed something to thaw inside Nicole and, like sections of ice broken free from the main, her thoughts tumbled out freely.

"He'd be right here with us," Sophia said. "You know how important this was to him."

"Maybe he is, even now."

"That's right, honey. In some way, I'll bet he is."

They drove along in silence for some minutes, allowing each to commune with the spirits let loose by these comments. Sophia was the first to break through their reverie.

"I've been wondering if you actually wanted me along for the ride with your activist friends."

Nicole knew exactly what she was referring to but wished she could plead ignorance. "I'm sorry I've made you feel that way. I can't really say where it comes from, either, but I'm glad you're here with me now and that we can share this experience."

Another brief period of quiet prevailed, and again it was Sophia who ended it.

"All these years of living have provided me a few lessons. The most difficult one has been realizing how little control we really have over anything. It's like when you left college. It wouldn't have done for us to be disappointed about it. We knew you had to follow your heart.

"Your dad's dying is of a whole other order, but then again it's not. The time working with Cindy and the other women has been good for me, an opportunity to feel good energy spread through me. But it did not really lessen the ache in my heart or fill in the great emptiness I feel."

"You don't have to explain yourself Mom. I know how much you miss Dad."

"And you know, too, that I'm still alive, and that I should find ways to affirm this life, even if I stumble looking for the right ways to express it."

"Of course I know that." Mother and daughter both felt the tears now, falling down their cheeks to the same river where all tears flow.

"I wish I could hug you right now," Nicole said, "but I'm sure we'd crash if that happened and then what would we do?"

"And poor Artie. How would he deal with us wrapped around a tree?" Sophia said, admitting she had observed his anxiety. "Seems he already has his hands full." They both laughed deeply, an experience that had been absent for so long that its reappearance felt alien.

When the buzz subsided, Sophia felt the need to share one more observation.

"This is my path, but it is not the same as yours. I've been watching you, seeing your struggle without talking to you much about it. This demonstration is part of the answer for you. Maybe Bountiful is too. But don't let what I or anyone else do stop you from pursuing your own personal path."

"You really are trying to crash the car, aren't you?" Nicole said, and they both shared another wonderful laugh.

Carloads of people did, in fact, arrive for the rally. Artie's mood improved as the numbers swelled. Some stayed in their own knots of interaction, others reunited with friends, and a few struck up conversations with strangers. There were about one hundred and twenty-five in all, which was more than a respectable number.

They lined the sidewalk around the City Hall's entrance and held up their signs. Cars drove by and occasionally honked. These were greeted with half-hearted cheers from the crowd. Mostly, there was nothing to do but wait. Sophia went off to greet her new cadre of friends while Nicole stayed behind and shifted around aimlessly. She carried on small conversations with a few people close to where she stood, mostly about what brought them here, but that became repetitive and felt false. Again, there was the problem of most of the protesters being at least twenty-five years older than her. She hated herself at one point when she mentioned her dad's death. As soon as she said it, she regretted sharing something so raw with a stranger, wondering if she had brought it up simply to revitalize a flagging conversation.

A local musician started singing songs on the steps of City Hall, bringing the group back from the street and focusing their attention. The march began after a few songs. They were headed to the office of Field Resources at the Old City Hall building, the company pushing hardest to get into the Loyalsock State Forest. Chants began and provided the assembled group with a sense of unity.

Nicole and Sophia reunited when the march began, and they walked together along the sidewalk, enjoying the clear, sunny, early spring day. The chant generating the most enthusiasm was, "Stop fracking in the Loyalsock" with the word "stop" screamed the loudest and "Loyalsock" dragged out into three long, syncopated syllables. Nicole and Sophia shouted all the chants with gusto. People on the other side of the street, unaware of this planned activity, stood and stared, reading the signs flickering in the air.

Sophia motioned to the small package containing the cookies. Nicole, who had abstained to this point, peeked in. Only three of the thirty-six cookies still remained. The two women laughed and Nicole plucked the one closest to hand. She began nibbling and delighted in its flavor, one that seemed impossible to grow tired of.

When they reached their destination, only five blocks from the starting point, they congregated around a makeshift stage which contained a podium, microphone, and portable sound system. Again, there was an extended period of standing around and waiting. When everything was set up and ready to go, Artie stepped to the podium, greeted everyone, made some comments about what brought them here, and introduced the first speaker. He continued performing this function and led the group in chants to reinforce the points made in the prior speech. He knew better than anyone that each participant needed to be lifted up by the crowd and making some noise was a damn good way to do that.

The speakers talked about a variety of topics. Some of the information was new to Nicole and very disturbing. Word-pictures were created of entire communities changed for the worse: water wells gone bad followed by a total lack of accountability from drilling companies and government, and doctors who couldn't talk to other doctors because of a gag order placed on them by the state government, forbidden to talk about illnesses they believed were fracking related.

The main speaker was a state senator from outside Pittsburgh. He spoke passionately about resisting the current push into the state game lands, particularly the Loyalsock State Park. He gave detailed accounts of the road-blocks placed in front of anyone trying to slow or stop the intrusion of the gas companies into Pennsylvania, mostly into its rural communities.

It was then that Nicole noticed a small group of eight at the periphery of the demonstration. They dressed all in black, and covered their faces with Guy Fawkes masks. No matter how often Nicole saw these masks, they always provoked something in her she could not quite formulate; it was the dangerous quality lurking behind the smile, at once placid and out-sized, the wire-thin moustache and goatee, and the eyes that saw everything but expressed nothing.

She was sure the eight had not been present before or during the march and wondered where they'd come from. They appeared to pay close attention to the speakers but, because their faces were covered, it was impossible to determine the effects the speeches had on them. Their black shirts contained skeletons or other images intended to shock; desolate faces with lashes cut into the skin, and human heads with machine parts sticking out of them. Everyone at the demonstration was angry, but they were expressing it in an altogether different way, a darker, more elemental way, and this intrigued her.

Nicole was surprised to see someone else walk to the podium after the featured speaker—a girl of about thirteen. Hailing from the Scranton area, the young teenager had written a report for her eighth grade civics class. Having her speak last was a stroke of genius, because the truth she spoke summarized everything that was stated before in the simplest possible terms. She described how the water in her town's reservoir had been drained to critical levels to feed the drilling wells. Family members had contracted skin and respiratory diseases along with many of her neighbors.

She ended by saying that her parents had taught her to not let fire stay unattended in the wild, and then cited the frightening methane burn-offs that were occurring in the deep forest around her. Here was a young girl's apocalyptic vision, and one she would have been spared but for the gas companies, which came into her community and had their way with it.

The crowd's mood grew increasingly dark and angry as Artie took the microphone back and addressed the crowd. Two big, burly security guards had come out of the building during the speeches and were positioned in front of the door. The demonstrators did not have a permit to enter the building, but Artie was free-wheeling now and said they should go and visit the Field Resources office to demand some answers to questions raised that morning. Continuing to embolden the crowd, he sang "We shall overcome." The crowd joined in, marching slowly towards the entrance of the building. When Artie got to the front door, it was blocked. He demanded from the security guards that a company representative come out of the building to address their concerns, but none appeared.

Members of the masked group suddenly charged to the front, yelling and cursing at the guards to let them in, threatening them. They spanned out along the building and banged on the windows they could reach. The focus shifted from the well-disciplined larger group to this militant faction. Nicole was captivated by their actions, which felt more real than anything she'd seen.

She still stood beside her mother and looked at her now. Sophia had not been focused on the main event but instead studied her daughter's reactions. Nicole, returning the look, saw her mother's conflicting emotions. Sophia's deep concern gave way to a partial smile and a slight nod of her head. She placed her hand on Nicole's head and stroked her hair a couple of times before lowering her arm and turning her gaze back to the group. Walking away from Sophia in the direction of the one member of their party who had stayed back, Nicole spoke to the stranger.

"Who are you?" Nicole asked.

The woman she was addressing knew what she meant.

"Why do you want to know?"

"Because I've been looking for a group ready to fight back," Nicole said, voicing a thought she had not fully admitted to herself.

The woman considered what to do for a moment before responding, "Can you meet me at the Cornerstone Café tomorrow at 4:00 PM?"

Nicole said she could. The woman, whose face remained covered, said she would find her.

The other members of her group were yelling threatening taunts to anyone within the building. A member of the group pulled out a spray can, tagging the building with the letters "2 Degrees." From beneath their clothing, two others pulled out bags containing a red liquid. They threw them against the doors, now covered with what seemed like blood. They then executed a well-orchestrated retreat.

The woman with whom Nicole had spoken, and who was serving as a lookout, she suspected, ran with them and disappeared around the corner and out of sight. The rest of the demonstrators were stunned silent. This was not what they expected, and each was left to consider whether or not they approved of the tactic. They marched back and wondered what they would say if questioned by the media and police. A new option in the struggle had been placed before them. Most would reject it, but the majority felt emboldened by this show of outrage.

———

Nicole arrived at the coffee shop early and sat at a small table, positioning herself so that she faced the main entrance, paging through a copy of the Sunday *Williamsport Gazette*.

"You won't find anything there," said the woman who appeared in front of Nicole's table. She had long, wavy, dirty-blond hair, and a shawl draped across her long body. By any standard, she was beautiful, but she expressed her beauty casually, as if there were many things more important to her. As she extended her hand, which unwrapped the shawl, Nicole saw a couple of tattoos on her arm, though she did not have time to inspect them. The woman asked if she could sit, a request Nicole granted while she swept the paper aside.

"So what did you think of the demonstration yesterday?" the woman asked, not introducing herself.

"It was good to see so many people show up," Nicole said. "I learned some things from the speakers, and then it got better when your crew acted up. Nicole returned the rueful smile that had greeted her, and studied the woman intensely. The woman was older than her, Nicole figured, though unsure by how much.

"After you left, there was a lot of confusion," Nicole said. "It felt like you let the air out of the balloon. I think everyone was trying to figure out how they felt about your tactics and actions."

"Good," came the response. "That's the best we could hope for, because nothing else really will come of it. I saw you looking at the paper. Probably for an article about yesterday. Don't bother. The local TV news had nothing. They try to keep us invisible, and we keep trying to push our way into the public eye and demand our voices be heard."

They sat and drank their coffee. It was a comfortable place to hang out. There were a few small tables to sit at and a medley of cast-off living room furniture pieces on the other side of the room. Assorted art work and message boards filled the walls and offered interesting diversions. Nicole had chosen a table next to a window and the one most secluded from the others. There was a lazy quality to the café, and they were grounded by its charm.

"How did you get involved in the rally?" the woman asked.

Nicole considered the question and chose not to respond at length. "Was tired of the multi-nationals coming in and telling us how to live our lives, I guess."

"And now that we've had our demonstration, do you feel better?"

"Why are you condescending to me?" Nicole said, snapping at the woman, who was now peering at Nicole in not quite the same way. She held her coffee cup in both hands rotating it slightly, obscuring the lower half of her face, and making it difficult for Nicole to discern the woman's expression.

"Because I need to know you a little bit before I decide what I will talk to you about. I have to be careful. You have no idea. The government has issued statements that their agencies should use counter-insurgency techniques against anti-fracking activists. Do you know what that means?"

"Iraq seems to be all about counter-insurgency, and the military and politicians are all about it, but do I know what it means? I can't say I do."

The woman's response came quickly. "For one thing, it means infiltrating opposing groups, reporting on their activities, and creating dissension in them if they pose too much of a threat."

"So the enemy is not just the multi-nationals."

"Not by a long shot."

"And you think I might be one of them? A *plant* or a *mule* or whatever they're called." Nicole spat the words out, angry that such a thing would be considered.

The woman smiled for the first time, "Not a *mule,*" she corrected, "but you have the right idea. I'm sorry if you are offended, but we need to be super careful. I don't want to make it sound like we're some heavily radicalized group. The truth is, we're getting our asses kicked, but we're trying to kick back where and when we can."

It was Nicole's turn to consider what she wanted from this conversation, what direction she wanted her life to head in, and what she was willing to share.

"My father died of a heart attack in the middle of his farm, watching fracking fluid from a blown-out well overrun his land. It came from a rig he couldn't stop from being built because he didn't own the mineral rights, something he didn't even know about until the drilling company came knocking at our door."

Nicole looked away, sharply feeling the loss of her father and the way he was taken from her. Although she liked this woman, she was angry that she had caused Nicole to divulge this private piece of herself. She felt vulnerable and considered getting up and walking away from the conversation.

"I'm sorry for your loss. The way it happened is terrible." Her eyes softened and became unfocused for the first time, turning her gaze inward. "My journey towards activism was different than yours. I'm an English professor at a local college. Reading great books is what I always did and probably liked to do more than anything else. Sharing this passion came easy to me, so teaching was the natural career choice. I've been at this school for five years. The first couple were fine, and I loved what I did.

"Then the drilling started, the truck traffic, the noise. Then reports of wells being contaminated, reports of sickness, gag orders put on doctors. All the things I would have liked nothing more than to not have to deal with but found I could not ignore. My books, the love of my life, the things that defined me and sustained me, no longer could be counted on. Questions like how the Victorian novel gave way to a modern idiom no longer had quite the same importance to me. History had intruded, and what was going on around me left me feeling hopeless. A sense of history, that is missing from so much of the literature of the last century, like the other arts, put a big lasso around me and dragged me towards it. And I am still being dragged in that direction."

"There's nothing wrong with your old life," Nicole responded, seeing this other person for the first time, entwining the strands of experience from their pasts. "We still need stories to help define who we are, where we've been, and what we can aspire to."

"I suppose that's true, but the problems I became aware of were a gathering cloud that led me to question whether I was willing to throw myself into the gears of the machine causing all the destruction, or fight against those forces destroying not just the local environment but the ecology of the whole world. That is the question I ask you: Are you ready to fight? Are you ready to take risks? Are you committed to charting a course to a more just world?"

Nicole looked down at the table and stared blankly. She was monitoring the sea change stirring inside her. Her blood coursed warmly through her body, rising in pressure as if her menstrual flow was upon her. There was the force of gravity, the need to be attentive to this surging power that was undeniable but not all together pleasant.

"I would probably not have stayed involved if all there was for me was the group I worked with to organize the demonstration. Don't get me wrong. They are good, well-meaning people, but they were satisfied with the demonstration, until your group came along and hijacked it."

They both smiled and laughed quietly.

"But it's not enough," Nicole said. "Nobody's listening. Nobody's talking about improving the economy for the long term around here. Five years from now—maybe more, maybe less—the gas will have dried up. The only thing left to show for all the drilling will be the devastation it caused; the water will be polluted, but neither the fracking jobs nor the fracking businesses will still exist. We will only have contributed to climate change and the wealth of the few at the top.

"The people I was working with are old. I can't think of any other way to say it. I respect them and recognize their contributions, but for all their talk, they're not going to lead the fight in new directions. Not that I know what direction we need to move in yet. I want more than a Saturday afternoon rally that takes a lot of effort to organize, and when you're done you don't feel like you've accomplished anything. Yeah, I'm ready to do more than wave a sign and sing to the choir."

The woman let Nicole's final comments linger in the air for several moments before responding. "Glad to meet you. I'm Sherri Beck," she said, and reached out her hand.

"Nicole Marshall."

They warmly shook one another's hand. Some unspoken agreement had been reached and a friendship started. Moments later, they resumed their conversation and began making plans.

———

Nicole was instructed to go to Trucker Bar and Grill, a rough bar on an otherwise barren road, to enter as if she belonged there, and to walk to a room in the back of the bar.

Inside were a handful of stools lined up along the bar, a few booths, and a couple of pool tables. Nicole couldn't make out anyone's face through the dim light and smoke haze. She was glad for this, because it meant she couldn't be easily identified either.

She found the back room and entered. Six people were in the midst of a heated debate. She knew Sherri had informed the group she'd be attending, but the conversation barely paused after she entered. She took a seat next to Sherri, who welcomed her in a friendly way, but she wasn't acknowledged by anyone else. The room was an office and had a desk to one side. Fluorescent lights were mounted within sections of the dropped ceiling and were covered by sheets of plastic.

"Jensen says there are times when it is necessary to take out your opponents. If they are enemies of the people, they must be stopped. Do you think the world would have been a better place with or without Dick Cheney in control?"

"This isn't a binary decision or argument. There are lots of people I disagree with, but that doesn't mean I want to *off* them all."

The woman questioning Jensen's tactics was Lia, who apparently was responsible for vetting would-be volunteers in order to retain a more militant core. This conversation was an example of her tactic. She would expose the timid and show them the door. Miles, her adversary in this discussion, had sparred with her before.

"Better than sitting around in the back of some dirt bag barroom, jerking each other off," Lia responded provocatively.

"Who's going to decide who makes the cut and who doesn't?" Miles shot back. "You? Who's going to pull the trigger once the decision's made?"

Nicole wondered who decided it was alright to kill her father. When she decided to join this group, she realized she wouldn't be satisfied with half-measures.

Lia knew she wasn't yet ready for that degree of direct action, and wasn't happy the discussion had jumped to this end point so quickly. Even if she felt she was ready to follow this course of action, she would not proclaim it publicly. There was a range of activity between assassination and inaction she wished to explore, especially now that a newcomer had entered the room.

Lia turned to Nicole. Both were wiry and sinewy—a recently acquired look for Nicole.

"How about you?" Lia said, "What do you think of our little discussion?"

"Is this a test?" Nicole said, surprised to be confronted in this way so soon after arriving.

"It's whatever you want it to be."

"OK. I think there are different ways to be effective without pulling a trigger; other, less lethal ways to confront evil, but sometimes the actions you suggest may be necessary if they're all that's left," Nicole said in a no-nonsense tone.

It had, of course, been a test, and Nicole passed. Lia smiled at her in a way that guardedly suggested her hope that she'd found a new comrade in their struggle.

"The problem is we've all been anaesthetized," Lia said. "Pick your poison. Drugs and porn are the easy targets, but there are others just as effective. Look at the way these oil and gas companies have marched into our towns and changed the way we live. There are no jobs here anymore, so the few they're offering to the locals is a way of buying our silence. Then, they get the so-called community leaders in line by signing a check for improvements at the schools and hospital. Everyone's on the dole, not that they need to be. Almost no one cares about self-determination. It's a dangerous notion that can get in the way of *progress,* so it needs to be extinguished, and that can usually be done in a quiet, unassuming way, at little cost to the corporate powers, and anyone who dares to speak out can easily be marginalized and intimidated."

The group members called themselves "2 Degrees." Their guiding principle was to do everything in their power to stop the imminent annihilation of the world caused by the over-heating of the earth's atmosphere. "2 Degrees" was a reference to climate scientists' loosely held belief that the earth could absorb that much additional warming. After that, the descent into a hellish environment would be swift and, at some point, unstoppable.

Several more people joined the gathering, and after they got settled, Lia was back at it.

"This is no place for middle-class pretensions. We accept that we are out-numbered in every way, but we also know the forces aligned against us will fail eventually, that what they are constructing is a house of cards. That it will fall to pieces is inevitable and it is our job to push events towards that eventuality as effectively as we can. We, along with our comrades across the country, are pushing against this cataclysm inch by inch. When the existing controls start to unravel, the walls will come tumbling down with unstoppable force and at tremendous speed. And we will be there to embrace it, midwife to a new order based on justice and fairness."

The conversation continued, spreading into a general discussion of tactics and methods. Nicole was able to determine that the group ran a web site dedicated to airing their grievances against the fracking industry. One woman spent most of her free time videotaping fracking activity and posting it on the site. She also managed the site, but had not been heard from for some time.

Nicole listened to the conversation and recognized some of her own thoughts being articulated in ways she'd been unable to before. She was surprised it did not leave her feeling better, more included in this group. Except for Sherri, no one knew her or made any effort to introduce themselves. They were in the struggle together, maybe, but she did not yet feel connected in any other way. *I'm not here to make friends,* she reminded herself. *I'm here to find a way to take action.* Seeing an opportunity to lend her experience to the group, she spoke up.

"I took some web design classes in college. It's been a few years since I used those skills, but I can work on the web site if that would help."

The two groups she had recently contacted were different in most ways, but their response to news of this kind was very similar: The circle opened itself to her because she had something to offer it.

The meeting returned to the main order of business. Another demonstration was planned at Loyalsock to protest the drilling expansion. Work was scheduled to begin in one month, and two male group members were to arrive early, climb trees, and fasten themselves to them.

They spoke about how they would lash themselves to tree trunks and bring enough food and water with them for at least a week. They were prepared to go to jail. If that happened, they would need to raise money for bail and legal fees. Nicole was brought into this discussion because the call for money would be made through the web site, so the logistics of setting up a fund were discussed. As soon as the men were in the trees, the online campaign to support them would begin.

After the meeting, Sherri asked Nicole if she would like to stay around in the bar and have a drink. The setting didn't appeal to her, but she agreed. They grabbed one of the booths and relaxed for a few moments.

"Don't be put off too much by Lia," Sherri said. "She is very committed and expects the same from everyone else."

"I thought the last time you and I talked was my job interview. Part of tonight also felt like one."

"What they are doing with you they do to everyone showing an interest in our group. You passed with flying colors, though."

"If that's what has to happen for me to be accepted, then I'll deal with it."

The color faded from Nicole's face as she gazed into her glass, shades of amber reflecting back to her.

"You're thinking about your father, aren't you?" Sherri said, deciding she would broach this sensitive topic.

Nicole considered the question before responding. "I suppose, yes. I probably would not be here if it wasn't for what happened to him, but it's not the only thing. The community is under attack and needs to fight back in whatever way it can."

"But that's not all there is . . . fighting. We need to live too. There are other ways to liberate yourself besides fighting."

"You think Lia would agree with that?"

They both laughed and Sherri answered, "Probably not."

"But you may be interested in something else some of us are involved in. It's called 'Fire Calling.' We're a loose collection of people spread across a few neighboring states. We have three or four festivals, gatherings really, during the warmer months, and one is next weekend. You're welcome to come if you like."

Nicole considered the offer, which she had not seen coming. These days, she did not think much about enjoying herself, so such weekend getaways held little appeal.

"Is it a group against fracking, a time for meetings and strategy?"

"No, nothing like that," Sherri said with a bit of laughter in her voice. "Most of the people are not politically active, and the agenda is very loose. We gather to reconnect and try to remember how to live in harmony. If you know anything about Burning Man out west, you've got some idea of what we are trying to accomplish, but on a much smaller scale."

Nicole told Sherri she would consider the offer, and let her know the next day. But even after they stopped talking about the Fire Calling event, Nicole's thoughts still moved in that direction. She kept these thoughts to herself—this idea that it was time to let good things in, to diffuse the anger.

CHAPTER 17

The previous night, Joe pushed himself a bit too hard during his gym workout. He always slept well after heavy exertion, so now he entered the office ready to deal with anything that came his way. He worked up itineraries for the senator and managed any conflicts. When done, he dove into the senator's mail, separating those requiring immediate attention and forwarding the others appropriately.

By mid-morning, Joe had completed all his routine work. Everything was accounted for, so the day should be a smooth one. He went back to his own email and saw that they'd been dinged with the same security audit they'd been hit with each of the last four months. Each time he emailed the responsible party—actually an entire department—with simple instructions for fixing the problem. He took remediating action and forgot about it until the next month, when the same alert showed up in his inbox.

Deciding it was past time playing nice, he used a heightened tone in his response to the audit. It started with, "Come on, people! How difficult can this be?" And ended with, "What do we have to do to get off this treadmill?" He copied the senator and the department head of the offending staff, considered the possible ramifications, and then threw caution to the wind and pressed the *send* button.

"Quite a letter," Senator Bain said with a smile on his face, starting the one-on-one meeting he'd scheduled with Joe. "Someday, you'll find someone who can figure out what you're saying about them with the front part of their brain, and they're not going to like it.

"Before we get onto what I'd like to discuss," Senator Bain continued, turning the meeting to his intended topic. "I'd like to return to that conversation we had a while back about fracking. You seemed pretty upset and concerned about your friends up north."

That was true, although Joe was not so in touch with these feelings anymore. "They've been through a lot, but we've sort of lost touch. I hope things are looking up for them."

The senator allowed a bit of relief to pass across his expression and responded, "I hope so, too. They've had more than their share of heartache, but I need to know that experience has not clouded your perception and made it difficult for you to do your job."

"Sir, I've always been a team player, and you can count on my loyalty to you."

"Good, that's what I needed to hear, because we have a tremendous opportunity before us, and I want to tell you what's being considered. The people I serve have a once in a lifetime shot at greater prosperity. Forget about what I told you before—my plan to initiate a bill to allow more drilling. There's so much gas being pumped right now that prices have dropped through the floor. But the drilling companies can't slow down production because they've leased all this land. If they don't develop it within a certain timeframe, they lose their rights to it. So the price will continue to fall, and no one will make any money from all this gas coming out of the ground. The industry is essentially cannibalizing itself."

Senator Bain stopped a moment, letting the consequences of what he said sink in before continuing. "The next step in this gas revolution is to find ways to export the gas to foreign markets. That can't be done economically in its gaseous state. It needs to be converted to liquid gas. This is the final stage of technology that will make the whole system work and make a difference not just for Pennsylvania, but for the country and the world. The gas markets are reeling. Europe is being held hostage by Russia, which has the lion's share of gas on that side of the Atlantic, and they would jump at the chance to trade with us, a more reliable, friendly partner.

"This is a game changer, the thing that can propel my district into the 21st century. They need to build a gas to liquid conversion refinery somewhere, and we are going to do everything we can to have it be built in my district. This will be a multi-billion dollar expenditure. We're talking about a huge number of jobs and investment. A couple of industry execs have already contacted me and said they are considering building it in our backyard. We need this. This is just the thing to set us on the course to the future."

Joe had never seen Senator Bain so excited. Joe felt susceptible to the same contagion.

Senator Bain continued, "The Governor would like a dog and pony show for the company, Rockwell Oil and Gas, proposing this, and I would like you to be in charge of making this happen. In fact, I want you to be the lead liaison between the state and Rockwell."

This news was sobering to Joe. He realized immediately that this could be a coup, not just for the senator and his district, but for him personally. If you were a staffer and wanted to move up, you got yourself assigned to projects with a lot of attention. He was surprised this was not being handled by the Governor's staff, but kept this thought to himself. Doing this for the Governor and Rockwell would open doors for him in both the public and private sectors.

The senator made it clear that whatever he needed for the event would be available. In addition, Joe would be working closely with reps from Rockwell by helping them compile the data for the research they were performing.

"We'll have to think about the itinerary," Senator Bain began, allowing his thoughts to unwind. "Christ, not twenty years ago, we had some sizable textile plants, but they're all gone now. Still have some large distribution centers and small manufacturing sites, employing 50 or so people. Downtown Williamsport has its charm that we can put on display. I'll give you some more parameters and then you can come up with a recommendation. This is being fast-tracked. It will probably happen in about three weeks. This is your top priority. Start by reading up on Rockwell so you know who and what we are dealing with. There is a meeting at three this afternoon to kick this thing off. Plan to be there."

Joe got right to work. He googled Rockwell. Rockwell was part of a group of companies that were outsiders in the oil and gas industry, all of whom were unheard of twenty years ago. Rockwell was valued at about twenty-five billion now, but they had been fending off bankruptcy just a few years ago, and it seems like it had been on quite the roller coaster ever since its inception. They were wildcatters, a term harkening back to a distant era of American history, not buttoned-down, Ivy League types. Most were from in and around the Dallas area. A couple of the lead geologists hailed from Oklahoma prairie land, but their unifying theme was a belief in the deposits of oil and gas in the rock beneath the US of A.

While the big oil and gas companies searched for deposits overseas, they felt a driving force to make America so energy independent it could stop coddling corrupt regimes abroad with large energy production and reserves. They saw themselves as patriots who would engineer their way out of any problem that came along. And if they got rich as hell, there'd be no apologies offered because they were risking everything—time, money, and prestige, over and over. If their gamble proved they held the winning hand, then the rewards should be commensurate with the wager.

Right now, with a glut of gas on the market that could not be easily transported or marketed, the fracking companies were looking to build a refinery and convert the gas into liquid. The fact that such plants cost billions of dollars to construct was viewed as a detail to be worked out, just as others before it had been. The heads of these companies were consumed with this vision.

Rockwell's CEO was the quintessential oil man of this generation. David Cunningham had emerged from every crisis stronger and more confident. He was in his late 40s, but his biography suggested someone who had weathered more storms than could possibly be compressed into so few years. His gray hair was longer than you would expect from the CEO of a major corporation and was wavy, almost frizzy, as if it had been touched by the fires of some awesome power.

Cunningham would be at the event Joe was planning. He'd be getting a lay of the land, measuring the people and whatever else went into the calculus of billion dollar investments. Joe sensed his heart racing, and felt his sweat rise to the surface of his skin. He realized Cunningham was the main attraction and that the Governor himself was nothing more than a salesman in this era of casino politics. Joe went back to work with a renewed sense of purpose.

The meeting convened precisely at 3:00 PM. Senator Bain, with Joe beside him, sat across from their counterparts from Rockwell. The senator had spoken with the older man, Simon McMahon, a couple of times, and this meeting was the upshot from that communication. The younger man, Reid Gemstone, smiled along with the rest, but had his laptop open the whole time and busily typed away with eerie, multi-tasking ease. Margaret McBride, the Governor's top aide, rounded out the group.

The introductory remarks were made by Simon, and covered the same territory that Senator Bain had shared with Joe. The only new nugget of information was that a decision would be made quickly and, after that, work would begin almost immediately. It all seemed surreal to Joe, and he struggled to keep focused, rather than wander into thoughts about how quickly things were evolving.

When Simon was done, Senator Bain picked up the thread.

"For the next few weeks," the senator said with his eyes fixed on Joe, "your primary and overriding duty will be to provide Rockwell staff, and particularly Reid, with the information they need to make a proper assessment of the state's ability to be the refinery's location. Anything you can't answer, you let me know, and we'll track it down together."

Reid removed his hands from the keyboard and the chattering background noise vanished. Much to Joe's surprise, Reid rose from his seat and extended his hand to Joe, who also rose, a couple of beats behind, and grasped it.

"I'm looking forward to working with you," Reid said, smiling broadly.

Joe sensed Reid's charm and charisma immediately. There was an exuberant quality in the offer that made Joe smile to himself. *Maybe there's still a good-old-boy quality to the oil business I'm being let in on.* There was a pedigree here that turned your head.

"Me, too," Joe said.

Senator Bain went back to laying the groundwork. The clattering keys once again recorded every nuance.

When the meeting ended, Joe and Reid left together. The senator had secured a conference room for Reid to work in, and Joe's first task was to show Reid around and get him settled.

"So, how long you been with Rockwell?" Joe asked, interested to learn more about the company. Joe left the meeting sensing that Reid was more comfortable than him with handling the tasks before them, and was unnerved by this. After all, this was Joe's turf.

"Not," Reid responded, as he matched Joe stride for stride even with the laptop over his shoulder and a briefcase held at his side.

"Not?"

"The senator was mistaken. I didn't think it was my place to correct him. Truth is, Simon and I work for Distincture. We have a contract with Rockwell. We'll do the financial analysis for them. Then Rockwell decides what to do with it—in this case, where to build a refinery. You and me, we'll just be feeding the numbers into Distincture's software, and watching the analysis documents flow out the other end."

Distincture was an off-shoot of one of the Big 8 accounting firms of the 1980s. Not only had its reputation not diminished since then, but it retained the same conservative approach to business that had led to its success.

When they were seated in the conference room, Reid flipped open his laptop and began searching and talking to Joe at the same time, doing both with total fluency and, it would seem, attention.

"I'll send you a list of things we'll need. This is data that, for the most part, you can probably get your hands on pretty quickly."

Reid then asked for Joe's email address. Reid handed Joe his business card, which contained more contact information than Joe would ever need.

Joe returned to his desk, having felt dismissed by Reid after discussing the next steps in the process. Reid was cordial enough, but more attuned to the tasks before him than interacting with Joe or anyone else. A sense of purpose defined his behavior; it drove him on to each new endeavor. He exuded youthfulness and gravitas, a mix certain to garner both admirers and adversaries.

Joe looked at his email and opened the one from Reid. Its intent was to strip down Senator Bain's district into a set of metrics that could define it in rational business terms: trends in the economy and population, rail and highway routes and capacity, salary and cost of living information, levels of worker education, real estate values, and demographics like race and age.

Nothing like this had ever fallen into Joe's lap before. His tasks had always been mostly administrative—around the office type of stuff. Now he was being asked to dig deep and define a region in a way that could lead to a multi-billion dollar expenditure, if the sales pitch he cobbled together was well received. He looked up from his computer and stared vacantly at his surroundings for several moments. When his attention returned, he shut his laptop, exited the office, and roamed the hallways looking for a way to think about and analyze everything rushing past him.

Reid and Joe worked closely together for the next week. Within three days, Reid began churning out impressive PowerPoint presentations and PDF documents.

Joe reviewed the reports before they were sent to the senator and Distincture management. He looked at them, awed by their presentation value, even beauty. Graphical representations were embedded into the documents to corroborate the narrative of the piece, while background colors and various fonts helped carry the reader along to the conclusions.

Here he was, a top aide to one of the leading senators in the fifth largest state in the most powerful country in the world, and he felt reduced to being a go-for, always several steps behind this well-orchestrated business machine. He thought about the skirmish he had over the security breach a week before, reconnecting with his sense of accomplishment and daring at the time, and the embarrassment he now felt over its pettiness.

After reviewing the first batch of reports, Joe sat down with Reid to discuss them.

"Not a pretty picture you're painting of Senator Bain's district," Joe said, summarizing the message contained in the documents.

"Not me, us. I mostly fed in what you provided to my templates and let the story tell itself."

This was not true, Joe knew, but he appreciated Reid's attempt to share ownership of the process with Joe.

"The report shows all the indicators are down. Most of the economic drivers have left the area, and those remaining are limping along," Joe said, returning to the report's findings.

"There are only a few ways to grow a region, and they all require a base," Reid said. "You can either take advantage of natural resources, or use them to make something. Large cities can also become centers for government or financial institutions. There are a few other ways to grow, but not that many. In the recent past, the area we are looking at has seen all those indicators trending downward."

"What are you saying . . . case closed, pull down the tent, and move onto the next location and see if it has more to offer?" Joe said, his voice sounding a little frosty.

"Not saying that at all. Actually, I'm not saying anything really. Not my call. I doubt whatever we're showing is something Rockwell hasn't already considered. I don't know exactly what drew them to this area, but I can guess. Williamsport is a small city with reasonable infrastructure. Good to very good college and universities in close proximity. It also has, most importantly, good rail and highway access to notable sea ports. Getting the gas to market would be feasible, and more straight-forward here than in most places."

"Well, it's good to know we aren't compiling all this information just to have it shredded and forgotten."

"That could happen, too," Reid said. "I've seen it play out that way more often than not, and the process is often not as rational as you would hope. I've seen entire systems, and I'm talking about big, expensive, and highly functioning systems, replaced by inferior competitors at tremendous cost because of nothing more than personal dislike between the vendor's and client's senior management, or because of minor but intractable disagreements in contract negotiations."

"It ain't over till it's over," Joe said.

"Yogi had it right," Reid said. "And don't assume that a sagging economy is a negative. That might be just what they're looking for. Gives them the chance to swoop in and be the knight in shining armor. They could expect fewer roadblocks in an area hungry for an infusion of jobs and capital."

"So negatives become positives."

"They can and often do. If I catch wind that that is what they're looking for, you can bet that is the way I will bend the report. My mama didn't raise no fool."

Reid raised his hand and Joe slapped it. *Were they becoming friends?* Joe allowed himself to wonder. He wasn't sure, though he doubted it.

After work, they went out for drinks and wings, meeting other Distincture consultants and other state staffers. To Joe, class differences were readily apparent. The consultants were all graduates of top colleges with tough technical programs, or working on advanced degrees, all while working gargantuan hours for Distincture. Smiles never faded from their faces. The state workers, not so much. They contributed to conversations, but Distincture-types provided the final, authoritative word.

Joe had run for various offices in high school, but rarely won. There was usually someone a little smarter or more charismatic. He learned the sad lesson of his limitations early on, as most people do, but he learned something different as well. He learned of his talent for brokering concessions and defining terms of agreement. He also learned how to recognize winners and to align himself with them, to make himself a key component of that winner's success.

Joe graduated from Penn State. He had an unremarkable academic career there, but cultivated several reliable and useful contacts in both political parties during his college years. Mostly this was the result of grunt work like putting chairs around a room for local political events or delivering campaign literature door to door. As a result of these connections, he landed a job as a staffer and worked his way into the office of the Republican's third highest-ranked state senator, Jeff Bain.

Even among this cadre of Distincture go-getters, Reid's star shone most brightly. The others deferred to him, sensing a Type-A charm that it was hopeless to mount a charge against. They continued their revelry, drinking and eating more, all paid for by Distincture credit cards that flashed a step or two faster than the state employees' personal plastic. During the get-together, they played a game: Tell something about yourself the others might not expect from you . . . Distincture-style ice breaker. Joe was surprised his mind darted to unhappy periods in his life, like experiences of personal failure. These got self-censored, though, and all he was left with were the pictures of Ronald Reagan in his family's finished basement, which were met with appropriate, scattered laughter.

When it was Reid's turn he started talking, he was interrupted by a B-level Distincture type, who cajoled him into divulging an aspect of his lineage. Reid resisted at first before admitting that yes, his great, great uncle was none other than Albert Einstein. This connection was received with an elevated silence.

They moved on with their bar crawl, found some pool tables, and co-opted them. Joe was a natural. He had better hand/eye coordination than anyone with Distincture, and kicked Distincture butts three times consecutively before laying down his stick. *Not as impressive as sharing a gene pool with a certain wire-haired dreamer, but not bad either,* Joe reasoned. Pool skills, after all, are important.

Sitting back again with Reid, somewhere just barely within the safe zone of inebriation, they talked for the first time in a space away from the State House.

"Another week or so and we'll have this thing wrapped," Reid said, clinking beer bottles with Joe.

"Never thought we could do it," said Joe. "Seemed insurmountable." Then, putting his guard down, he admitted, "I wouldn't have known where to start."

"No one does," Reid said quickly, taking a big swig from his beer. "Distincture has a template for every type of project you can think of. Sometimes we merge templates together, but we always have a way to design a plan, and then it's just a matter of plugging in the data, following the plan, and producing the desired results."

"Project Management like no other," Joe said.

"Yep, we do it better than anyone else."

In his mind, Joe kept turning over these seemingly innocuous comments, trying to understand why they made the hair on the back of his neck stand straight up.

"How do you know these templates will produce the desired results?"

"We don't," Reid answered. "We report our results to a project design team that manages the project template library. They, in turn, refine the plans based on this feedback, which is reviewed by several levels of management. It is our version of continuous improvement. I could pull up the template for it if you like," he said half-jokingly.

Reid's answer only partially satisfied. Joe.

"So you never start fresh with an idea?" Joe asked, casting around now.

"Right, never. It would take too long. Why reinvent the wheel? We take on new projects, new requirements, and translate them into defined work plans based on our experience of what works best. For instance, nearly every project is based on some variation of the ETL model: extract, transform, and load."

Joe's alcohol-fluid mind began to understand.

"So, if you are the project guys, taking on new work, blazing new trails. . . What does that make us, the people working for the organization, the state in this case?"

Without batting an eye and with a clear, direct tone, Reid said, "This makes you the guys who keep the lights on, the day-to-day guys."

And there it was. The clearest explanation of roles and responsibilities Joe ever heard. The clearest understanding of how work got done, how change was accomplished, and his role in the process. The realization that followed stripped him of his alcohol-induced buzz and reinstated his distrust of consultants, who he now realized would always be there to make the important decisions that it would be his job to carry out.

With chilling immediacy, Joe felt what he had observed at meetings between industry and government officials. He realized Reid was more his boss than Senator Bain. And even Reid was more hologram than real. ETL? Reid was right. That was what they did. Repackaged the known world in pursuit of a rational model. And now he knew the sacred texts underpinning the enterprise, a labyrinth of intersecting templates synapsed together by a phalanx of scribes certain of the ultimate truth they would someday present.

CHAPTER 18

Ted sat across from the help desk, where Pennsylvanians called to report water and air contamination problems, and to ask questions. Those answering the phones were non-technical staff, and therefore had to stick to the set of questions and answers displayed on their computer screens.

Ted observed how often the phone would ring without being answered. He thought about picking up the phone himself, but he wouldn't have known how to help the caller. Also, it was not his job, and as a state employee, you did what you were authorized to do—nothing more nor less. Finally, though, Ted decided to call in himself. After responding to a series of automated prompts and questions, he reached the tenth ring, after which his call just dropped into a void. It made him angry. He found it difficult to go back to work.

He began listening to the conversations when someone actually picked up the phone. The first question was always where people were calling from. After their placement was set, the questions followed along two separate directions, and Ted imagined a flow chart with divergent pathways. From what he could tell, callers from the northern part of the state needed documentation, which was not needed from callers in southern districts. If they complained about the safety of their water, they were asked for results of tests from prior to when the problem started. Ted, and everyone else, knew that virtually no average citizen performed water tests to provide that type of baseline information.

Ted ran into one of the women who worked the phones in the hallway, and decided to ask her about the hotline.

Lynette and Ted were not friends, but they were cordial, and he didn't feel uncomfortable stopping her to chat. He also had rank; he was salaried, and she was hourly, and he thought this made his inquiry more reasonable and professional. Her response surprised him.

"They've told us not to talk to anyone about the calls, saying that we could get in trouble if we discussed what people are calling in about."

"It's OK. I'm not going to ask for anyone's name or address or anything like that."

It was Lynette's turn to be surprised and a little annoyed too. "I'm obviously not going to tell you that type of information, but that's not all I'm talking about. No one outside of the office knows I do this, not even my boyfriend."

"Why is that?"

"Because it's confidential, I guess."

"But everything we do is confidential."

"Not like this. Have you noticed that no one works a full day there? I'm only on the phone about eight hours a week. Even got a raise when they gave me this to do. I don't even know which other employees are assigned. In that way, sitting across from the help desk, you know more than I do. But don't tell me. I don't want to know. We aren't supposed to tell anyone about the complaints coming in. We even signed some papers about it."

"I noticed you seem to ask different people different questions."

"It's all scripted," Lynette said, still calibrating her responses. "You type in an answer to a question and hit enter, and another question or set of questions come up on the screen, and you keep doing that until you're done."

"From what I can tell," Ted continued, edging towards his real interest, "you usually don't get to the end. Not many problems get resolved."

Lynette fidgeted and twirled her glasses in her right hand. She was bigger than Ted both in height and across the shoulders. He heard her get mad a few times and on occasion chew out whoever caused her displeasure. It didn't seem to matter the level of the person either. He figured she was one of those Perry County girls, rising long before dawn to milk the cows or whatever they do on those farms he heard so much about. He liked her for all these reasons, but they were also what made him a little wary of her.

"I could say I know what you are getting at, but I won't. Look, I usually work in the secretarial pool. I don't know anything about all this fracking." She blurted this out, and Ted wondered if she had intended to divulge this bit of information.

"What happens when they can't produce baseline reports?"

"How should I know?" Lynette responded. "All I know is the status for all these claims is the same, 'In Process – awaiting validation.'"

"And that is probably where those complaints will stay, too?"

"That's my guess, but I didn't tell you that."

Ted pressed on now that he understood better how to manage the conversation.

"I'll bet people's wells are getting messed up. I'll bet they call this hotline and about 50% of the time no one is there to take the call, and I bet if they don't have documentation up the wazoo, they get told to pound sand."

"I'd say those are pretty safe bets," Lynette said. "I'd also bet that people who call too often are told to stop calling, and doctors calling are told they lack the proper authorization to receive answers to questions about whether there are spikes in things like nose bleeds, asthma, and allergies in their area. I'd bet the whole system is rigged to make the gas companies look like they're not doing anything wrong. These are just guesses, you understand. I did not give you one shred of information about what is going on up north based on what I've heard on the phones. Just one more day in the rumor mill from the mouth of some Admin Assistant Level 3."

"That's right. Thanks very much, Lynette. This is helpful and won't go any further. You know how it is around here. No one talks about what's really going on. It takes some guts. It's what I've always admired about you."

"Listen," she said, all of a sudden more introspective. "I had one girl call over and over. Got to the point she was asking for me. What could I do for her? Nothing at all, but she had sick babies, and she knew it was because of what they'd done to her water. I was told to hang up on her. Can you believe that? I couldn't do it and wondered if I'd get reprimanded, fired maybe, if I spoke to her. Then, finally, ten months after it started and after multiple tests confirmed elevated levels of nasty stuff in her water, the test looked OK. At which point they slammed her case shut. Did things get better for her? I really don't know, but she had ten months of fretting, and all that time, the state turned a blind eye to her until they could hoist their victory flag without caring to find out if her children got any better."

They went quiet, knowing there was nothing left to say except good-bye. She started first, then Ted left; paths following different directions, but tied to the same disquieting thoughts.

When Ted returned to his office, he remained distracted from his usual work. He wandered onto the internal DEP website and navigated to the Complaint Tracking System, which managed calls from citizens. He entered his ID and password and was surprised it let him in since he had no business in this system and knew accessing it could get him in trouble. He went into a different application that showed him the LDAP roles assigned to his ID. There was one called Tracker Admin, suggesting he had wide-ranging access in the tracking system. He knew he should stop there. It had been drummed into all DEP employees that they should only have the access that was necessary to do their jobs. Anything other than that should be reported to the Security Department. Ted had already proceeded down a path that might have consequences, but if he logged out now and reported this inappropriate access, he would have nothing to worry about.

Instead, Ted returned to his Complaint Tracking System session and clicked on the main menu. As he expected, a wide range of sub-menus opened. He studied them for a minute before opening the Workflow menu. He recalled Lynette's comments about the scripted nature of her conversations. The initial branch of the decision tree was based on county of residence. Callers from northern counties and some western tier counties—the ones with fracking operations—were sent in one direction, everyone else, another. Decision branch followed decision branch. When the caller complained of water problems and linked them to fracking, a list of legal and scientific questions followed. Each one represented a stop in the workflow, meaning progress on the call could not be made until this bit of information was entered. A quick review showed twelve such decision trees for water complaints in fracking communities, five in non-fracking areas.

Ted searched the menus for a reporting function but found no data mining features at all. This was an old mainframe system, which was not uncommon at the state. One by one, they got mothballed and replaced by systems with a modern interface, but this one had not yet been upgraded. Even in the old systems, there were some reporting features. With this one, nothing.

Ted got on the phone and called Bill Johnson, his main contact in the IT department that supported the DEP. Bill had worked for the state a long time and probably could retire if he wanted to, but it would be hard to see him doing anything else, Ted decided, and Bill knew it. Despite their thirty-year age difference, Ted and Bill had hit it off immediately. They not only recognized the passion each felt for their work, but didn't take themselves too seriously. Another thing they had in common was a fondness for a good cigar.

"I think it's time, Bill. I'm willing to spring for a couple of CAO Flathead V660 Carbs if you've got some time after work. Got a couple of questions to ask about a system I'm working with, too."

Bill did not need to be coaxed. "I was looking for an excuse to close up shop early, and you've just handed me one. How about we meet at the Cigar Hut at around 5:30 this evening."

Ted gave a short laugh. This was well after the normal end of the work shift, but it was all relative. "That works for me. See you then."

They sat at one of the few tables outside of the Cigar Hut savoring their Flathead V660s. At $11 a pop, this was top-shelf stuff, or as close to top shelf as Ted and Bill ventured. It was also one of the few unhurried occasions in Bill's life, and he felt obliged not to intrude upon it. Eventually, he asked the question he'd been wondering about since Ted called him.

"It sounded like you had a system problem earlier. What was that about?"

"I was in the Complaint Tracking System and looking for some reporting capabilities, but I couldn't find any."

"And you won't," Bill said without missing a beat. "We had a batch reporting cycle that used to execute weekly, but that was stopped a couple of years ago."

"Sorry to hear that. Any idea why it was stopped?"

"Not really. I remember some emails about recovering capacity on the mainframe, but it never made any sense to me. This is a small system that doesn't take any real processing power to run."

"Would it be possible to run that cycle again?"

Bill sat back in his chair. It was not the first time in his career he had fielded such technical questions. The suits at work really had no idea what could and could not be done, though he tried not to take advantage of their ignorance.

"I designed the CTS system," Bill began. "It's written in IDMS, which is a mighty powerful database engine. Thing is, you need to know how to code to maintain it, and the data has been designed for a data model that renders rational access if you know what you're doing. It's like a pit bull–give it the attention it deserves and it will perform at exceptional levels and be quite affectionate. If you don't, you may be in for trouble." Ted could see Bill lavishing attention on a pit bull the way he did his software systems.

"But IDMS went the way of the dinosaurs when relational databases came along. Unless you're careful, these relational databases turn into a mess pretty fast. It's too easy to add tables. Nothing gets modeled properly. Systems store the same information in multiple places, and they become inconsistent. The *coup de grace*? End-users generate their own reports without knowing how the data is structured, but regard the output like it was gospel.

"I remember being called into a meeting a couple of years back. Some consultants were brought in to work on the CTS. It pissed me off that I didn't get the assignment." Bill smiled and laughed gruffly. "They were trying to understand the internals of the system, and I probably could have made it easier for them than I did . . . Oh well. I kept tabs on what they were doing. They added a feature to delete complaints more than two years old unless they were deemed required to retain. Not sure what the criteria is for keeping a case longer, and I doubt that information was communicated to those working the system. If that switch wasn't set on a case, it was deleted two years after it was opened. I mean gone."

'That's weird," Ted said. "Have you ever seen that before?"

"Never." Bill was way ahead of Ted. "We have projects on the books to archive data that would really help processing our batch cycles. Databases containing twenty-to-thirty-year-old data, but no one will pony up the money to get this work done. That's not the weirdest part. No one *deletes* anything around here. If you remove data from a primary source, you retain it in a secondary source. The minimum is seven years, but most systems with sensitive data retain that data for at least thirteen years, and this is sensitive data."

"Someone doesn't want that data hanging around," Ted said, arriving at the only possible conclusion to Bill's narrative.

"When I asked a department head why this information was deemed confidential, his answer was: 'Don't want to cause alarm.' By confidential, he meant not be made public in any way, shape, or form."

Bill no longer wore his happy face, but still, when talking about his systems, he remained in a space he preferred to most any other. When his attention turned back to the current conversation, he smiled at Ted and continued in an encouraging way. "What exactly are you looking for?"

Ted described the specific and aggregate data he was interested in. In the middle of Ted's explanation, Bill pulled a mechanical pencil from his chest pocket, opened a writing pad, and jotted some notes. The conversation became a question/answer session between end-user and programmer.

When they were done, Bill closed his notebook and commented, "This should only take me a couple of days to put together. I'll just need to pull out the data model and sharpen my IDMS skills again. Haven't programmed in that language in a lot of years—too many, really. And I haven't enjoyed programming as much since then. There was a certain order that's been lost." He was rubbing the tips of his fingers together unconsciously, as if preparing to relish a gourmet meal. "But I sound like an old guy. I'll let you know when I have something."

They went back to their cigars, drawing in, then puffing out smoke that hovered around them before dispersing into space.

———————

Ted and Joe sat in a burrito shop on 2nd Street. The high volume of business and commotion around them established a wormhole for their private interaction.

"So, you've been playing Deep Throat, have you?" Joe said, aware of some of Ted's investigations.

"I never thought it would come to this," Ted said, uncomfortable laughter lacing his response. "Here, this will pretty much tell the tale." He slid a manila envelope towards Joe as his laughter stopped, aware of the clichéish secrecy he was now part of, but also aware it was putting his future at risk.

"I tell you," Ted said, "it's a total scam. You got a water problem and try to report it to the government? Forget about it. I don't work on these complaints, but I know this data, and I can tell you the analysis is flawed and inconsistent. Positive determinations of fracking found to be the root cause in one complaint, but not for neighbors in the same circumstances. And that's all the time. No explanation of why or how the different decisions were made. Shit, the DEP allowed gas companies to throw out its own pre-drilling tests and replace them with post-drilling results. They come out looking pretty good when they compare two sets of numbers that are exactly the same."

Ted paused and let this sink in. Joe felt a vise tighten around his brain as he absorbed the Catch-22 quality of this tale.

"What do you want the numbers to say?" Joe's voice had a dream-like, surreal quality.

"And you can forget about people getting accurate medical information," Ted continued. "There are calls from doctors looking for trends in conditions that may be fracking related, but they're denied access to this data. There's even a gag order not allowing them to talk to other doctors about what might be fracking-related illnesses. There's more, much more, but the only conclusion is that the DEP is at war with the people they're supposed to protect."

Ted's voice rose as he said these last words. He was angry again, which reminded him of why he took this action.

"Well," Joe said, trying to introduce some levity into the discussion, "companies are people, too, according to some here in government, including the highest court in the land. Sounds like they're the ones being protected."

"Right. Of course they are, and individual citizens hardly have the same resources as these jokers. They can pack a court proceeding with a roomful of lawyers, who can work around the clock on any annoyance they care to, like people complaining of illnesses they swear were not there before the drilling started. Just try to prove that once the lawyers start picking your statements apart."

Joe sat back in his chair. He had been watching his friend unravel for a while, and knew something about the problems in Ted's marriage and his daughter Evelyn's sickness. Now the job he loved left him feeling dirty. He looked at Ted and the wormhole tightened. The change he saw should have scared him. Normally it would have, but he was touched by Ted's honesty. That was the one trait that he could still recognize.

"What do you want me to do with this?" Joe asked, barely placing his fingertips on the package, as if not yet taking ownership of it.

"Don't know. I guess I should apologize for dragging you into this."

"That's all right. We're old friends."

Considering Joe's question, Ted waited to respond. "Go home and read this when you have a chance. Make up your own mind. If you think there is foul play, you've got some friends on the legislative side of the house. Maybe you can generate some interest in this, in these people's stories."

Ted did not know that the state senator Joe worked for had become a leading supporter of fracking, and Joe did not mention that to him either.

"That'll work. I'll get to it soon. I'll let you know what I think."

Ted felt relieved and showed it. Bearing this by himself was one thing he couldn't take right now.

"Thanks, I appreciate it. More than you know."

"That's cool. It's what I'm here for. Why we're here for each other."

"The final straw came when I tried to make the numbers sync." Ted said, his anger rising again as he tried once more to explain his motivation. "The online system admitted to 260 cases of water contamination, but my contact provided me with over 2,300 complaints. They're all here, printed out and on a CD. Even this is only from less than half the affected counties. He couldn't get the rest because the DEP offices responsible for them use a totally different tracking system.

"I analyzed what he gave me, and saw that whenever the company and resident settled without the government's involvement, the case was given a status of "withdrawn." No follow-up by any inspector, with the outcome remaining a mystery to the agency responsible for monitoring these types of harmful events. Then there are the cases moved to other departments for no reason, just so they don't get counted as positive impacts. All of this is collusion, plain and simple. The government is no longer interested in protecting its people. Everything is done for the gas companies' benefit. It's got to be stopped."

The food came and they tried to enjoy it, but the conversation had ruined their appetites. They only picked at their food before getting up to leave.

——————

After work, Joe went back to his apartment. He opened a beer, closed the door in his bedroom behind him, sat down, and began reading. What he saw was a consistent pattern on the part of the government to hide the issues raised in complaints. Everything Ted had said was correct. The ones that got to him the most were those that were practically next door to each other, with just about the exact same degraded water quality.

How could one receive a positive impact result while the other got a non-impact result? He wondered if the difference was caused by cruelty or incompetence. He also wondered what effect this had on relations between these neighbors. He marveled at all the cases where the department claimed the problem had existed before fracking, without citing sources to corroborate such a claim.

By the time he was done, Joe felt something break inside him. He was an operative in his job. He was not called upon to think for himself about matters of ethics. In fact, doing so was a liability. If his boss staked out a position, he was expected to conform to it in lock step, but here there were all these cases of abuse, and if he walked away from them, he became an accessory to that abuse.

Which was odd. His time at work during the last couple of weeks had been among the best he ever had. Word spread, as it always does, about his role in organizing potentially the biggest road event of the administration. He could sense how it changed the way he was perceived by both his peers and elected officials. He was being given a chance to lead and make a name for himself, and he embraced this opportunity. Truth was, he had drunk the Kool Aid, something he found was surprisingly easy to do.

Senator Bain's district had hemorrhaged nearly all of its good jobs, and here was a chance to reverse that. Joe had become a cheerleader, and he chafed at the revelations Ted had brought him. The refinery was going to be built somewhere, and there was no alternative to joining in the frenzy once the business elite deigned to show even cautionary interest in your piece of turf. If the senator had any reservations, expressed them publicly, and the refinery was built elsewhere, his political opponents could likely run him out of office as a result. Everyone had their role, played their part, and became an advocate.

It was not mere subterfuge that had drawn him to think the refinery would be beneficial. There was a logic to what was being proposed, and there was no reason to demonize the people he'd be hosting. The staff from Rockwell were as pleasant and professional as any he'd dealt with. They had a mission, and were committed to it, along with the success it would bring their company. It was not that complicated.

But now Joe was forced to deal with the reports laid out before him: stories of abuse of power, an uncaring for the lives of the citizens affected by the transformation of their communities. Several hours and beers later, he did what he knew he had to do almost from the first moment he started reading. He had only one point of direct contact with the reality of fracking, and had never been able to shake free from the effect Nicole had on him. He tried on multiple occasions to contact her by phone and email, but she always pushed him away. He gave up, finally, pretty sure what had started between them would never be recovered. Thinking about this now saddened him. It was a sadness that started with him and Nicole but inevitably included Gabe, whose death continued to haunt him.

He dialed the number and was surprised when, after the fourth ring, he heard Nicole's voice saying hello to him. Even if she had hung up after her greeting, it would have been worth it to him. Instead, he found himself saying something that was not rehearsed but conveyed how he felt. "There are others like you. Lots more."

Nicole was not expecting something so vague from Joe. That was not his style, and she was so puzzled by it, she prodded him—something she had been unable to do since her father's death.

"How do you mean?" she asked, allowing him to make his case before reacting.

"I've got the caseload from the DEP. Complaints from fracking related activities. So many of them showing disregard for the people's well-being. Here's one," he said, reaching from the pile still laid out in front of him. "Organic farmer in Sullivan County. Major spill onto his property of fracking fluid onto his farm. Estimated at 10,000 gallons. Lost his organic accreditation as a result. All under review. Another, the mother of a farming family came down with cancer soon after fracking came to her community. No history of cancer in her family. No compensation yet, and this happened over a year ago. Try proving cause and effect in a court of law with these corporate lawyers lined up against you. And another—unexplained outbreaks of nausea and skin problems in Berwick County. No progress on this one either. It's all a game, and the cards are seriously stacked against people like you . . . and your dad."

Nicole was saddened to hear this report, but grateful too, and heartened.

"I know. I've made a lot of contacts in the anti-fracking movement. It's opened my eyes to a lot of things. Things I'm still working out."

"That's good," Joe said. "That's the best thing for you," Joe said. And then after a pause, "Damn, it's good to hear your voice."

Nicole laughed a quiet, contented laugh. "And it's good to hear yours." She felt herself circle her emotions, conversing with them in a way that felt fresh, expressing sentiments that had long been absent.

"I'm sorry for how I've treated you," Nicole said. "Pushing you away."

"It's OK," he said. "I can't imagine what you were feeling and what I represented to you."

"You're a good man and a good friend," she said, and these words radiated through him, swelling his heart.

They spoke some more, filling each other in on what they'd been up to. She told him about how she and her mom were struggling to keep some part of the family business alive.

"I'd like to see you," Joe said. "Maybe I could come up and help out around the lodge. I'd also like to show you the file and talk to you about what to do with it. I don't know who else to discuss this with."

"I'd like that," Nicole said, comfortable with her decision.

They made plans for the weekend after next. He'd hoped to see her this coming weekend but was told that she would be away with a friend. He would take Friday off and spend the long weekend at the lodge. They both looked forward to getting back together and discussing all that had happened to both of them.

CHAPTER 19

For more than two hours, Nicole and Sherri had been in the car taking them to a stretch of the Pocono Mountains near Scranton, PA. They had plenty to unpack, but Sherri was so excited to be there that they left it all behind and started looking around. As they walked, Sherri provided more information about the place where they'd be staying.

"Jake Miller owns this land. On the other side of the mountain is a campground he runs as a business. He's an old guy, and I guess he makes enough from the fees he charges others to get by. Not sure how he and our group made contact, but he took a liking to us and lets us have our gatherings here. For no charge. All we need to do is walk lightly on the land and, before we leave, make it look like we were never here. It's not as easy as it sounds, but everyone does their part until the work is done."

Before arriving at the area where the tents were set up, they were greeted by two men and a woman, all of whom said they worked for a traveling circus. The woman was a tattooed aerialist, one of the men worked as a magician, and the other as a roadie. What's more, they were part of the gathering's steering committee, which was more event structure than Nicole realized.

"So," Sherri asked, "what do you have planned for the weekend?"

They shifted around for a moment, and then one of the men spoke up, "We decided we should shake things up a little. Include an Ordeal Ritual or two."

Sherri looked puzzled. To her, this was the sort of activity normally reserved for the summer solstice gathering, which had long since passed. "Any reason you're changing things up?"

"Different people have been complaining about bad things happening to and around them. Overall, a lot of bad karma. We just felt it was needed—the right thing to do."

Nicole was thrown by this comment. She'd recently had plenty of shitty karma in her own life. She and Sherri left the group and continued their walk around the grounds. There was an old structure with a large stone fireplace and walls constructed of knotty pine boards. Several tables were set up, but not enough for all the people attending the gathering. Nicole estimated about fifty people had already arrived, and it was still early.

They continued on to their next destination, the fire circle.

"This is where the main activities are held," Sherri said. "They will start tonight. People will drift in and out. I'll be here for you, but get from it what you can and do what feels right."

Nicole liked it here. The building reminded her of an old camp structure, and she enjoyed the busyness of camp life. "What was Bart talking about?" she asked. "What are *the Ordeal Rituals* he mentioned?"

Sherri considered this before responding. "Guess you could tell I was surprised. Usually, we conduct those ceremonies only when the community is sufficiently energetic, because it takes the most trust, the most focused attention. It is a chance to confront your fears and do things you never imagined you could do. Things that may seem crazy in the light of day, but perfectly reasonable within the magic the circle provides. The idea is, if you accomplish these things, you're better prepared to vanquish your own personal demons."

"There are a couple of more things I want to share with you now that I see you'll be involved in our rituals. Most are derived from traditional, Indigenous practices. The blood of several tribes flows within the bodies of some in our group. We are grateful for their presence and let them guide us in the proper preparation and experience of these ceremonies.

"Another thing I want you to be certain of is that there is nothing haphazard about the way these rituals are administered. Precautions are taken to minimize injury and harm, or transferring disease from one participant to another. Members of our group are trained in traditional and western medical disciplines and are ready to assist if the need arises.

"But most of all, if you choose to take part in any of these rituals, make sure you feel grounded in them, that you trust the good spirit of the group, that you trust it will guide you through the ceremony you've chosen to enter into."

Nicole pondered Sherri's words as they began unpacking things back at the car. They looked for a place to set up their tent and found a flat spot nestled in pine trees. The pine needles blanketing the ground would make things more comfortable for them.

As more folks arrived, it seemed that Sherri knew most of them—she seemed to have only one degree of separation from them. The group setting up next to them was up from a small town outside of Richmond, Virginia. Nicole was warmly greeted into their company. They consisted of two couples. The younger ones were about Nicole's age, named Seth and April. The older couple, Martha and Dale, were probably in their late forties.

"Looks like you guys are traveling together," Sherri said, by way of greeting them and showing an interest in what they were up to.

"Traveling and living, right now," Martha responded with a clear sense of pleasure in her voice. "Off and on since last summer, we've been lucky enough to have Seth and April stay with us. They've been helping out around our property. Dale is usually busy with work, so a lot of what we need to do around the house has been left wanting."

Seth and April were equally upbeat about the living arrangement.

"We've put in a garden and are building chicken coops right now," Seth said. If we have time, we're going to build a shed for farm equipment Martha and Dale want to buy. They got three beautiful acres of land backing up onto state game lands. We can grow a lot of food and raise some animals too. That's the plan anyway."

Nicole was intrigued by everything about this arrangement and asked Seth and April, "Do you two have any experience doing this type of work?"

"Not really," April responded. "We're just a couple of city kids looking for something different. We talked to Martha and Dale at a gathering last summer. Told them we were thinking of signing up with a program where we could work at different organic farms for room and board. One thing led to another and before you knew it, we were heading to their place to do pretty much the same thing, but with friends. Good idea all around, we think. Google and Youtube are wonderful teachers. What we can't learn that way, we can get by tapping someone in the Fire Calling community."

Soon they were back at the task of setting up camp and Nicole was left with her own thoughts. *Is such an Eden possible? Can a community of this kind really exist? How far does it extend, and how do they cope when people or events push against those limits?*

She wrestled with the images and energy she had already been exposed to. A couple of young people, Seth and April, with nothing to do find an easy way to spend their time, she told herself, but there was more to it than that and she knew it. Wave after wave of authentic good feeling washed over them, and her anger screamed back, but less effectively. Still, she felt a shortness of breath, a constriction in her chest.

Several tents down, a commotion was brewing. Friends were greeting each other with screams and peals of laughter. Cries of "I love you, man," echoed through the woods. Young men and women, but mostly men, hugged each other until they went down in a heap, rolling together in their embrace. Laughter, pandemonium. Nicole watched the outsized emotion and wondered if it could be real. In the midst of these reflections, drums, djembes mostly, were unsheathed and the playing began. Most everyone in close proximity dropped what they were doing and heeded the drums' call. Sherri wrapped her arm around Nicole's shoulder, and they were off to Nicole's first impromptu drum circle.

"Does this happen often?" Nicole asked.

"They'll use any excuse to pull out their drums," Sherri said with laughter in her voice. Up ahead, twirling dancers accompanied the drums, their bright swirling garments flickering in and out of the sun's rays.

The drumming lasted longer than Nicole expected. At first, she felt good watching so much spontaneous joy, but as time stretched on, her feeling of being an outsider took hold, pulling her away from the web of emotion that had initially drawn her. You were either in or out of what Nicole decided was a contrived *happening*, and it no longer enthralled her. She thought about the greetings again: big, hairy guys rolling around on the ground, reminding her now more of wrestlers or football players than men with true affection for one another.

Sherri moved off to greet old friends, Nicole declining the offer to go with her. It no longer mattered if Sherri, her lifeline, was there with her or not. Nicole turned and walked away, removing herself from the circle, retreating with no other purpose. Each step allowed her to breathe a little more deeply, though she still felt uncomfortable and alienated. She walked as far as she could, to the point on the property where she could go no further, and stood nestled in a small wooded cove.

Even here, she experienced feelings of claustrophobia and paranoia, and she dropped to a knee. The tree in front of her was encased in vines: no longer willing to share space, but determined to overwhelm the host. What trigger causes imbalance? Escape, but to where? From herself. Impossible even if she'd brought her car. . . . She had become unreachable.

After several minutes, she was able to move again. Rising unsteadily, she walked back to their campsite and looked about furtively for something to do. It wasn't long before such tasks presented themselves, and she was thankful to be busy.

When Sherri returned, she sensed the change in Nicole, who continued looking for and finding tasks to occupy her. At that moment, she was rigging up a rope and a bag on a tree, in which she would place food items so that they could be hoisted high enough to be out of a bear's reach. That it provided her some distance from the campsite, and Sherri, was a calculated benefit, but once it was done, she had no alternative but engage Sherri.

"You should have come with me when I went over to talk to Marge and Jim," Sherri said. The idea of being confronted with new faces, the vertigo-inducing introductions, and small-talk unnerved Nicole.

"They just got back from a month in Denali National Park. Nothing but open wilderness. They described a few bear and moose sightings. They even saw a mountain goat."

Nicole knew this should interest her, but they were words without meaning. It scared her how disconnected she felt and she wondered how she'd make it through the weekend.

Instead of feigning interest, Nicole decided to express what she felt, at least partially. "This is all pretty overwhelming. So much happiness, so much of a sense of belonging. It's great you feel that way. I wish I could be there with you, but for me it feels false, and if you're not feeling the energy everyone else is experiencing it can be really hard to be around. I feel like the perfect malcontent. I know these feelings all too well and don't like them, but they're what I feel, and there's no use denying them."

Sherri was sitting in a camp chair, the seat made of scooped-out canvas, a book in her lap waiting to be read. Her response came quickly because Nicole's comments were not unexpected. "I think you should know that probably everyone here has been where you are. We don't live in this blissful state all the time—most of us anyway. We have our jobs, our struggles to find meaning, and lives away from these gatherings, but this is our reminder of community, caring, and safety. Our rituals are real and they connect us, but they aren't always accessible, ready to be touched and experienced.

"Let yourself feel what you need to feel, but don't exclude yourself from the possibility that what we have to offer is real, not only for us, but for you, too."

Nicole received these words and felt their kindness, thankful for them.

Hectic camp life proceeded around them: the setting up and airing out, adjustments to tents and air mattresses, nothing ever completely right, but good enough, especially with the fresh air and the clear sky. Soon they were starting a fire, upon which they would cook their meal. Nicole gave herself over to these tasks, enjoying working together with Sherri. The dread Nicole experienced was replaced by a washed-out feeling that she did not find disagreeable, for it allowed the world to flow in and out of her without much interference.

The drums started again as the sun descended. A different source of light came from the fire circle, a large bonfire crackling and sputtering like an adolescent with something to prove. Gradually, the campers headed toward the fire. They came in small groups, and their boisterousness lessened as they drew closer to the gathering. Sherri and Nicole were joined by the two couples camping beside them.

There were about ten drummers sitting together, and another fifty people were dispersed around the fire. The beating drums accompanied the spidering flames, their magic restrained for now.

The music stopped as a woman named Nel, standing off to the side, strode to the center and addressed the group.

"It is a joy to see all of you here—both those who are regular attendees to our Birthing by Fire ceremony, and any who might be here for the first time. A blessing to you all. May the source of your power be restored to you. May your beauty brighten the sky as does this fire upon which we gaze. . . . Before the drums are reawakened, please join me in a simple devotion."

Nel raised both her hands and the group fanned out, slowly widening until a single circle could be discerned.

"Let us begin with our prayer that calls upon the spirits from the four directions, and then from the earth and sky themselves, so that we can draw their sacredness to the ground on which we stand."

Nel proceeded to turn in one direction and then another, invoking the spirits of each. She called upon these powers to assist in shedding unwanted energies, showing the way to live beyond anger, fear, death. She spoke to the elders, those among them now and those departed, summoning their wisdom. Finally, turning eastward, she shared a vision of the rising sun and the birthing of a new day.

The evening was just starting.

CHAPTER 20

Ascending the driveway to Bountiful, Joe first saw them around the first bend—the fracking drill pad and apparatus. The land had just been cleared when he had last visited, and now that he saw the derrick close-up, he was surprised at how ominously it towered over the surrounding landscape. He stopped his car and continued to gaze out.

Five acres of farmland lay fallow between him and the drilling pad, but even at this distance, the monstrous machinery was all he could see. His other senses registered change. A whirring, hissing noise and a foul rotten-egg smell competed with the sounds and smells he was used to being greeted by.

Nicole came out to meet him, soon joined by her mom. After their initial hellos, Nicole wasted no time addressing the topic they couldn't ignore.

"How do you like our new lodger?" Nicole asked, while pointing in the direction of the derrick. She refused to turn her gaze towards it, an act of defiance she knew was ineffectual.

Joe briefly hesitated, then admitted what he felt. "It's worse than what I thought it would be," he said, grimacing. He knew he wasn't directly responsible, but he couldn't help feeling connected to the people who were. "It's all I could see as I was coming up the driveway."

"What a mess it made. There was noise and dirt all the time; trucks coming and going," Nicole said.

"Maybe it's better Gabe didn't have to live to see it, much less every day," Sophia said soberly, considering the subject closed.

They walked up to the porch and continued their conversation over a cup of coffee. Joe learned that five of the eight cabins were vacant that week, which, they said, had been pretty common this summer; other years at this time of year, they would have been full to capacity. They had two cabins booked for the following week, and then that was it for the rest of the summer.

Joe felt his heart fill with sorrow as he saw how hard it had been for Nicole and her mother without Gabe, and wished there was more he could do to help.

"I don't see it getting any better," Sophia said, sighing with resignation. "Not sure what the future holds, at this point."

"I hate to say it, but we'd be under water right now without the money coming in from the well," Nicole added. "Blood money of the worst kind."

Joe let this sink in for a moment and then, trying for something a little more upbeat, responded, "Well, I'm here to help out any way I can. Been sitting in my office too much and could use some honest manual labor."

Even though the season was slow, and there was no hope of business picking up, Nicole and Sophia were keeping up appearances as best they could. They were in the midst of sprucing up a cabin, something that would normally have been done months before, but because there had been no need, the project remained lost in the malaise that Nicole and Sophia inhabited. This past week, Nicole had cast off the gloom and thrown herself into the process of making it available for use. She believed the cabin still served a purpose, even if she wasn't yet able to define quite what that was.

Nicole took him at his word and put him to work. Joe was assigned to cleaning windows, and after a couple of hours of trying unsuccessfully to keep up with Nicole, he paused and, with a smile, suggesting he was happy to be bested by her rigor, asked what had gotten into her.

"What do you mean?" Nicole responded with mock surprise, keeping her face as neutral as possible, but the twinkle in her eyes betrayed her and the fact that she knew *exactly* what Joe had meant.

"When we spoke a couple weeks ago, you were stuck in neutral, maybe even moving in reverse. Now, I watch you, and you're doing four things at once and getting them all done faster than I could do any one of them."

They both laughed. She scanned his work on the windows and agreed with his observation. She emitted a *hmmm* drizzled with sarcasm, a reaction that caused them both to laugh again. "Maybe you're just not in as good shape as I am. We're going to have to toughen you up," she said, giggling.

Then her expression became more thoughtful. "I woke up last weekend. I'd been sleeping since Dad died, and now I realize all the things I need to get done."

It was the first time he'd heard her refer to Gabe as "Dad" and not "my dad," and it made Joe feel closer to her and Gabe.

They moved from the indoors to the porch and sat down next to each other. Nicole was ready to tell the story of what had happened to her—a story she had not told anyone else. "I went to this festival last week. Not a music festival, but a gathering of people who have been doing this for a long time. At first, I didn't think it was for me. Everyone was so happy—not that that's a bad thing, but it freaked me out because I didn't feel connected to it. I was still too much in my own head. I was with a friend, who was really digging it, so I stuck around. It got so my brain felt like it was in a vise.

"Everything changed in the evening. They had some rituals to set the mood, giving thanks to the four directions as we stood around this enormous fire. I resisted, but the mood was irresistible, and I decided to open myself to it.

"There were dancers and hula hoops, and the drums always building and cresting and ebbing. People came and went for what seemed like hours. I don't know if anyone was doing drugs, but it still felt like we were all on psychedelics. Time was warping, and once I let go of my anger, I took part in the journey, becoming one with the ceremony.

"The energy shifted when a man entered the circle, dancing and chanting from some place deep within him, almost like an outside force had taken over his body. He radiated positive energy, gliding from one section of the circle to another like a hummingbird, but instead of extracting nectar, he dispensed it. Then a guy in the circle extended his hand and this humming bird of a man grasped it lightly as he continued to dance and move like he was in a trance. He guided the man to a device strapped to a tree. Its purpose was unclear to me until I saw him being strapped to it. They hoisted him, but then I realized the straps were only for backup. The real support was from two hooks, and those hooks were inserted into the guy's back!

"I thought I'd go crazy when I realized what was going on. I thought everyone watching and allowing this to happen was crazy. They raised him and he screamed . . . and whimpered and cried, but then the pain didn't seem to consume him. The drums guided him and everyone in the circle. His smile was unearthly . . . He stayed up there for a couple of minutes, the serene expression never leaving his face.

"Two others followed with similar experiences. I then felt my own arm raise, and I was escorted to the pulleys. My guide was the same man who had escorted the others. He danced around me in a way that was both mischievous and confident. I felt safe. The fear was greater than the pain, and the pain, when I was first pierced, was extreme. I screamed and cried when I first lifted off the ground. Everyone controlled the height to which they were raised, and once I got up there, I felt driven by something—I don't know what—to keep ascending ... towards something.

"If I could have risen above the trees, I would have done so, but then at the top, twenty feet off the ground and suspended by hooks inserted into my back, I felt a break in consciousness. At that moment, all bodily sensations vanished, and I found what I was looking for. I saw Dad—no, not saw him, but he was there, with me, inside me. He was radiating all his goodness, all his love. He was saying goodbye, telling me that all was fine with him and in the world. He told me to always listen to the drums, and I've been feeling better ever since, like an enormous weight has lifted off of me."

Joe listened, speechless, but heard a story different from the one Nicole thought she had told. His mind stopped taking in information when she explained the device that had hoisted her up. He just kept thinking about the pain involved, the barbarity of it. He wondered if she had lost her mind, if her grief had caused a break in consciousness different than the one to which she alluded.

"Why would you do that to yourself? Inflicting pain on yourself? That seems masochistic to me."

"It's a way to confront your demons, in my case, of dealing with loss. I've done some research on the practice, and it has ancient roots. American Indian cultures used this as a rite of passage and in their ceremonies."

Joe knew next to nothing about primitive, pagan rituals, and this verbal introduction did nothing to further his interest. They did not seem like prerequisites to happiness, and after hearing Nicole's story, he felt this even more strongly, and he was willing to argue the point.

"I suppose there are lots of ways to get to the same place. I would have thought you'd have found a gentler way to achieve this, or do you think you needed to experience something this painful and violent before you could get on with your life?"

Nicole decided she was done with the conversation. An opportunity to share with Joe how she'd reconnected with her father's spirit had turned into a chess match of a conversation cheapening her revelatory experience.

She gave him a steely gaze and asked the question that pushed itself through her current of competing thoughts.

"What? Do you like me better when I'm depressed?"

Joe found this to be beyond contemptible.

"I've tried to be there for you and will continue to be. I don't deserve that comment."

"Then try to be there when I have something good to say. Even if it means I'm changing in some important way."

Again, Joe was unable to hear what Nicole was saying, and his words spoke to his lack of comprehension, "What else has changed? Are you still interested in the fracking information I brought with me?"

"Of course," Nicole responded, bewilderment and annoyance saturating her tone, "What does that have to do with anything? I'm as committed to that as I ever was."

"OK, I'm glad that hasn't changed," Joe countered, already regretting his last comment. He blamed himself more than Nicole for how the conversation had deteriorated.

They sat in silence—an uncomfortable silence—for a couple of minutes, and when Nicole announced there was more work to be done, they were both glad to return to action.

This time they found themselves in different parts of the cabin. Nicole scrubbed the floor in the bedroom with renewed vigor, but was fueled by hurt and anger. The experience she had conveyed to Joe represented a deep cleansing, and he was unable to see this or chose not to. She had been looking forward to telling him about it and sharing the closeness she had felt to her father, thinking he would be able to understand the transformative power it had on her. Instead, he had reacted aggressively, as if he wanted to tear it all down. She wondered if all that bound them together was her grief. The conversation caused her confidence to falter because the thing replacing her sorrow was still elusive and undefined.

Joe's recoil would not loosen. He couldn't get beyond the image of Nicole suspended in the air on a couple of hooks like a hunk of meat. *What am I supposed to do with that?* he wondered.

He now thought about the information he brought to show her, and the proof of government abuse it represented, but compared to what he'd just been told, that world didn't look so bad. Not all government and business was evil. Most of the people he worked with were motivated to do good for the people they represented, as well as the general populace. The alternative of hanging out in forests re-enacting primitive rituals did not signal a better life or a higher form of being.

Joe was under no obligation to work, and this fact lessened his desire to do so. When he was done cleaning a window, he announced that he was taking a walk down to the stream.

He found a rock to sit on, relieved to be alone. He hoped to not think of anything and just experience the beauty of his surroundings, but his mind would not allow it.

He would never admit that he liked her more depressed. That was wrong and simplistic, but he did prefer her feistiness to the starry-eyed quality she had just displayed. Things had gotten so complicated for him, particularly in the last week. He had been swept up in the excitement of the business venture being considered. The energy and buzz were palpable, and he liked being a part of that. He knew that people were being hurt by the drilling. And the industry had quite possibly contributed to Gabe's heart attack and death, but people needed energy, and here was a way to provide it. The true Luddites of the world were few, and the rest should get over it, make their best plans, and move forward.

It would be easier if Ted had not dropped his bomb about abuse in the DEP, but even that could be dealt with without shutting down a project with enormous potential benefit for a large number of people. The fact was that the majority of people in this area were in favor of both the drilling and, based on initial polling, the gas to liquid plant. Call it casino economics, or being bought off, which is how the liberal media always framed it. Whatever it was, there was clear support in the community, and it was his boss' job, and therefore Joe's job, to satisfy their wishes as best he could. He was getting tired of feeling guilty about it all.

The next morning, Joe rose early. He headed out to a bakery, about five miles down the road, and brought back pastries for Nicole and Sophia, hoping they might enjoy them after preparing a meal for the few lodgers. Nicole and Joe had gone to hear music at a local bar the night before. They had a good time dancing and having a couple of drinks, but the romantic spark was clearly diminished by their earlier conversation; neither could find a way to overcome what had gone between them.

"How did you know my favorite was sticky buns?" Sophia asked, as she broke off a piece of the gooey pastry and carefully brought it to her mouth so the threads of dangling goo only touched those things for which they were intended, and then she let out a contented sigh.

They ate and sipped their coffee quietly while sitting on the porch looking out.

"This is probably our last season," Sophia said after finishing the final bite. "No one wants to come to a place in the woods and have to look at and listen to that thing," she said, motioning at the drilling rig. "Nicole talked me into keeping things going this summer, and it's probably good we did because it kept me from getting too down about Gabe and kept me in touch with him, the things that he loved and we loved to do together."

She paused to think. She knew Gabe's touch, his laughter, when she was here, performing the tasks that had defined their lives down through their years at Bountiful. Now, as she considered a different lifestyle for herself, her primary fear was that she would no longer be able to sense those qualities.

"But we're losing money, and most of those who came this year are long-timers who felt a sense of loyalty to us. Most of them probably won't want to return next year."

Sophia and Nicole had had this conversation before, and Nicole had always offered some resistance, but this time she could not find the words to suggest an alternative, and so her silence was received as a type of surrender.

Again Sophia spoke. "I know you two have things to talk about, and I have some tasks to get to. Mostly I need to work off that sticky bun, for which I want to thank you most heartily, Joe."

Joe and Nicole were alone again, and their differences seemed attenuated by the gentle sadness of Sophia's words; her great sense of loss was palpable to both of them. It allowed them to discard their differences, a chance to repair what had been damaged the day before.

"Would you like to see the information I brought with me now?"

"I thought you'd forgotten about that," Nicole said with a cagey expression Joe was happy to see.

"I wanted to wait until I didn't think you were going to bite my head off."

"I think you're safe. For now, anyway."

Joe went out to his car and pulled the folder containing the reports of fracking-related complaints and negligence on the part of the DEP. When he returned to the porch, he pulled a table in front of Nicole and took a seat next to her.

"It's all here," Joe said, slapping the folder down. "Hundreds of cases of water contamination and the resulting illnesses. In almost all of them, the DEP put up roadblocks, so they never got categorized as wells contaminated by fracking. If a base line test wasn't taken, no contaimination was found.

"Then you have a large number of complaints because the royalty payments have dried up or property values are tanking. For some reason, they started to push fees, like transmissions costs, onto the well owners. All very legal . . . and underhanded, if you ask me.

"The third large category of complaints relate to the general degrading of the quality of life. Lights shining into houses from drilling sites in the middle of the night, destructions of landscape and infrastructure, constant noise, and diesel exhaust from a constant stream of trucks."

Nicole leafed through the documents while Joe spoke. When he was done, she looked up at him with a stunned expression. "I'm surprised at how widespread this is, and how much information you've got here."

"That was also my feeling when I first looked it all over. When you read through this, you can just see the state folks searching for flaws in people's stories. The method of data-gathering is designed to invalidate complaints—stop them dead in their tracks."

Joe guided her to a few reports that confirmed his comments. After she finished reading them, she asked, "Do you have any idea what you're going to do with this information?"

"Wish I did. It would not be good for me to be implicated as a whistle blower right now. Never is a good time, but right now is particularly bad." Joe had no interest in being more specific.

Nicole paused. "I've gotten involved with a group up here recently," she said.

"You mean another one, different than the one you told me about yesterday?"

"Yeah, that's right. . . . I've been busy." They both laughed, signaling that a relationship repair was at least possible. "They're an activist group working against fracking. I've become their webmaster and can use their site to broadcast this information."

Joe didn't expect this. To that point, he'd expected the information to stay in the shadows. He got up and started pacing. Scenarios too numerous to differentiate burst through his thoughts. If he agreed to this plan, he would lose control of the data's dissemination and its impacts.

The pacing did not help. He could collect the papers and walk away, back to his everyday life, and slowly distance himself from the times spent here.

"Just remember," Joe said in the midst of these reflections. "If this gets tracked back to me, it will mean the end of my career, and maybe worse." With no clue why he was taking this path, he was now an accomplice to a crime he could not give name to.

CHAPTER 21

Nicole pored over the reports after Joe left. Names and street addresses had been redacted, but everything else, which was in plain text, provided a sweeping indictment, a true narrative of the problems the gas industry had brought to the Commonwealth. She had not seen information like this before, and wondered how much of it had ever been seen by the public. Exposing this data was her one shot at slowing down the machine, maybe even damaging it a little, she thought.

The next morning, she considered how all the pieces were falling into place. 2 Degrees' website provided her a forum, and now she had combustible information to post. She had no idea of the legal ramifications, but knew the surveillance state could easily find out who posted the information if it wanted to; she didn't have the skills to hide herself, so everything she did on the internet would leave a trace, but realizing this did not dampen her resolve.

And then, to her surprise, she pulled out her phone, found Artie in her contact list, and called him.

"Hi Artie."

Without missing a beat and responding as if he was expecting this call, Artie responded, "Well, if it isn't our sign raconteur," he said, going all French on her on the final syllable. "The woman who can single-handedly portray all things diabolic, fracking-wise, on a 4x6 cardboard canvas. To what do I owe the pleasure of this call?"

Ever the jokester. Not like her father, exactly, but she understood why she was seeking out Artie's advice before all others.

"I've landed on a gold mine of information. Complaints from people around the state related to fracking that the DEP is doing its best to not only ignore, but to bury from view. Hundreds of them, almost all of which the agency has found a way to put on hold for one reason or another."

Artie, who knew all too well how hard it was to get raw data of this kind, deliberately asked who had provided it to Nicole.

"You pretty sure this is reliable?"

"Without a doubt," Nicole said forcefully. There were things about Joe that annoyed her, even made her doubt his character at times, but he was nothing if not reliable. She laughed to herself at how defensive her last comment might have sounded.

Artie didn't say anything at first. He flitted through the catalog in his brain that contained forty years of pushing back against the forces of big business and a complicitous government, with nearly all of those actions ending in failure of one kind or another.

"Sounds like this can be a powerful tool, and an unprecedented one. What are you planning to do with it?"

"I've got access to a website for an anti-fracking organization. I'm planning to put all these cases out there. Probably lay them into a spreadsheet and make them sortable by date, type, location, and whatever else makes sense."

"What organization owns the website?"

Nicole could see no way around it. "2 Degrees."

"Haha," Artie roared, a response Nicole was grateful for, and she let her own laughter merge with his. "Yes, I seem to remember having some contact with them recently. They hijacked the demonstration very effectively, not that I minded. They got the blood flowing and kicked the conversation into a different gear, at least for a little while.

"After you put this stuff out on the web, what are you planning to do? You can't just release this into a vacuum. We need to actually do something with the information, or it won't have an effect. We need to make it *matter* to people and to corporations."

Nicole did not have to consider her response for long, realizing instantly the other reason for contacting Artie. "That's where you come in. You're better connected to anti-fracking groups than anyone I know. If you would spread the word to all your contacts, this thing might build some momentum."

"I see . . . tapping the experienced rabble-rouser who can still rally the troops. I might not be as spry as I was in my youth, but I still come in handy sometimes!"

"That's what I was thinking. I'm hoping you'll be willing to help—I don't think I can do this on my own," Nicole confessed.

"Of course! I'd be more than happy to do what I can!" he boomed, and then grew more serious. "You know, if this is as big as you say, it can really shake things up in ways no one's seen before. The powers-that-be don't like folks like you and me gumming up the works. You can't really keep information like this anonymous, not when the government and big business are involved. They could come after you, and I mean *really* come after you. Once you're in the crosshairs, they can make your life real unpleasant. I've been through the ringer once or twice so I know what to expect. I'm willing to risk that again because I know our cause is noble, but I want to make sure you're ready for the practical ramifications."

"I know. I've given that some thought," Nicole said. "It won't stop me, but I'd like to talk more about it with you so I can be totally ready for whatever they might throw at me."

"You bet. I'll do anything I can to get you prepared, and if you need help defining the message you want people to take away, I'm pretty good at that too."

'I'll keep that in mind. Thank you for offering to jump into this."

"With both hands and feet."

Nicole next contacted a few 2 Degrees members and told them what had dropped into her lap. One of the members, Adam, ran a PC repair shop. He hooked Nicole up with a maps-based software that Nicole installed on her PC. Within a few hours, she refined the application she would build. It contained a map of Pennsylvania which recognized all of its townships and boroughs, more than enough specificity for Nicole's purposes. She would load her database in such a way that complaints were categorized by health, quality of life, water contamination, status, event date, and whether fracking was specifically mentioned in the complaint. A single complaint could be put into more than one of these categories.

It took most of the day to configure the software. She turned to Joe's folder and pulled out the first complaint. The data entry form allowed a description, and she paraphrased the nature of the complaint. After hitting the save button, she returned to the map and saw in Sullivan County a red pushpin icon for the entry she'd made. The experience, the recognition, was thrilling. She clicked the icon and read the description of the event she had just entered before returning to her folder and going back to work.

It took most of a week to enter the data. At the end of the fifth day, she sat in front of her PC, sipping a beer, spinning through the various sort options. It was cruder than websites advertising vacation spots or available real estate, but functioned in much the same way and was just as intuitive. She had entered all 2,300 complaints that were included in the report.

She filtered the health complaint data into two-month increments during the prior year, and observed clusters of pushpins returned from some of these searches, most in the Marcellus fracking areas. The majority of all complaints were in the Marcellus area, the majority of resolved cases were not. She lost herself in this analysis, marveling at the story it conveyed.

The next day, she devoted herself to installing this application on the server that housed 2 Degree's website. After copying it, she put a link to it on the website's home page, built with a freeware tool she'd been using to perform simple maintenance to the site. She entitled the page, "The Health of Pennsylvania—Water and Air Problems Reported to the Pennsylvania Department of Environmental Protection." Below, she typed in these words: "The data contained in this map was derived from archival DEP sources."

She updated the home page with the new link at 9:00 PM. It had been a long day of work, but she felt a sense of accomplishment she had not experienced in a long time. She needed to share what she'd done, so she sent Artie an email with the website's URL and called him.

"Didn't catch you at a bad time, I hope. Not too late," she began.

"Quite alright," Artie said, "just warming some milk and nuking the hot pack."

"Got something to show you. You near your computer?"

"As a matter of fact, I am."

"I sent you an email with a link in it. Take a look."

"What have we here?" Artie said, performing his own analysis. It did not take him long to recognize what this amounted to.

"This is amazing. Not only are the analytics dead-on, but the details you've captured on the individual cases will validate them."

"That's what I thought too. It's good you feel the same way."

"Nicole," Artie said, deep concern registering in his voice, "I don't think you understand what you've got here. For a very long time, environmental groups across the state have been clamoring for a public registry of the health effects of fracking. The DEP has stone-walled this, giving all kinds of excuses, partly related to funding, but their main defense is that the information is stored away in some antiquated computer system they can't get information out of. Stupidest thing I ever heard, but I could pull up plenty of press clippings where they say just that. You're showing them and everyone else they've been lying to us."

"Wow! I figured this could get some attention, but had no idea how significant it was."

"It could go viral. You're probably breaking some laws. You could delete this post now and walk away from it. I wouldn't fault you if that's what you decide to do, but if you follow through with this, you need to be ready for a lot of pressure. You could be living in a shit-storm for quite a while."

Nicole paused before responding. She'd have been a fool not to. "Artie, when I first told you about this, I wanted you to make other groups aware of this information. Now that I heard all you had to say, I want you to blast this information from the rooftops."

"OK, darling," Artie said. "You'll get your wish. The hot pack and warm milk will have to wait. Don't expect to catch much sleep tonight. Got some agitatin' to do."

Immediately after they hung up, Nicole began to wonder what the morning would bring.

CHAPTER 22

Nicole slept poorly that night. Unconsciously, she swept her arm in the direction of the alarm clock, which was pounding through the layers of sleep suspending her. Her lurch into consciousness ended with a slap at the snooze button, but full consciousness occurred rapidly once the events of the previous day and her talk with Artie pierced the ether. She sat up in bed and didn't feel as driven to get to work as she had since her project started. Instead, she felt good in her aimlessness—good because she had done something important and courageous.

There were chores waiting to done, ones her mom had been kind enough to overlook. It was only during lunch when she took a break and opened her computer that she sensed the unfolding chain of events.

Artie rampaged across the state with his dispatches to environmental organizations, many of which she'd never heard of. She jumped over to 2 Degrees' website and accessed the hit counter that, on most days, barely registered a pulse. Today, there were 112 hits, and that sent a shiver through Nicole, validating her effort. It wasn't much in the grand scheme of things, but it meant their impact was growing.

She returned to Artie's emails and the threads spawned by them. In the latest, he called out the head of the DEP, and put his face inside a wanted poster. The caption called him a liar for saying this information was unavailable and said there would be groups of people tracking him wherever he went, demanding a response and an apology. Artie might not have become a member of the cloth, but he'd spent enough time in their service to learn how to do righteous indignation with the best of them.

She went back to work, but lacked focus and intensity; the afternoon dragged on until Artie called her.

"Well, it's started," he began.

"What has?" She had her suspicions, but wanted it spelled out for her.

"The powerful responses to your post. I sent you an email with links to blogs that are lit up with discussions about what you revealed. Also, I got an email from a reporter I know in the Scranton area. She's written a lot about fracking for the Scranton Times, and she'd like to interview you about your findings."

"Not sure what I'd have to say, except study the data and draw your own conclusions."

"There's plenty to say, and I can coach you if you'd like. More than anything, this is our chance for some mainstream coverage. That doesn't happen often, and is something we need to take advantage of when it's handed to us."

"OK, let's talk."

Artie told her about interviews he'd given the press, including tips on how to keep them on topic. He relayed sound bites she could fall back on if things were not going well. After they hung up, Nicole read through the blog posts he had sent her. These were on anti-fracking sites, so the comments were largely lauding the findings, validating long-held suspicions. When she was done, she picked up her phone and dialed the number Artie had given her.

"Hi," Nicole said, "I'm trying to reach Cheryl Leonard."

"Yes, this is Cheryl speaking."

"Hi, this is Nicole Marshall. Artie Landon suggested I call you."

"Oh yes, I'm glad to hear from you," Cheryl responded. Nicole thought her tone did not seem as glad as her words suggested, but maybe that's just how reporters were.

Cheryl was intent upon finding out whether this story was worth pursuing.

"Artie sent out an email that I was copied on. It contained a link to your post. Some very interesting data. Not sure if you realize it, but it's setting off quite a fire-storm." She had a direct, rapid-fire delivery that focused on the facts.

"When we spoke earlier, Artie compared it to a different type of storm," Nicole said with a chuckle. After a moment's hesitation, she added, "And I'm really glad to be the one stirring the pot."

Cheryl, an experienced beat writer, had been turning out a lot of copy about fracking in the Scranton area. She wasn't happy with the rapid growth and lack of controls at the drilling sites, and would jump at the chance to have hard data like what Nicole purported to have discovered, but how could it be accurate when so many environmental organizations couldn't pry the lid off the container concealing the information?

"I'm glad to hear that, because you may have to defend yourself against some tough questioning by powerful people who aren't happy you made it public. Artie's a good one to give you pointers on how to respond to confrontations like that." After drawing in a breath, she continued, "But, the real reason I asked to speak with you is I may want to write an article about you and the information you've posted. First thing I'd like to know is where you got this data. Who supplied it to you? This is definitely inside information."

"Sorry, that's something I'm just not going to divulge. I'm not going to put my sources' careers and welfare in jeopardy. I'm sure you can understand that," Nicole said firmly.

"Then, you can't substantiate it, and without that, it has no value," Cheryl shot back, jarring Nicole from her seemingly sure footing. She was playing Nicole, and Nicole didn't have the experience to rebuff or divert the challenge. But what she had was better.

"I don't agree. My report is gaining attention because it resonates with people. It reflects what people are experiencing in their lives and in their communities. If you say it's invalid, I say read the blogs, talk to the people making the comments. This is substantiated by the impacts that people have had to deal with! If the government has proof that my data is bad, let them make *that* public. Until then, there isn't a person alive that can discredit me or what I've posted."

Cheryl made her decision then. All of her journalistic sensors screamed this was an important story. Nicole was an unknown, not affiliated with any of the environmental groups she knew to be operating in the state, so she was something of a wild card, but her attitude was sincere, and she'd dropped a bombshell out of nowhere. Cheryl proceed with the interview, teasing out the back-story to help determine the direction of her reporting.

"We'll table the question of your source for now. What can you tell me about the data itself? What system did it come from?"

"All I'll tell you is that it came from a database in the DEP."

"OK," Cheryl responded, chafing a little, but resigned. "We'll go with that for now. So, when did you come in contact with the data? How did you decide to share it?"

"No real mystery there. After I looked it over, I knew people had to see it, because they needed to know they weren't alone. Their problems weren't all inside their head, as the government would have them believe."

"You're right about that," Cheryl said. "There's nothing like it. People all over Pennsylvania have been trying to break down the barriers to get to this type of information, to substantiate the anecdotal information, which is all we've had until now."

"So I've been told. Artie explained the trouble people have gone to."

Cheryl reflected on what she was hearing, allowing the structure of her article to come into focus. "It will be fun seeing the boys at DEP dance when I question them about what you've published," Cheryl said.

After a few moments of shared, quiet laughter, Cheryl continued, "What about you? What can you tell me about yourself that would help draw the reader into this?"

Nicole had already decided to not link her father's death to her activism, but saw no reason to not describe the way a fracking rig was set on her parents' property. She provided an overview of how it happened, and Cheryl viewed it as dramatic counterpoint to the information contained on the web site.

"The last thing I'd like to know about is your involvement with 2 Degrees. I'd never heard of them until I looked at your post. Read some of the other articles on it, followed its links. They seem a little out on the fringe . . . radical environmentalist types. Can you tell me something about them?"

"Not too much. I've just recently gotten involved with them. Haven't been in the anti-fracking movement that long, actually. They are more radical than most and are willing to perform acts of civil disobedience, but I can't give you a definite answer on what they've been engaged in. My guess is there's a lot of tough talk by some members, mostly because they don't have the power to do anything else. No one in power listens to them, so it's natural they act out a little."

"How about you? Have you performed acts of civil disobedience?"

"Only in my mind," Nicole said. "All talk to this point. Like most people."

Cheryl jotted notes. She could see 2 Degrees being a liability, but there was little to be done about it. She accepted that Nicole was innocent of any crimes, and still partially innocent of what she had stumbled into. It was one of the big draws of this story, and one she kept tossing around in her mind. She had worked with Artie on a few articles, and noted that she should call him to see if he could fill in more details about Nicole.

"Look, Nicole, this story's hot. Today is Tuesday, and I am going to push to get something in this Sunday's paper. Probably don't have the time to do the type of investigation needed for a full exposé. We're also looking at a lead editorial. Once it hits the street, there could be a lot of heat from those wanting to discredit it. This is all public record now. If I don't break this, someone else will, and they could be a lot less sympathetic than I am."

"Thanks, Cheryl. I get it. Artie said some of the same things. The answer is, I want this information to be publicly available, and I want the government to answer for it. If that means gaining some notoriety, I guess that's the price I have to pay."

Days passed. Nicole monitored the responses to her post on several environmental blogs. She sensed that the outrage had peaked and the response was trending downward. She didn't know what to expect, but this wasn't it, and she realized there was a degree of vanity in her response that she wasn't happy about.

Nicole and Cheryl did not speak after their initial conversation, which surprised and disappointed her. She came to expect she'd only be contacted if something developed with the story, and went about her normal business. Sunday came and she purchased a *Scranton Gazette*, almost as an afterthought. Nothing on the front page or local section. She turned to the editorial section, and there was a picture of Cheryl, older than she expected, beneath the heading, "Fracking Concerns Raised by Unofficial Health Registry."

She scanned the editorial before reading it again more carefully. It was all there and then some. Cheryl had attempted to get a statement from the DEP, but they refused to respond to data they said was either fabricated or illegally pulled from government records. Cheryl reported on several people who claimed they recognized their own complaints in the archive. They were all glad to see their cases represented here, because the government's response had been woefully inadequate, they said. They now felt some type of validation.

Cheryl identified Nicole as the author of the report and drew a personal profile of her that was so complimentary it made Nicole blush. She was described as brave and on the side of government transparency. But she didn't much like the discussion of Gabe's death, for it contained one critical mistake. Cheryl had reported Gabe's heart attack occurred while fighting with the fracking workers at the time the well blew out. *Who the hell told her this?* Nicole fumed.

She had not given Cheryl permission to include anything about her father. She straddled her fury with her overall positive feeling about the article. Then it hit her. It didn't matter what permission she gave. It was all out there. She was fair game. She was a target, and even in this friendly portrayal, there was an egregious error that probably would never be corrected.

———————

The first article was followed by others. The demands for information made to the Governor and the DEP escalated, and they still declined to respond to the assertions made by the data she published.

Surprisingly, Nicole remained a hot commodity, a rising star, at least in environmental circles. Her family's fracking-related tragedy resonated with the public, and she became inseparable from that.

The local media not only sought her out, but so did those in larger media markets. She gave interviews to alternative outlets in Philly and Pittsburgh, and then the mainstream networks followed. Her name was mentioned in direct questions to the Governor, questions like, "Why can't you provide an official health registry like the one Nicole Marshall supplied?" The attention was exhilarating, and Nicole needed to remind herself of her original reasons for exposing the information.

Today's interview was a special occasion. She was being interviewed by John Nichols, a young, charismatic documentary filmmaker. His first film about fracking, *Indecent Energy*, had garnered a reasonable level of success, but was eclipsed by other films that had come before his and covered much of the same material. He told Nicole the new film would not focus on the science or ethics of fracking, but dig deeply into the impacts of fracking on individuals and communities.

Most of Nicole's other interviews were conducted by phone, but John came out to Bountiful. Talking to the media had felt increasingly artificial for Nicole, and talking about the fracking rig, the data she posted, and the harmful effects on her community became topics she addressed practically by rote. In order to set the record straight, she breached her decision to not talk about Gabe's death, and now it was part of the cavalcade of questions she responded to. This topic, too, was losing its potency and charge, which scared her.

"As I mentioned on the phone, we're making a sequel to *Indecent Energy*," John explained. "I also told you we were more interested in the human impacts this time around. So, Nicole, if you wouldn't mind, we'd like you to take us for a walk around the property. Tom will follow you. He'll have a camera and record our conversation," he said, pointing to his lone companion. "We'll get to the health registry later, but first I'd like to learn about the events here at Bountiful that people have heard led to your activism."

Nicole studied John and determined he was a strange brew. His eyes had an easy going, even lazy quality, almost as if they could have been the inspiration for an R. Crumb poster, but his speech was clipped, in control. He had started his crusade as a victim of fracking, like many others in his community, but his years in front of the camera, in the midst of the debate, had caused him to internalize the attitudes conducive to the twenty-four-hour news cycle. Nicole considered this dissonance, then let it go and began their tour.

They started by the cabins. It was late summer, the normal time for them to be shuttered. There had been rain the night before, and the clouds still partially shielded the sun. Dew-wet melancholy, the patter of condensing drops from eaves and leaky gutters. A chill. The smell of pine. Nicole could sense these things whole that so recently had been shattered.

"The cabins were empty more than 50 percent of the time this summer. Something that never happened before," Nicole explained, as they stood in front of one of them. The camera panned the front. A small porch beside the entrance, rustic clapboard siding that needed a coat of white paint every five years, a roof standing beneath towering pines sprouting seedlings that needed to be dislodged each year.

"We won't be able to continue this way, and we're not sure what we'll do instead. Even if we wanted to sell the land, we couldn't get much of anything for it. Not since the well went in."

This interview felt different to her. It was being here, walking the grounds, that allowed her to loosen her grip on her emotions, re-experience the deep memories this place held for her, and with John's able guidance, letting her thoughts meander down these byways.

They stood admiring the simple structure, the stillness in the air that provided a deeper focus and appreciation.

"So what was it like up here for you before fracking moved in? How would you describe the change?"

"Summers were always hectic when I was growing up. My parents worked all the time, and I guess I would have liked to have had more of their time, their attention. I had more surrogate parents and adopted brothers and sisters than I could count."

She was lost in her reverie. The camera panned to her and her expression showed the nearness of her memories. "So many of the same families came up every year when I was young. We'd play in the pool, in the woods and stream, from morning till night. They'd take me on day trips to see the sites in the area. It was a good life, one I thought I'd inherit when I moved back up here, but that's all gone now."

They walked the horse-shoe dirt road along which the cabins were situated. Nicole recounted stories of times past, things she had not considered for many years, and unearthing this buried treasure sent a swirl of emotion through her that was difficult to contain.

The road led back to the fields and the fracking rig, a towering, menacing presence.

"This is the path my father took the day he died. They came in after the fact and removed the top layers of dirt that had been covered with fracking fluid and replaced it with better dirt, or so we're told. My dad had been watching them drill from the house. He sensed a disturbance, but couldn't have known right away a blowout had occurred."

She was caught up in Gabe's final moments, coming as close to them as she'd ever been.

"He loved this land like it was one of his children. It's hard to explain. As he walked towards the chaos at the rig, the fracking fluid flowed toward him. Desolation and rage—I'm sure those were the things he felt. So much that it burst his heart."

Verbalizing this overwhelmed Nicole. She broke down standing near the spot where Gabe had fallen. John motioned to Tom to stop the camera and directed Tom back to their van.

John approached Nicole, who had squatted to touch the ground. He stood by her for a minute until her crying subsided. He took her hands and guided her to her feet. He put his arms around her and gave her a deep hug. He pulled back enough so that they were able to look at each other.

"I'm so sorry, but hearing you tell that was overwhelmingly powerful," he said, moving in tentatively to kiss her.

His action confused and then infuriated her. "That is not what this is all about," Nicole spat out. Or was it, for him?

The interview was over. She pulled back from the embrace and walked towards the house. As far as Nicole was concerned, he could do with the footage whatever he wanted.

Nicole was ushered into a room at a local TV news station where a microphone was promptly strapped onto her. When the time came, she would be told to look into the monitor. The room was dank, and she suspected mold grew behind the fake wood paneling covering the walls. Graham, the technician at the news station, assisted her, proceeding with the setup without uttering one more word to Nicole than necessary. She was to be interviewed by Don Lemon, the breathy and earnest news anchor on CNN. She hoped this would be the end of it.

Two minutes before the interview started, powerful lights were turned on and directed at her. Surprised, she turned to look at them and was blinded momentarily. Graham, behind a glass enclosure, interacted with his CNN counterpart.

"Time to look into the monitor. The interview will start in twenty seconds." Two full sentences from Graham. Astonishing!

Don introduced Nicole briefly. She only had an audio hookup and the lack of visual cues was disorienting. Don then went on to introduce the other members of the panel, which was alarming to Nicole because she had been unaware she'd be part of a panel discussion.

"Also joining us is Ralph Ditmer from The Sustainable Gas Drilling Coalition, a consortium of gas companies working in the Marcellus region looking to pursue their business in responsible ways. He will help flesh out some of the questions raised by the publication of Ms. Marshall's findings. Also joining us here in the studio is Jeffrey Toobin, CNN's lead legal analyst.

"Let me start with you, Nicole. Your posting of water-related complaints in Pennsylvania has stirred up quite a ruckus, and gone viral in the environmental community and elsewhere. The response can't be attributed solely to the content. People have also responded to your story, and the story of your family. The flip side is the Pennsylvania state government's response, or lack of one. They refuse to comment on the legitimacy of your findings."

"That's right," Nicole responded. " I think that's because they know my data is correct and they have no way to respond and not look like they're hiding something."

"That is flat out wrong," Ditmer interjected. The screen flipped to the two remote panelists, split side by side.

"The state did not respond because they did not want to validate you and what you posted. If they did that, they'd have to respond to every crank caller and doomsday accusation. They are not going to do that—no way, no how—nor should they."

"This is different," Nicole said, utilizing one of Artie's talking points. "The response from people has been overwhelmingly in favor of disclosure by the government, of making this information available in a transparent way."

Don Lemon reasserted himself in the interview. "Now, Nicole, we are all aware of the," a pause to sniff at a passing scent or spirit, "tragedy experienced by your family recently. A fracking rig placed on your property against your will and the accident that occurred on it, the downturn of business at the resort your family runs on this property, and of course your father's death that may have been, at least in part, caused by these events."

He stopped again, a slight smile suggesting he was pleased with his deconstruction of events. "What would you like to say about these experiences? How have they shaped your current actions?"

"I'm sure my life would be different had those things not happened, but they did and I'm here now. People have responded to the information I made available. It has grown larger than me. I'm happy to have contributed in this way."

Lemon spoke again and the screen shifted back to the studio. "I'd like to bring in Jeffrey at this time and ask him about the legal implications of Nicole publishing this information."

"Well," Jeffrey began, "there are concerns for sure." He paused to consider, performed his characteristic eye roll, and pushed back a lock of hair that had dislodged from his carefully coifed, upwardly extending mane. "The fact that so many people see their own cases in the data is something I would worry about. That could lead to lawsuits if privacy rights have been violated. I know the Pennsylvania state government is looking into whether the extraction and publication of confidential data was performed illegally. If they find any infractions, I'm sure they will prosecute. The fact that Ms. Marshall has not been forthcoming regarding the source of her information does not help her cause, either."

"I expect the government to do what they can to discredit me." Nicole said. "What else can they do? But they're the ones that should be put on trial. If we can't get them in the courtroom, people can voice their concerns in different ways. Look at the discussions on the internet. People are really scared that fracking is degrading their health in a number of ways, and no one can put the lid back on the box now that it has been opened."

"I'd like to get back to your complaint about the state not providing this data to the public.," Ditmer broke in, trying to veer the discussion in a direction he could control. "That is coming. They are working on that, and did not need you to tell them to do so. I'm not sure how your *overwhelming* public support squares with recent poll results. Most of the complaints I saw on your report are about things like too much dust in the air. People get over things like that. What is relevant is that 71% of people in your area are in favor of continued and expanded gas drilling in the Williamsport area. Or don't you care about what the people in your community want?"

"Of course I care. They're my neighbors. Where do you live?" Nicole continued without waiting for Ditmer to respond. "When the only jobs left are flipping each other's burgers, you're forced to make decisions you might not want to make."

"Do you care enough about getting your way to break the law and perform acts of violence to promote your cause?" Ditmer pursued.

This was the first time Nicole hesitated, and it said as much about what she believed as anything that would follow. She displayed a thoughtful expression a more accomplished interviewee would have disguised. The eyes of the other panelists and the viewing public were focused on her. When she finally responded, she said, "No, I wouldn't do that," in a way that was not altogether believable.

"Had to think about that, didn't you?" Ditmer was absolutely gleeful. Game, set, and soon, match! He had deflected the conversation from its primary topic to one of Nicole's personal beliefs, and her uncertainty glistened like an open wound. In the world they inhabited, ambiguity equated to failure. His goals were within reach.

"Well, it's good to hear you're not planning to break any more laws, at least not right away. The reason I asked is I read some of the articles on the website where your data was posted and found them very disturbing. I also noticed the banner on the page with your data contains the phrase, 'Live Above the Earth.' What exactly does that mean?"

"For one thing, it means we should stop all the toxic underground mining being performed every day and exploit above-ground sources of energy like solar and wind."

It was Ditmer's turn for an eye roll, which was quickly replaced by an avuncular attitude. "There are so many problems with that whimsical notion, I'm not sure how to respond. To start, where would you get the material to build the solar panels and wind turbines? You need metals mined from beneath the ground."

"Not sure that's true. Have you looked in the junk yards across the country? I bet there's enough metal and other raw materials in them to create all the solar panels and turbines we'll need for a very long time."

"Well, that's a new one. Transforming our economy and energy supply by picking through garbage," Ditmer was dismissive, condescending.

"Not so new. Do the research. This is the world of the future. The idea that you can continue growing forever is a thing of the past, and we need to replace it with more sustainable ways of thinking."

"Which I guess explains some of the incendiary material on your website," said Ditmer. He had found his target and dropped his payload. "Like links to interviews with Derrick Jensen, for instance. That guy is a nut-job. He advocates violence to overthrow western civilization. One of your original Luddites. Is this the direction you think we should move in?"

Again, Nicole hesitated. "I don't know. When I figure it out, I'll tell you. What I do know is the world you promote is not the one I want to live in. You self-satisfied, high-paid lobbyists for the gas industry are a cancer with nothing better to do but discredit the legitimate concerns of people who don't have much of anything, including power. I would rather stand with them than alongside you and the sleazy business elite you're a lackey for."

"OK," Lemon said. "I think we need to shut this thing down before you two turn this into a barroom brawl."

That was it. Lemon offered some parting lines of thanks, then the phone line went dark. Graham disconnected her and wordlessly exited the room. She was empty, shaken. The news cycle had chewed her up and spit her out. She could not remember the contents of the discussion, but had a clear feeling it had been diverted from the important topics she wanted to discuss. What good had she accomplished? And at what cost to herself? She stood up shakily and walked out the door. She felt totally exposed and the fight was drained out of her.

"You done good, girl," said Artie, who called early the next morning.

Nicole, asleep when the call came in, managed to get the phone to her ear.

"Hi, Artie," she mumbled.

"You helped to put our cause on the map," Artie said, ever upbeat.

"It didn't go the way I expected."

"Never does. You try to keep things on track, but the people on the other side have different agendas and try to move the conversation where they're most comfortable." Artie paused and let out a big laugh. "Happens every time. That guy last night was so desperate, all he had left was to attack you personally. Most people will see through that."

"I hope so," Nicole said, not sure she hadn't squandered a big opportunity.

"Anyway, take a look at your email," Artie said, on the move again. "This is just the start. We need to capitalize on this. Organize another rally. Strike while the fire's hot. Don't know if you're aware of it, but they're talking about building a refinery in Williamsport that can transform fracking gas to liquid gas. Huge, crazy project. We have got to come out in force against it."

"If you say so, Artie," and she smiled for the first time since the debacle the night before. The exposure she felt would heal, but first she would roll over in bed and let sleep pull her back down, away from this next wave of activity that she seemed destined to be carried away in.

Nicole hopped onto her computer and navigated to 2 Degrees' website, curious to see the level of activity after her interview. Her credentials failed when she tried to access the admin page. She tried a couple more times, unsuccessfully, and wondered if the site was partially down. She called Lia to see if she knew what was going on.

"Hi Lia, I tried logging into 2 Degrees' admin page but couldn't get in.

Could you login and see if my account is locked?"

"It's locked alright," Lia said in a cold, threatening way. "Permanently."

"How's that?" Nicole asked, incredulous.

"You know, after your performance last night, we can't take a chance with you."

"What does that mean? You make it sound like I sold us out. You think it was fucking easy, getting out there in front of everyone, talking to those clowns?"

"Not only do I think it's easy, but it's something I would welcome and would have done a much better job given the chance. More than anything, you let the discussion get personal. Don't you know this fight is bigger than you? Bigger than any one of us? We are all just agents of historical forces that we try to bend towards equality, justice. How dare you allow it to be trivialized with the insignificant circumstances of your own life?"

"Sounds like your biggest problem is that it wasn't you being interviewed. It's all about *the movement* as long as your ego's being fed. You're jealous, and just making up activist nonsense to hide it. . . . But the report is mine. The data is mine. I have the right to manage it and respond to questions."

"Sorry, I'm the moderator of the website, and I decide who gets to work on it and who doesn't. And you've lost that privilege. In fact, your attendance at 2 Degrees meetings will also cease immediately."

"Who gave you the right to banish people? Who gave you that power?"

"I'm warning you: Don't show your face at one of our meetings. If you do, it won't turn out well for you."

The line went dead. Nicole couldn't believe she was now being threatened by those she'd considered her allies.

CHAPTER 23

"How's our dog and pony show shaping up?" Senator Bain asked Joe.

"So good," Joe replied, "that if Rockwell doesn't build the refinery, I might just do it myself."

The senator gave Joe a querulous look, but it did not register with Joe, who was lost in the plans he and Reid had devised. He continued, oblivious, "In less than two weeks, we'll be hosting some of the most powerful people in the energy industry. The CEO of Rockwell will make a speech, as will the Governor. As the state representative from Williamsport, you'll be expected to offer your perspective on why Williamsport is the best place for the plant. And Bill O'Brien, the Chamber of Commerce president, will hit the same themes from the business side.

"Some of the major businesses in the area have agreed to give their employees time off to attend. The high school marching band is even coming to start things off; it'll be a community affair!"

"Sounds like you've thought of everything," the senator said, though his tone suggested ambivalence.

"Just about. Still looking for some babies for you to kiss as you wade through the crowd," Joe said, joking.

They both laughed easily, giving them a pause, which the senator used as a segue to what was really on his mind.

"What was it you said?" Senator Bain asked, slouching back deep in his chair, an unusual position for him, "You know, about building the plant yourself if Rockwell doesn't do it? Where did that idea come from?"

This was an unexpected question, one Joe needed to consider before answering. "It didn't come from anywhere, really. Thought maybe I'd get a laugh out of it."

Senator Bain took a moment. "That's what I figured, Joe. Probably not worth worrying about. But for weeks, I haven't been able to get rid of these gas guys and their consultants. Now, during the last few days, they've gone dark; they won't answer their phones or return my emails. Just when we should be charging towards the finish line, they've disappeared. How about you? Your access cut off?"

"Reid told me a couple of days ago he'd been given an urgent new assignment. I didn't mind because I knew I had things under control. I expected to get some feedback on a couple of loose ends, but you're right, I haven't heard a word. It started annoying me."

They looked at each other for a moment but then looked away. Neither wanted to consider the questions expressed on the face of the other.

Later that day, Joe sat at his desk reading Harrisburg's local newspaper, *The Patriot News*. The front page lead article addressed the possibility of a gas to liquid plant being built in Williamsport. It conveyed the basic facts reasonably well and contained a discussion of the event demonstrating local support for the project. The location for both the proposed refinery and event was an industrial site west of Williamsport.

A picture of what remained of Shenandoah Industries was provided; the unoccupied buildings there showed the decay you'd expect from twenty years of abandonment. They would be razed and replaced with an industrial complex containing the latest fuel conversion technology. It would sit alongside a Norfolk Southern train line used to transport the fuel after it was liquefied. The estimated cost for the project was $2.5 billion.

The article did transition to the growing popular resistance to the plan. The resistance to fracking in general had spiked since the publication of, as yet, uncorroborated data related to the health impact from fracking in Pennsylvania. This had proved to be a springboard for environmentalists, who coalesced against the plans for the refinery.

Joe had been only dimly aware of the growing backlash from the opposition. He became drenched in sweat as he considered a nightmare of his own making. He walked into the hallway and, without thinking, pulled out his phone and called Reid.

"Sorry, I've been incredibly busy," Reid said before Joe even had a chance to voice his complaints. Joe hadn't expected Reid to answer; he had planned on leaving a simple voicemail, but now had to figure out how to express what was on his mind.

"I'm not in Harrisburg right now. Still down in Maryland on an account needing urgent attention," Reid said. "I'll be back tomorrow night. We have a lot to talk about. You available for dinner tomorrow?"

Conversations like this with Reid pissed Joe off. This was by far the largest project Joe had ever managed. He and Reid had been working side by side, and then *poof*, all of a sudden he was flying solo, forced to make decisions he was uncomfortable with. Then, when Reid decided to acknowledge him, he was back directing the exchange between them, undervaluing the difficult position he'd placed Joe in.

"I suppose. Yeah, we can meet for dinner, but I have some critical issues I'd like to run by you regarding the logistics of the event in Williamsport on Tuesday."

"I understand, sure, but let's hold them. I think we'll be able to clear them up over dinner."

"OK," Joe said. He wasn't going to beg for the man's attention.

"How about we meet at The Hill at seven? I'm buying."

Joe's eyebrows rose. This would not be the normal 2nd Street bar run dinner. More upscale than he could afford, which is why he had never eaten there before.

"OK, I'll keep things rolling until then."

"Great. Looking forward to getting together."

The phone clicked off before Joe could even utter a goodbye.

For an emergency meeting of 2 Degrees, eight members sat around in the back room of Trucker's bar. Lia called the meeting to order at the appointed time, 7:00 PM.

"I scheduled this meeting to discuss recent events and our options moving forward," Lia said. She chose not to explain her other reason for the meeting. The group had grown flabby, which Nicole's free-wheeling antics had proved. Discipline needed to be reasserted.

"The name of our group is known to more people than ever before, and we need to take advantage of that. Other groups are planning a big counter rally at the site of the proposed gas-to-liquid refinery. We need to make a statement. The impetus for the demonstration came from information posted on our website, so we need to clarify who we are, and differentiate ourselves from those afraid to see our adversaries for what they are. We need to call out the evil in our society and make clear we're prepared to fight against it. 2 Degrees has recently been coopted by media attention, and we can't allow our thoughts and actions to be filtered."

Sherri broke in. "Not following you, Lia. You must be talking about Nicole's interviews. She held her own on CNN. That was an experienced lobbyist she was up against. She did OK."

"She sounded like a school girl and made 2 Degrees look like any of a hundred other environmental groups out there playing nice with the existing power structure. We all know where that leads: becoming coopted and inactive. We need to remain pure."

Purity was Lia's mantra and, in her obedience to process, she resembled the capitalists she abhorred. Metrics catalyzed both, and reasonableness was a sign of weakness. Lia personally suffered from what she called chronic Lyme disease. Each day, she woke to the tightening grip of a disease that the medical establishment denied existed. She had fought with the doctors, but now realized they were just as culpable as all of the other power brokers and eschewed their advice, preferring to consult every source of alternative medicine she gleaned from her internet odyssey. Her joints ached a little more each day, her energy diminished, and it was only her determination to struggle and fight, that kept her from being defeated by the disease's determination to overwhelm her.

"What good are we if we act like every other environmental group pandering to the elites?" said Craig, one of Lia's main supporters. "Nicole and her health registry," Lia said, diminishing their relevance, and continued the attack. "Most people only get involved when they're affected personally, and then they disappear when that threat fades from view. That's not who we are! We recognize the larger societal injustices in play, and are motivated by them, sacrificing ourselves to correcting these misdeeds."

"Where is Nicole, anyway?" Sherri asked. "I, for one, would like to congratulate her, so I'm glad she's not here to listen to this."

"She won't be joining us," said Lia. "We spoke on the phone a couple of days ago. She's become a real diva with all this media hype. I told her this was no place for that. She got more upset and told me she was finished with 2 Degrees. Just as well from my point of view, considering how poorly she handled the CNN interview."

Sherri remained quiet after that. She would follow-up with Nicole, but for now watched and listened. She had been reluctant to consider something she now couldn't deny. Those sitting around her did not want alliances—not with ordinary people anyway. They were cloaked in their separateness, purity, and absolute certainty that they knew what was best, not just for themselves, but especially for those sitting outside their circle. This circle was constricting, hardening like a reptile's spiky armor, expelling impure modes of thinking. Sherri shrunk away from the group as they made plans that would disrupt not only the event, but the larger counter-demonstration.

On her way back from the meeting, Sherri called Nicole.

"How you doing, girl?" Sherri asked.

"OK, I guess. Trying to get back to normal." Since her talk with Lia, Nicole had turned her back on the world. She avoided the internet and only answered calls from people she knew and wanted to speak to. Instead, she threw herself into the work around the lodge, including painting one of the cabins.

"Just got out of a 2 Degrees meeting and couldn't believe what I heard."

Nicole considered the various ways to respond and then merely said, "I think Lia's upset it wasn't her being interviewed."

"I'm sorry. I know how she can be. I think the struggle is all she's got, and that's become unhealthy for her."

"I agree, but there's nothing I can do about it. I don't feel bad really. I don't think 2 Degrees was a good fit for me. Something else would have happened to cause me to part ways with them."

"I know what you mean. I expect I will be following you through the exit door," Sherri responded thoughtfully.

Half in jest, Nicole said, "I'm surprised I wasn't shunned . . . that you're allowed to talk to me."

"Very nearly. You can relax. No fatwa was placed on your head by our supreme leader," Sherri said, glad to make a joke of it.

Nicole redirected the conversation to an idea she'd been considering the last couple of days, one which she had already passed by her mom.

"Actually, I've been thinking of giving you a call to run an idea by you. The demonstration is scheduled for the week after next. Do you think the Fire Calling folks would be interested in attending? The cabins are empty right now. They could stay in them or camp out on the property if they prefer. I keep thinking about how great the festival was for me. I could use being around that spirit again."

"That's a great idea, Nicole," Sherri said after giving it some thought. "I'm sure some people will be interested. Let me think about how to get the word out. I'll give you a call in the morning and we can work out the details."

"I really appreciate it," Nicole said. It pumped her up in a way that was unfamiliar. It wasn't driven by politics, but she was engaged in a way that felt real and substantial.

The other side of the river had all the appearances of a rundown strip-mall. Route 11/15 abutted the Susquehanna River, strangling access to it, and making it easy to forget the natural beauty that had been sacrificed. Joe surveyed the other side of the road that contained the mash-up of fast food, car parts, and assorted businesses residing in the half-emptied malls. Acres of unused parking space, cracked and in disrepair, separated him from these places of commerce.

Then he made a quick turn up an incline and was met by a different atmosphere: high-class, elite style dining. The Hill served the best steaks around; scallops in exotic mushroom sauce, the edgiest item on the menu; and more martinis and Manhattans than at any restaurant in the vicinity.

All of this made sense to Joe. Every seat of power needed such places.

Sufficiently out of the glare, they provided big-time players the safe havens where they could consider and discuss options outside close scrutiny. They were places of understated wealth that fed the egos of those who'd acceded to power, and ignited a thirst in those in pursuit of it. Joe wore a charcoal gray suit, understanding perfectly what was expected.

Reid sat waiting for Joe and motioned to him when Joe walked through the entrance. Reid rose from his restaurant seat as Joe walked through the entrance and approached.

Joe's animus for Reid quickly melted away. It was hard to hold onto ill feelings for him. Reid had on a dark blue sports jacket that accentuated his blue eyes, which seemed like an opening to an expanse of sky or sea. His curly black hair fell easily about his head. His smile radiated as he welcomed Joe.

"Sorry to have been out of touch the last few days. I was called in on a really high profile account. Been working day and night on it," Reid said, again, offering this as an apology. A bottle of wine sat on the table. A glass of it had been poured for Reid, but it did not appear to have been touched yet.

"I get it. You've got competing assignments to attend to like the rest of us, but there are a couple of things I would like to run by you. I'm hoping we can get through them tonight, or at least set the groundwork for what needs to get done."

"Sure, sure," Reid laughed, "we'll get to that, but let's enjoy our meal a little first." Reid motioned to the wine, and Joe nodded his head.

Joe avoided bringing up the current status of their activities, but that was how they interacted, and he wasn't sure what else to talk about.

"Get whatever you want," Reid said, "This won't show up on any Distincture expense report." Joe took him at his word and ordered the filet.

"The last time I was here was with the Governor and a senior VP at Distincture," Reid said. "You should have seen how they ran up that bill. I would not have wanted to be on the hook to pay that one."

The wine had started to send its warmth through Joe's body. It was different, better than any he'd ever tasted. He was tempted to describe the experience, but realized he didn't have the vocabulary to do so. This clumsy statement from Reid was not like him at all, and Joe looked at him quizzically, unable to stifle a condescending laugh.

"You're right," Reid said, "Stupid comment. Not sure where that came from."

Then Reid rallied, "Actually, yes I do. There is something I want to discuss with you." Reid took a long draw from his wine before proceeding.

"I've been down in Cove Point, Maryland the last few days. Ever hear of it?"

Joe shook his head slowly, his interest engaged.

"Cove Point is a port town on the Chesapeake Bay. We finished up a deal for a pipeline. It will bring the gas from all points north to the shipping terminal there, and that is where it will be converted to liquid."

Reid waited for the news to sink in. He did not need to wait long.

"So the plans to build the refinery in Williamsport or any of the other Pennsylvania locations are dead?"

"Correct."

"Now I understand your lack of interest in our project the last few days," Joe said with caustic laughter.

"I just do what they tell me," Reid said unconvincingly. "Rockwell got some major concessions for this plan. They've been looking at this a long time, but both Maryland and Pennsylvania were placing road blocks on the pipelines."

The cells of the Rubic's cube spun into alignment for Joe, even through the wine haze. "I'm starting to get it. All the planning, the rising expectations. It was all a ploy orchestrated by Rockwell to get what they wanted all along."

"I really can't say. No one expressed that to me, and it was not my place to ask."

Joe understood the rules of etiquette to which Reid alluded.

"But think of it from a business perspective," Reid said by way of explanation. "If you can get the gas to the terminal without requiring the transition to rail, you're saving a ton of money."

This rang true to Joe. The logic was inescapable. How he had not seen it coming was something of an embarrassment. He drank from his glass again, but it lacked all depth and mystery this time.

The food came and little was said. Joe resolved to eat and enjoy his meal as best he could, and then get out of there. Midway through dinner, Reid sent the conversation in a new direction.

"I could have called you to give you this news. Hell, I could have not said anything and let you find out when it was announced tomorrow."

This was true, and Joe felt some appreciation for Reid's actions.

"Truth is, I've enjoyed working with you," Reid said. "You might think you needed to confer with me on some issues you're sorting through, but you don't. I've watched you sit in meetings where people get long winded and say way more than necessary. With a line or two, you bring it back to where the discussion needs to be. Then you go out and do what needs to get done."

Reid paused and drank deeply again from his glass.

"I won't be doing this work much longer," Reid said. "They've got other plans for me." There was no boasting here, but plenty of power rippling through each word. "Usually, you can't teach what you're capable of doing, and I'm going to need people with your skills. People who can make sure things get done unobtrusively, the way they need to get done. . . . What are you making now? Sixty grand or thereabouts?"

Joe shrugged his shoulders in a way that neither denied nor confirmed Reid's assertion.

"How about you take a job with Distincture. I can offer you 120K to start. Things work out, there will be another twenty grand in a year. You'll work hard and travel a lot, at first anyway. Some of it will be grunt work, but you'll be in the middle of things, big things."

Joe sat back in his chair. Staffers dreamed of conversations like this, and now he couldn't find a single word with which to respond.

When Reid realized Joe was stunned silent, he spoke again, "It's OK. Take some time. I won't be able to make an actual offer for a month or so. Things are being put in place for me now so I won't need to know your decision for two, three weeks."

Finally Joe responded, "You're right. We did good work together, and I enjoyed it. Whatever happens, I want you to know I appreciate the compliment and the job offer."

They both got something from the conversation, not necessarily what they wanted, but enough so that when they turned their attention back to the meal, they fully appreciated it. Even their conversation resumed the bantering quality they were used to, avoiding the explosive topics crowding their minds.

———————

The next morning Joe arrived at work and booted up his laptop. He was not surprised to find an IM from Senator Bain, asking Joe to come to his office.

"I always try to maintain a degree of healthy skepticism," Senator Bain said, expressing his unwinding thoughts after Joe took a seat across from him, "But that's not really who I am. I'm a dreamer, and I let this dream take hold of me."

Senator Bain sat a few feet back from his desk, his legs spread lengthwise as if a strong wind had pushed straight into him, with his heels anchoring him against further blowback. An email from Reid's boss had been opened. Joe sat across from him and marveled at how shell-shocked he looked.

"I know. I found out last night. Reid told me." Joe had rehearsed what he would and would not say to Senator Bain, and modulated this when he saw what state the senator was in.

"Says they will be pursuing as yet unspecified alternatives for transforming the gas into liquid."

"Reid specified it for me," Joe said, replying cautiously. "They are sending the gas all the way from the fracking regions to Cove Point, Maryland via pipeline. That's a shipping port, and also where it will be refined."

Bain took a minute to let this settle in and follow the logic of Joe's comments.

"Probably what they wanted all along."

"Apparently," Joe said, agreeing without wanting to.

"So they've been playing us."

"It would appear so."

They were both left feeling foolish while Joe sheltered one piece of information—the job offer—from his longtime boss.

Word of the gas-to-liquid plant quickly reached the Williamsport com-munity. The scions of business were lining up behind it. On the other side, the fervor Nicole had kicked up had not abated. Calls for government trans-parency peaked and continued to find new outlets, resonating in different organizations.

Artie was spearheading a counter-demonstration. He produced flyers with slogans like, "We need to overwhelm them." And, "If they get a thousand people to come out in support, we need two thousand telling them we're not interested in their dirty technology." He painted a vision of hell in his emails, his rallying cries. He described pipelines from all over the state funneling combustible gas into their community, providing clips of pipeline explosions erupting into mushroom-shaped fireballs.

Other themes were the pollution dangers the refinery would bring, and the desolation left behind when the gas dried up. This was the moment when the moral fiber of the community would finally rise up and push back against the aggressive overreach of the multinationals. It was not long before the news of the event and counter-demonstration gained statewide and even national attention.

Artie had stayed on top of the news feeds, but like everyone else of this era, siloed himself within those news outlets corresponding to his own point of view. He felt totally unmoored when the news arrived.

He'd won. The corporate interests were beaten back. He read the news accounts coming across the line. Each one talked about Rockwell stepping away from their plans to build the refinery in Williamsport. The primary rea-son given was the widespread and growing opposition of the local population.

Artie, who had never seen them flinch, could never claim victory. For the people he served, things were either not quite bad enough that they'd turn and bite the hand that controlled them, or their circumstances were so bad their concerns never ventured beyond life support. He never wanted for things to get worse, but he was tempted to think about what that might mean every time a union vote went against him, or a demonstration or Saul Alinsky workshop was poorly attended. He went where the fight took him, and environmental activism was where the resistance was now. Even if his allies were mostly white and middle class, the adversaries were the same, and he knew them well.

He was embarrassed by the emotion. There were even a couple of tears. *What was that about?* he wondered. He cradled his head in his hands, feeling something like redemption.

"We did it, young lady," Artie said.

"What's that, Artie?" Nicole responded.

"Guess you haven't heard: Rockwell and its cretins have pulled away from building the refinery."

"Wow, that's amazing news."

Artie filled her in on the details of Rockwell's decision before saying, "You had a lot to do with this. The information you published galvanized people together. We need to capitalize on this! I'm wondering if we can still have the demonstration, but with a different theme. Maybe we go after fracking altogether."

Instead of gearing up, Nicole was looking forward to backing off, looking around her, reassessing her options.

"Can't see how you do that," she responded without speaking to what she was feeling. "The demonstration's just a week away. You can't refocus it on a new topic and expect it to work. The threat we were fighting has disappeared. People are looking to celebrate, not go to another demonstration."

Within moments, his brain waves were synapsed along different pathways, "You're right. That's what we'll do. We'll turn this into a huge victory celebration."

The further Artie went in this direction, the further Nicole moved in the other. She needed a break. Her energy for planning events such as this had left her, and she would not commit to being actively involved. She listened to Artie recharging his batteries by looking for new ways to rally people, and sensed how distasteful the prospects of taking part in this felt to her.

"So why didn't you call and tell me the news?" Nicole asked, feigning annoyance.

Joe, on the other end, was at work and got up from his seat.

"Hey, Nicole," Joe said. "Wait a minute while I find some place where we can talk."

He wasn't looking forward to this conversation and walked out of the office and into the hallway, remaining quiet until he rested his back against a wall in a vestibule he used sometimes to clear his head. They'd stayed in contact after he'd given her the health registry information, talking on the phone frequently. Their disagreements were replaced by a bond of trust that nurtured their affection, and a deeper understanding between them, but this was onerous beyond imagining for him. He did not know how to break the news to her.

"It was all a sham," he finally said when he collected himself.

Nicole, assuming he was referring to how disingenuous the gas companies had been, still did not get it. After hesitating, she said, "They were all ready to barge in and we sent them packing. Not sure how but we did it."

"There's more to it than that."

"What do you mean?" Nicole said, beginning to sense the possibility of a different narrative.

"All along, they were playing us—all of us."

"News articles say they wanted to look elsewhere because of community pressures."

In addition to what Reid told him, Joe was listening to his own silos of information, the stories spun in the mainstream media. News from those outlets provided a scattershot of reasons for Rockwell turning away, from the glut of fracking gas and the resulting downturn in gas prices to Rockwell choosing to pursue other business opportunities at this time. So there were at least three versions of truth and Joe, like the purveyors of those other narratives, was certain that his version alone was accurate.

"I've researched this company and I can tell you nothing much gets in their way once they've decided they want something. Truth is, their plan to build the plant in Williamsport was a bargaining chip for what they really wanted, which are pipelines from all over Pennsylvania down to Cove Point, Maryland. And guess what? They've secured concessions from Pennsylvania and Maryland to do just that. Going to build those pipelines over people's properties and public spaces whether those people want it or not. As I said, we were all pawns in their game."

Nicole was tired of being whipsawed around, but she was getting used to it. "That totally sucks. I mean really. What the fuck are these guys thinking?"

"They're thinking about making money and increasing their market share," Joe said, stating the obvious.

"And they don't care who they step on."

"There will be winners and losers, just like there's always been."

Joe had begun walking and now stood in the rotunda. He tried to look through the same eyes he had fifteen years before on his fifth grade trip. As a boy, he'd been taken in by the murals, the strength of the historical images, but now he looked at the words printed along the circumference of the lower balcony, the only ones visible to him, "that we may do the thing that is truly wise and just," and wondered what, if anything, they had come to mean.

Nicole took a couple hours to digest Joe's message before calling Artie.

"Hey Artie, I just spoke with someone in Harrisburg who works in the state government about Rockwell bailing out."

"This would be your Deep Throat?"

"It would."

"And in what way did this person enlighten you?"

Nicole recounted the information to Artie and waited for a response. This was certainly unwelcome news, and Artie took some time to shuffle the deck.

"No offense, Nicole, but I'm not willing to say I do or don't believe your source." Artie had a harsher tone than she expected. She wondered if she had made a mistake calling him.

"He has no reason to lie to me," Nicole said, a little defensively.

"No, of course not, I'm not suggesting that at all, but this is a win for us. They're not going to build the plant in Williamsport. No one is going to convince me that our efforts did not play some part in it."

Nicole stopped right there. Artie was one of the most honest truth-seekers she knew, and yet here she had found a limit to how much truth he would let in.

"I see what you mean, Artie."

"And further, I see no reason not to capitalize on it, to have our celebration, and look to our next steps in the struggle."

He jettisoned the first part of the conversation and was off again talking of plans and preparations, but Nicole mentally disengaged from the conversation, only occasionally offering perfunctory responses. Artie seemed not to notice.

Nicole went back to work on the cabin and painted for two days straight. If she thought at all about recent events, it was unconsciously. She put off the trip to Wiest Hardware until she was almost done with the paint left over in the barn. The hardware store was one of her dad's favorite spots, and having accompanied him there numerous times, she liked it there almost as much as he had. She thought of the scores of wooden drawers containing every kind of nut and bolt, and the smell of the wood and various lubricants. Progress had clearly been forestalled in this store. She tallied up her requirements and decided a five-gallon drum would get her through the painting she planned.

She walked through the door and was met by the room's stillness. It was years since she'd been there, but she could have navigated the aisles blindfolded. Her focus was drawn to the basket to the side of the register. The register itself had changed. Now it was computerized, and probably managed inventory and other business operations, but the basket was the same and more importantly, so were its contents.

Lollipops in clear cellophane wrappers reflected the fluorescent lighting back to her. Remembrance and ritual—as a little girl accompanying her dad, asking him if she could have one. Gabe instructing her to ask Mr. Wiest the same question, which she did. And then receiving a response from the wiry, six-foot-two-inch man who was cue-ball bald, in the mildest way he knew how, that of course she could, and instructed her to take two.

She soaked herself in this memory until she was ready to reset herself in the present, and then looked around. Mr. Wiest saw her but did not come and greet her as he had always done in the past.

"Hello, Mr. Wiest," she said after walking over to where he was restocking shelves with fall lawn care products. He turned his head and upper torso, but kept his feet facing the wall.

"Hi, Nicole. What brings you in here?" he looked away, back at the shelves and fidgeted, which was not like him at all.

"Doing some painting on the cabins and ran out of paint."

"Well, paint's in the same place it's always been. If you need any help, we'll get someone over there to help you."

Nicole looked around. There was no one else in the store. He made as if to go back to his task. Mr. Wiest's dismissal of her was bewildering. Before stepping away, she held out one more possibility for dialogue with him.

"How's John doing? Haven't seen him for years." John was Mr. Wiest's son. They'd gone to school together. Not the best of friends, but ran in the same crowd sometimes. He was smart, too, an engineering student at Penn State, one of the kids who got out and was "making something of himself," or so she heard.

This acted as some sort of catalyst. Mr. Wiest let go of the item he was stacking and turned fully towards Nicole.

"John's doing fine. Been working with an engineering company in DC." Mr. Wiest paused before continuing. Everything darkened around him. The air within the chamber of this store no longer forestalled time, but mocked it, drawing life from the hosts contained within it.

"He was following the plans for this gas-to-liquid refinery. Been telling us for some time he'd like to find something closer to home. Thought he'd have a good shot at something with Rockwell."

He was staring at her now, but more through her. The bond he had with Gabe and Gabe's family was swept aside by the tsunami of feeling caused by the lost opportunity to have his son close by, the rapture of casual gatherings for dinner, sharing a beer or cup of coffee.

"But that won't happen now. You environmentalists have made sure of that, and you more than any of them. Made Williamsport seem like just about the worst, most unfriendly spot for business on the planet. No chance of luring industry with that type of message."

Any response, any justification, was worse than none at all.

"I'm sorry you feel that way, Mr. Wiest." She stepped back and made her way to the door without buying the paint. Casualties everywhere she looked, and for what? Having gotten thoroughly and publicly enmeshed in the controversy, she would forever be reviled by some people living in the area. The fabric of the community had been torn, and the path towards repair was not evident. She pondered these unhappy thoughts in silence during her trip home.

Later that night, she made the one call that needed to be made.

"Hi, Sherri," Nicole said. "How's it going?"

"Really good. I've been keeping up with the news," Sherri said enthusiastically. "Seems like a big win for our side."

This response was why Nicole had not called Sherri before now.

"Well, I'm not sure Rockwell was ever really interested in building the refinery in Williamsport, but that's another conversation."

Sherri did not have time to ask her what that meant before Nicole diverted her comments to her primary interest.

"You know, part of the reason for the gathering was getting people to the demonstration, and now the demonstration is either cancelled or is morphing into a celebration. I haven't kept up with it. Whatever happens with it, I want you to know I still want to have the gathering at Bountiful next weekend. Not sure why, but it seems more important to me now than ever."

"That's good, because I'm getting a lot of response to your offer. You can expect a full house. Those cabins seemed to be a big draw."

They drifted into preparations, and after hanging up, Nicole was left to wonder why she was drawn so much to this gathering and what it represented for her.

CHAPTER 24

Joe turned off the road and onto the driveway to Bountiful. Nicole had invited him to this gathering, and he jumped at the chance to get away and see her. His attempts at returning to normalcy at work were made with varying degrees of success, and the process was tiring.

Tents circled the area reserved for ball playing and frisbee tossing. It was hard for Joe to feel comfortable, with everyone dressed in imaginative hippie garb; each pair of jeans was a colorful patchwork, threaded together. *A lot of work to project a lack of caring for material things*, he reflected unkindly, but he felt envy as well. The persona presented by his own unadorned jeans, recently purchased shirt, and short hair left him feeling excluded from the greetings and happy faces he saw as he walked the grounds. He wondered if he›d made a mistake in coming.

Then he made eye contact with Sophia, and she waved to him enthusiastically. He was the most considerate of Nicole's suitors, and Sophia favored him for this reason, among others. Nicole had her wild side, and Sophia could see how he anchored her. Opposites attract; that had been the case with her and Gabe, and it seemed only right that it would also be so between Nicole and Joe. The conflict with her parents ended abruptly when Gabe roared into their bucolic neighborhood on his Harley Davidson, rescuing her from their Philadelphia Main Line English Tudor estate. And, as she learned years after she was slotted on the back of Gabe's bike, her parents harbored an admiration for Gabe, especially when they realized how much he loved her.

Joe and Sophia's conversations had still not emerged from the shadow of Gabe's death, so they approached each other cautiously.

"Nicole told me business was off this summer, so this must be quite a change for you," Joe said, his eyes surveying the encampment.

"We haven't been this busy, or had this much fun, in a long time, and now that you're here, we're not lacking for anything," she said with a wink.

Sophia moved closer to Joe, grasped him, and gave him a hug that Joe was more than happy to receive.

"Come with me," Sophia beckoned. "When we heard you were coming, we rearranged who was staying where. Wanted to put you in a nice cottage." Joe grabbed his bag and followed with renewed enthusiasm.

This was the last of the cabins to be occupied. Sophia had been the greeter and was responsible for getting people settled in. The guests were mostly young, about Nicole's age, and she made sure they were accommodated as well as possible. They had all exhibited sincere and heartfelt appreciation for those accommodations, each interaction a reminder of what she and Gabe had accomplished during their years here. This sort of community togetherness was part of what had inspired them in the first place. The flow of people on the grounds was a joy after seeing them so underused this past season. She had been prescribed Zoloft to deal with her experience of loss, but this was a far more effective remedy. She could do this all day and night.

"Feels great to be up here," Joe said, avoiding mention of his personal conflicts and the ones that preoccupied Sophia. Instead, he breathed deeply the fresh, honeysuckle-scented air as they walked towards the cabin.

"Someone's been busy." Joe stood in front of the cabin he would stay in, the one Nicole had recently painted. He thought nothing could be more perfect than this newly painted clapboard sided cabin with the porch rimming the front facade.

"That's very true," Sophia said, pride emanating from her voice. "Nicole had to put some space between herself and all the news surrounding us, and her in particular. Found a paint brush was a good way to do that."

Joe continued looking, his admiration only growing. It was the smallest of all the cabins, intended for no more than one or two people, and for this reason special emphasis was placed on making it cozy. Joe passed through the doorway and looked around. A piece of driftwood, a country setting painted on one piece of wood, a hoot owl on another. The bed laid out on one side, the kitchen area the other. *What more could I need?* The rustic quality on the outside was replaced by a more modern feel within the cabin. It was winterized, as were all the cabins. The walls and ceiling were insulated and covered with drywall.

After Sophia left, Joe unpacked the few things he'd brought, but he wanted to get out and look around, to see if he could fit in here. He had not yet decided about Reid's job offer, and that made his work days longer, more tedious and irritating. Then there was the subterfuge he'd engaged in with Nicole that left him feeling dirty when interacting with Senator Bain. He knew change of some kind would occur, needed to occur, and wondered if being injected into this new-age enclave would inform his decision. The one thing he felt certain of was the strength of his desire to see Nicole.

Nicole was leading the charge in the kitchen, and he headed in that direction. He passed by the tents on his way, and, to his surprise, was warmly greeted by those he encountered. Three people worked together by the fire pit, which was where families could have communal fires. But these three were enlarging it, transforming it in some knowing, practiced manner he was unable to fully grasp. Mark, a tall, lanky man with a full beard, contemplative eyes, and an Indian styled handkerchief pulled through his hair to create a man-bun, organized their efforts.

Joe found Nicole in an energized state not unlike that of her mother. She was helping others navigate around the kitchen while mixing and preparing the ingredients for quinoa mac & cheese for forty. He paused inside the door, unseen by her, and observed the effect she had on her surroundings and those about her. She was laughing now, pushing back against some playful criticism of the variability of size and shape of some onions she had just chopped. She waved a knife shakily in the air and cautioned against unwise criticism of her onion-chopping talents. With her lack of control, one never knew what could happen, she warned.

Those around her laughed with her, and she held their laughter just long enough for the knife to slice through the air. Joe found himself wondering if she could still make him laugh like this thirty, forty years from now. If she could still put a charge in the air as she was doing right now. These were questions he had never before entertained.

He moved from his perch and walked over to her and tapped her on the shoulder. She turned and lit up, throwing her arms around him, grasping him with hands that still contained the residue of cheese she'd grated.

He had never before seen the kitchen in such full-operation mode. Three people helped Nicole, two men and a woman, so this was not the opportunity to catch up on all that was happening in their lives. Instead, he donned the last remaining apron and took his place as one of Nicole's minions.

He was assigned to preparing baba ganoosh with eggplants that came from the small garden they'd managed to put in. They had already been roasted, and the spongy vegetable was transformed into a frothy mash that he scraped into a bowl. The others worked along, making a salad of greens, baking bread, and the quinoa, which was the main course.

Gerry, a curly haired novice in the kitchen, asked a question to no one in particular. "Any idea when people will be returning from the demonstration, or celebration, or whatever it's turned into?"

"Supposed to go until 4:00, but knowing some of the people running it, I wouldn't be surprised to see it last longer," Nicole said.

"You mean they run on at the mouth?" said Marie, who was kneading bread in slow, rhythmic motions. Her dreadlocks were swept away, descending down her back.

"Didn't say that. They're just looking to rally support the best they can," Nicole said, wanting to project a positive attitude about the event.

"Which reminds me," Gerry said. Why aren't you out there sharing the spotlight? You're one of the main reasons for this whole shebang."

Nicole shifted uncomfortably for the first time since installing herself in the kitchen. She and Joe made eye contact, and their gaze shared the story they believed to be true.

"My fifteen minutes of fame are done, and I'm glad of it. Call me crazy, but standing here with the group of you, preparing this meal for our gathering, seems more real, more active, even more revolutionary than anything I see going on at their celebration. But that's just me, and I wish them all the success in the world."

This was a new bit of information for Joe to process, one he decided contained the quality of truth for the woman he knew.

Surprisingly, Nicole's admission helped to further unify the group. They laughed more and anticipated each other's needs more intuitively. They worked along until all the tasks had reached the stage of rising and marinating; when time, itself, needed to perform its part in the process. This was the opportunity for Nicole and Joe to be alone to speak to each other, sense the changes in the other since their last time together.

Joe placed his hand on her shoulder, and she led them outside, but their intentions were interrupted by what captured their attention. Mark's design was well underway as he had lashed three tree trunks together in the fire pit. It towered high in the opening, captivating the space in which it sat. It employed a teepee style, but was clearly not intended to be modeled after one. The structure was a replica of the drilling derrick on the far side of the property, the "elephant in the room" brought within their circle. Joe and Nicole stopped advancing forward, and she broke from his touch and continued alone, circling the structure slowly, taking it in from all perspectives, and saying nothing.

As she completed the circle and turned back towards Joe, he studied the expression on her face. She was transformed, not at all the person who had just been beside him. There was a coldness, a fierceness in her look and demeanor. Instead of walking back to Joe, she walked over to Mark, who paused in his work. She placed her hand on his shoulder and thanked him. They hugged and, when their embrace ended, she motioned for Joe to join them.

Still addressing Mark, she said, "I knew it was important for me to have this gathering here but wasn't sure why. Now you've given me an important piece of the puzzle."

They stood in the late afternoon sun. It was the last week in September, and daylight no longer extended deep into the evening hours. Thankfully, it would not be too cold this evening, but the air was crisp, a clarifying presence that paradoxically burst with mystery and possibility. They stood in a spot where they could look through the wooden structure and see the actual drilling rig performing its monotonous operations. Nicole had learned to turn her gaze from it, but it never left her thoughts: a constant reminder, frequented with anger and bitterness. The proximity of the replica diminished the scope, span, and authority of the actual derrick. In fact, the real thing now looked like a toy, and not something to be taken seriously.

Joe and Nicole walked again, this time along a trail towards the river. They found a spot to sit, a couple of long rocks carved out by glaciation, and dropped along the river bed for their pleasure and use on this afternoon. They sat in quiet among friendly river fronds, the patterns of nature, these two people the only things not completely in synch.

"I didn't expect that, the way Mark's structure affected me," Nicole said, a shiver going through her entire body. She re-experienced the vulnerability that can saturate the soul in a flash, even one in the midst of joy and playfulness.

"It's a powerful image," Joe responded. "I understand why you reacted the way you did."

"I wonder if I will ever get on top of it. Since my dad died, I haven't had much control of my emotions." She got up and walked to a late blooming toad lily. She studied its form, its jug-shaped cups that contained all the nourishment the plant needed, even this late into the season.

"You'll figure it out," Joe said. "You're smart, and you see things more clearly than anyone I know. Give yourself some time."

Nicole smiled, thankful for Joe's kind words, but was unconvinced. "I would have agreed with you a year ago. Nothing ever slowed me down for long. Even when I left school, I knew I had something to return to, but I look around now and can't find meaning or certainty. Not sure if the folks up there in the tents and cabins offer a clue. They're kind, wonderful people, but most seem pretty aimless. They work at things they don't care much about."

"It's all about finding our way," Joe said, thinking about Reid's job offer, but not wanting to discuss it now. Instead, their focus shifted to nature's cradle of sound, sight, and smell, and it comforted them beyond any rational explanation. Nicole noticed a hummingbird and motioned to Joe. It was the first one he'd ever seen in nature: darting, hovering, close enough for them to hear it hum like a small helicopter. Then another approached, engaging and challenging the other. The two swooped in and out of sight with precise, angular movement. Nicole and Joe laughed as the aerial display raised their spirits.

"Like *Star Wars* starfighters," he said.

"Thank God for hummingbirds."

"Indeed."

The air, too, lifted them, with its cool touch on their skin. The sounds of crickets and river underscored the intermittent bird call, both song-like and insistent. There was nothing for them to do but take it all in, say yes to the full experience it provided, and in which they became sheltered.

They heard the sound of cars arriving, returning from the celebration-demonstration. Nicole was happy for their return, happy with her decision to forego the event, no trace of guilt for having done so.

She got up and said, "Come on, let's go. We've got a dinner to cook."

He rose, and they looked at each other. "Not quite yet," he said and drew her to him. Their kiss was long and tender. No need to rush. They felt like the other animals in this place, conduits of a great spirit, a sense of inter-being to which they remained attentive in the midst of their embrace.

As they walked up the trail, while looking at a woodpecker assaulting the bark of an old oak tree, Joe said, "They never question their actions. Everything they do has purpose, and is exactly what they ought to be doing."

"You won't have to worry about that for the next couple of hours. I've got plenty of tasks lined up for you. I'll make sure you're not bothered by all this higher thinking."

This call to work didn't tarnish his sense of well-being or the connection he felt to everything around him, but the mood they returned to was not what they expected. Scheduled Fire Calling festivals were purpose driven. Each had a theme: the freeing of oneself from demons: stress, depression, fear; the uniting with one's energy: spiritual, sexual, creative. But impromptu gatherings like this one were usually times for fun and learning what was new in people's lives.

Generally, unscheduled gatherings took on the character of summer camp for young adults. So much depended on the mood of the place, and the carefree quality of the returning celebrants was at odds with those who had stayed behind, their contemplative attitude rooted in Mark's creation.

The sun's slanting rays cut like knives through the scaffolding's vertical supports. Those same rays found entry to the wooden replica and splayed to touch those recently returned. The energy points aligned. Stonehenge, Egyptian pyramids, Machu Picchu. Bountiful seized its place among them. Verbal communication attenuated. A deeper understanding. The broken spirit of this place was absorbed and would be repaired, its energetic state realigned and balanced and permitted to flow again. The Fire Calling would make it so, attune itself to the conditions present and midwife a new direction.

A stream of volunteers flowed into the kitchen, more than Nicole could find meaningful tasks for, though she tried. Food was laid out in a buffet and each attendee emerged from the line with a colorful plate of healthy, vegetarian items. Jugs of cheap wine and pitchers of iced tea were stationed at an adjoining table.

The group, brought together by the meal, gained coherence and purpose. Many were only casual friends, but used this time and space to deepen their relations. Joe was impressed by this, and it lent a character to the event like none he'd ever before experienced. He and Nicole waited until the line died down and then filled plates for themselves and found chairs on the porch.

"So what's new in the capital these days? Or should I be afraid to ask?" Nicole said with a laugh, but was concerned about the firestorm it might set off in her brain.

"It's weird, almost like a death in the family. Everyone's walking around like they don't know what to do or what to say. There had been a lot of hope and a lot of dreams wrapped up in this refinery, and now it's gone. *Poof.* The fact we were being played for fools doesn't help. Senator Bain's worst of all. Hardly comes out of his office and looks ten years older."

"Can't say I share their feeling of loss," Nicole responded, "but I can certainly relate to feeling like a fool."

"What's become clear to me," Joe said, "is that you can't win when your opponent has unlimited resources and is expert in the type of conflict you're engaged in with them. They've figured out all the moves and counter moves, and they're tireless."

Nicole couldn't find anything to add to this. Instead, she looked out at the collected gathering, sensed its powerful spirit, and considered these different realities, these different sources of power.

Joe ruminated, besieged now by the other issue he needed to confront.

"You're not going to believe this, but I got a job offer. It's with the consulting firm I've been working with to put this deal together. It would mean a lot of travel and nearly double my salary. It's what staffers hope for. The revolving door. At the State, most of the directors and above move often between business and government."

Neither said what they were both thinking, that this move would place a wedge between them that would probably never be bridged, that they would never again be together like they were now.

"Listen, Joe. Somehow we've grown close through all this," she said, and they both laughed because of the unlikeliness of their relationship, "you have to do what is best for you, and no one but you can figure out what that is. I'll always think of you fondly. You helped me get through a tough time in my life."

She touched his hand, and they looked out. They said little more and returned to their meal. The importance of the issues they considered weighed on them.

When Sophia walked up to them, both of them felt grateful, because their stress would not yield. She was much older than anyone in the assembled group and enjoyed the rank this bestowed upon her. Oftentimes, when Gabe was alive, she had been overshadowed by his garrulousness, and she was happy to let him take the lead most of the time. After he died, she found herself rudderless, unable to find meaning and direction. So her attitude now was all the more surprising and wonderful to observe.

Sophia had recently cut her hair short, which made her look years younger. She wore a white blouse she'd made herself. Embroidery rimmed the collar and sleeves. The front contained a design that included a sunflower and rose. She took a seat next to them and placed the dulcimer she'd been carrying across her lap.

"We've needed a good party and big fire, and it looks like we're going to get both." Sophia said, while looking at the structure installed in front of them. "If we can't tear down the actual drilling rig, let's burn it in effigy. I'm ready to light the first match."

This was just the thing that needed to be said, and Nicole loved hearing her say it.

She began strumming the instrument, at first slowly, but then with vigor. Old Appalachian tunes filled the tree canopy, bringing Joe and Nicole back into this enchanted space, away from intractable issues.

Darkness was settling in, and the drummers began their call to the others to join them around the structure that would be set ablaze. When the group was assembled, the ritual calling to the four directions was enacted. A flaming stick was placed within the bed of kindling assembled in the center of the wood phalanx. Smoldering at first, the flames then shot up in fits, bathing the flanks of each pillar and preparing their transformation.

Nathan, an elder of the tribe, stepped into the circle to speak.

"We know of great tragedy on this land, and we desire to heal that which has been harmed and damaged. We cannot separate the private and the public. What has been done on this land and to this family has been done to each of us. We share in that knowledge. We share in that suffering. We have come to consecrate this land and renew its purpose, and the purpose of those who call it home."

The first flame spidered to the top of one pier and extinguished before others raced up again and again along adjacent pathways.

The drumming started in earnest. The flickering lights and smell of the fire enveloped them. Nicole observed everything and felt saturated by all the wisdom imparted to her during her life. This was the land of her youth that had brought much joy and had brought her to adulthood. In the last year, their experience of the land had been toxic. An international corporate gas company had destroyed all that was good here. Others would disagree. Let them. She had grieved, been beaten down, and suffered long enough. It was time to fight back and restore what was hers.

Nicole got up and stepped to the fire. Others were already there, so her movements were supported by them. She raised her fists, letting out a scream that rose above the drumming and any other transient sound. She screamed her grief and rage, holding the scream as long as she needed to, and from this scream came the seed of a thought.

As she danced to the drumming, she felt Joe was there beside her. *When had he arrived? So unlike him, and while he is certainly here for me, maybe he's here for himself as well.* She embraced him passionately, a surprise to them both, and they kissed. They danced again, separately, aware of a larger embrace, recognition of something deeper, a charge linking them to the assembled group. All the while, her thoughts grew in the background, seeking out flaws, and growing in substance as each obstacle was brought into focus and then dispatched.

For hours, they danced, chanted, and gazed into the fire. The wood, eaten out from the inside, collapsed in on itself, as of course it must. The chanting gave way to exaltation—bowing and stretching and hugging. That is when the germ of her idea crystalized in Nicole.

Why does this need to end when the weekend ends? She looked around and saw the cabins. Light emanated from only a few, but signs of life were in all of them, so different from the energy they'd possessed this past year. A vision broke forth in her. In some future time, some few years away, first and foremost the rig on the far side of the property would stop producing and go the way of the replica that was now all but disintegrated—and she would be the first to climb its beams, blow torch in hand, but then on the other side, here in this space she stood in now, would be small groupings: couples, small families. They would be living in the cabins year round. Solar panels would provide them with electricity.

The farm would again be made to grow the crops her dad had planted. Artisan work would be conducted for commerce, and the well sitting across from them would be the key. It was producing gas, and they were receiving monthly checks because of it. It would be the seed money to jump-start this operation. It was all there, in an instant. She had a lot to talk about with her mother, but this could wait until tomorrow, to give some time for reflection, to see if what seemed so clear now would be so again under the scrutiny of daylight.

CHAPTER 25

Nicole and Sophia sat on the porch the next morning drinking coffee. Small campfires replaced the large central fire, and the mood this presented was more diffused and relaxed. There was also a feeling of benevolence, pulled from the turbulence of the night before.

"You've seemed distracted, Nicole. Everything all right with you?"

Nicole had been looking for a way to share her vision with Sophia, but couldn't find the door to open. Her mom now provided one and she stepped inside.

"You know, this doesn't have to end. Isn't this better than how it was before we started preparing for this gathering?"

Sophia took a long look at her daughter before responding to her question. It was a wise gaze that suspected where Nicole was headed, but she held back from saying too much, too early, wanting, instead, for Nicole to provide more insight.

"I've loved having your friends here. Yes, ma'am, got my blood flowing in a way I haven't felt in a very long time. I feel I can allow myself the joy it has brought me, and I have my wonderful daughter to thank for this." Then, after a pause, she concluded, "Your dad would be proud and happy to see how our land was put to use."

Mother and daughter rose from their seats and embraced, a couple of tears loosening from their eyes. Sophia wiped them from her daughter's cheeks with the palm of her hand, then did the same with her own. They joined their hands, and Sophia looked at Nicole, now as vulnerable as she'd been at times as a young girl, and wondered how many more times she would see her like this, being the one to provide the essential comfort she sought.

"Nothing makes sense, Mom. I'm not an activist—not like some of these people. That's not to say I don't agree with them. I do in almost all cases, but

I never feel satisfied with what we do. The small victories are only a little satisfying, and the defeats are overwhelming, and there's a constant flow of them, and the costs? Just look at how we've made enemies with some of our neighbors."

Sophia considered Nicole's comments. "I know that, love. Have for a long time, probably starting around the time you became a teenager. You needed to appear engaged, committed to the oppressed. A lot like your dad. You'd join this group and that one, wanting to do good work, but you'd always back away, hated the politics, and hated the changes it caused in you. Some people find connection with political groups, some don't. There's no shame in being someone who doesn't."

They paused again, and as Sophia began to speak, she released Nicole's hands and grabbed hold of her upper arms, tightening her grip slightly. "But this isn't why we're talking really. It's not really what you want to say."

Nicole agreed. She lowered her gaze and reestablished herself within the vision that had appeared to her the night before. She left nothing out and added embellishments that had sprouted since the original idea took form and now glowed with a hotter flame.

Nicole ended her comments with this thought. "We'll never beat them at their own game. The rules they impose are horrible. Rules like thinking our lives are all about self-reliance, hoarding money, and being able to engineer our way out of all the problems we create. Thinking this way just leads us to be alienated from each other and the world around us, when most of us know the way we live is deeply flawed, and we know with an equal strength how to fix it."

Throughout the telling, Sophia beamed, and her body felt the warm glow of a truth coursing through it.

"I haven't heard talk like this since your dad was a young man," Sophia said. "I wouldn't be surprised if some of these ideas were his, channeled through you."

The pause that followed was electric and wild.

"Of course you can do this. We'll do it together. It is exactly what your dad would like for us and for this land he loved so dearly."

Nicole shared her plans with Joe after they unfolded during the ceremonies around the fire. Bit by bit, as it came into focus, he was allowed into this unfurling vision, but his response was markedly different from hers. It was this difference he was contemplating while sitting on a large boulder at the side of the stream behind the lodge the next morning. In the midst of these thoughts, Nicole emerged down the path and stood before him.

"Why so glum?" Nicole questioned.

"Not glum, just thoughtful," Joe responded.

"Not sure which is more surprising," Nicole kidded, and took a seat beside him.

They had stayed together in Joe's cabin the night before, and only separated when Nicole set off to speak with her mom. Some of their relationship had been characterized by skirmishes between them, testing one another, but now they realized that was largely in the past. Nicole stroked Joe's back soothingly, waiting for him to speak again.

"Been thinking about all you're planning to do here. Amazing, really, and I think it may work. You could have everything you want right here."

"I just finished talking with my mom, and she's on board. She sees this as a tribute to my dad, all the work and love he put into this place. If all goes well, we'll be offering people the chance to stay on, maybe even extend some offers later today, but there are a lot of issues to work out. Things like do we charge rent, searching out business opportunities based on sustainable models, resolving problems that will arise, divvying up shared chores and revenue. We can use the gas payments as seed money, but that won't last. It won't be long before we'll need to stand on our own feet."

Joe heard more than the words. For the first time he saw how he could be useful, saw that someone would need to develop and manage the processes to make this place viable. His mind conceived of workflows that could be coopted for use here.

"One thing I found," Joe said, "is whatever rules you put in place, make sure they are aligned with what you are trying to do. At work, management publishes mandates daily almost. You become immune to them. They become meaningless, and you find ways to work around them unless they improve your performance, your work experience."

Nicole took this in and filed it away, and Joe felt good he'd said something that would help her. They got up to leave, and their movement caused a young doe standing across the river to stir. The doe looked at the humans in the way only a deer can. Its dark, piercing black eyes turned everything about them—their movements and intentions—into a question they themselves wished they could answer.

Various groups formed to accomplish tasks around the camp. Joe and two others cleaned the fire pit that had been doused the night before. As he looked around, he was impressed at how hard everyone worked to return the space to the state it had been in before they descended on it. He shoveled the charred wood into a wheel barrow, rolled it to the adjacent woods, and dispersed it around tree trunks. It was good fertilizer, he had been told. Much of the wood and ash were still sooty, and it wasn't long before Joe was covered with a darkened film; a good disguise, a filter. The smoky odor overwhelmed him.

He walked to the woods and, before depositing the wheel barrow's contents, brought his face to within inches of the sooty mash and breathed in deeply. It was the all-consuming burning and fire of the night before, all over again. He drew his head away and placed his hands deep within this substance that sources life, the grimy stuff of rebirth. He grasped its various textures and extruded it between his fingers. This was something he would expect others to do, but never himself. To his surprise, the rituals of the night before had not ended, and he continued hurtling headlong in an unknown direction.

———————

Word spread throughout the camp. Requests were made to Nicole by some people wanting to stay on at the cabins. The buzz was transforming. For some, even those not staying on, it was cathartic. These seekers pushed and pushed, desiring a community where they could live out their dreams of reestablishing connection to the whole world and to ancient wisdom. They pushed in the dark, pushed that boulder inch by inch up a mountain whose summit always seemed beyond reach. Now that it appeared, amorphous possibilities lay before them, even things that seemed impossible moments before, and when the boulder is freed and rolling downward, advancing at an accelerating rate, those who had strenuously brought it to the top are joyously running after it. As it bounds down the path, it divides and divides again, and those following pursue the individual path that best suits them.

But some people needed to leave and get back to their normal lives, for now at least. Four of the eight cabins were spoken for, and the occupants of two of these needed to return to their apartments and gather items they needed. Only those that had already been living nomadically, with only the barest possessions, could stop and stay.

These were two couples that traveled together mostly. They were only in their late twenties, but their commitment to the road had allowed them to pack a lifetime of experience into their short lives. Now they looked around and saw an opportunity here, and seized it the way they did all opportunities presented to them. They were not afraid of hard work and lived for adventure, making them the ideal companions for this fledging experiment.

As the day wore on, the euphoria became muted. People left with warm wishes and embraces, but left. With each departure, the focus of where they were headed at Bountiful became more directed. Twelve people settled into the large living room in the lodge to plan their next steps. The discussion ranged over a variety of topics, all important but disjointed.

After about thirty minutes of free-form discussion, Joe suggested they try a storyboard technique he'd used during brainstorming sessions. An easel was brought up from the basement, and they were fortunate to find markers that had not dried out. He drew a twelve-month time line across the board. They found Post-its and started putting tasks and goals on them placing them along a month divider. The Post-its were moved as plans developed and became more coherent. The visual representation of what was said greatly improved the effectiveness of the discussion.

Joe took an active role for a while, but then found it difficult to stay focused. He walked out to the porch, sat in a chair, and watched dust motes carried in the slanting rays of light that the day's advance bestowed upon them. The chill in the air crept into his bones and announced the approach of fall. Soon, Nicole came out and took a seat beside him.

"You got quiet all of a sudden," Nicole said.

Joe considered what to say, uncertain of his own feelings. "I guess I'm trying to figure out why I believe I'm better suited to sling politician shit than cow shit."

The comment could have been funny but wasn't. It left both of them saddened, looking out onto the darkening terrain.

"We could use someone here who can make sure things get done. That's something you're good at."

"I tried to see it that way. Even did a little while earlier. What you are doing is right. I stopped trying to deny it. It's what we all should be doing probably, and I love it here and have never felt about anyone the way I feel about you."

They sat this way for several moments, considering their own and each other's thoughts until Nicole broke the silence.

"You're making a compelling case for moving on," Nicole said, and this time they both laughed. She placed her hand on his leg, and he placed his hand over hers.

"No . . . I'm not, but what I realized, sitting in there with all of you, was that this would never be enough for me. I feel fucked-up for saying that. It is enough. Maybe all there is, but that doesn't change the way I feel."

"So you are going back there. Back into the belly of the beast."

"Looks that way. It will continue to be there whether I'm there or not. Maybe I can humanize it a little bit."

"If it doesn't gobble you up first."

"That's a distinct possibility, but I might not even get a chance, because I've decided something else. I'm going to level with Senator Bain. Tell him about you and me. Tell him about the information I gave you. Hopefully, he'll want me to stay on. Hell, hopefully he won't press charges against me, but I can't keep working with this hanging over my head. It will destroy my soul." He laughed when he said the word "soul." It was not the question of whether or not he had one. It was, instead, his using it to describe some core part of himself that felt so foreign.

"What about the consulting firm and all that money they're offering you?"

"Fuck them. The only things consultants are good for is to give you an excuse not to make your own decisions. I'm not starry-eyed about them anymore. My goal from now on will be to keep them the hell out of my business as much as I can."

Their hands parted, and they embraced each other, not joyously, but deeply, with a passion they knew would be fleeting.

"I'll be back to visit."

"Don't say that, but, of course you will."

They embraced again, but already the flame of their union was beginning to dim.

When their arms returned to their sides, they peered into each other's eyes, resigned to what would come next.

"I think I'll head back to the cabin, clean up, and pack my things."

"Would you like me to come with you, give you a hand?"

Joe hesitated briefly, a part of him wanting to make a clean break from Nicole now, but there was never any doubt what his answer would be, "Of course I'd like your help"

They walked in quiet towards the cabin, the approaching darkness hurrying their steps.

"It hit me when Will and Max were in there clowning around, getting all excited about getting started first thing in the morning plowing the land," Joe said. "I thought they were going to wet themselves. It was like they were setting off on the greatest adventure."

"And how did that make you feel?"

"Other than like shit, you mean?" Joe said.

"Yeah," Nicole laughed, because the comment was funny, and because it made her uneasy.

"I saw myself out there on the tractor feeling . . . feeling tortured, wondering how I'd gotten there, each minute passing more slowly than the last."

"Guess it's safe to say you're not farmhand material."

He stopped and faced her.

"The only reason I struggled with this decision was to see what could happen between us. That was almost enough to change everything."

"I know," she said, raising her hand to Joe's cheek and stroking it tenderly. "And that's very sweet. When I wasn't caught up in all the activities going on this weekend, I was watching you. Even before this idea of people staying on here took hold, I had a feeling this would be the time when you and I figured out what we were about."

After a pause when emotions, strong and active, needed to be given space to range across the connection between them, Joe responded, "And now, I guess, we have. I had thought about asking you to come back to Harrisburg with me before all this talk of communal farming swept through the place."

Before Joe could unwind the rest of his comment, Nicole completed his thought. "Which makes about as much sense as you moving up here," she said.

"What I figured."

They entered the cabin and began packing his things and tidying up. These tasks did not take as long as they would have liked.

"Will you stay for dinner?"

"No, I don't think so," Joe said, each moment now drawing them towards a separation unlike any they'd ever experienced before.

"What about my mom and the rest of the crew at the house?"

Joe considered this before speaking, and then, deciding he did not care to test his resolve any further, responded, "If you don't mind, I think I'll pass. Could you say goodbye to them for me? Tell them to keep the passion alive that they're feeling now, that there's no reason they can't be successful. Tell them I will do what I can to make sure the legislation put into law has an inkling of humanity in it. That it promotes sustainability, has a conscience. Tell them I will be back to visit, and that they will always be close to my thoughts, my heart."

"I can do that if you like. They'll understand why you didn't say goodbye yourself. I'll make them understand. You've set a tall order for yourself, especially with those bobble-heads running the state government right now. Seems to me farming a piece a land would be a lot easier than what you're returning to."

He responded with a coda to all their conversation on this topic, "For you, maybe."

They carried his belongings to his car and stood there for a moment.

Joe began to speak in a plaintive tone, "We could have—"

Nicole placed a hand over his mouth. It was the only warmth he felt. He touched the hand with his, and kissed it at the same time, and then returned it wordlessly to Nicole's side.

They hugged one last time, and Joe entered the car, beginning down the driveway. The headlights flickered across the land and lit up the gas derrick. Previously, it was a woeful sight, but now he saw it as the bridge it would provide them. His mind leapt to the future: He could see the derrick, old and in disuse, rotting and rusted, the land around nurtured and healthy and thriving, children, artisans at work, the name of this place, Bountiful, again deserving its name by providing for those living upon it.

He would do what he could to give these notions a wider berth, because not everyone would live on a farm and do handy work, but everyone needed to provide, and everyone needed to question how their life's actions benefitted those who shared the bounty of their place and time.

Should he beep his horn as he exited the property? This was his final question to end this chapter of his life, and it gave him a fit of giddy laughter. The horn pierced the air: a long, celebratory arc of sound like noise makers on New Year's Eve.

CHAPTER 26

The air in the office, though heavy, did not feel burdensome to Joe. In fact, as he returned to his desk, he realized how much he enjoyed it and how comfortable he felt in this setting. Crowding out this feeling was the foreknowledge that he would have his sit-down with the senator today, and that his future here, or anywhere, was in jeopardy.

Senator Bain made time for Joe at 10:00. Joe took a seat across from the senator, who looked more like himself today, sitting upright, commanding the space around him. He'd cut his hair and, instead of it being slicked back as usual, it stood up in spots, giving him an edgy quality, not like the image of a used car salesman he sometimes evoked.

"So, what can I do for you, Joe?"

Joe fidgeted. For all his attempt at crafting his lines, he was unable to figure out what to say. What came out of his mouth was, "I've got something to confess."

The senator's demeanor changed. He sat back, dropped his day-to-day workload mentality and began a conversation more difficult than the one he'd expected.

"Sure. What's up?"

"You know back in March, when we were up in Williamsport, and I got a date with that waitress?"

"Yeah, I remember."

"Well, you're never going to believe this but her name is—"

"Nicole Marshall," Senator Bain blurted out before Joe could say another word. "The fractivists' Erin Brockovich."

Joe's thoughts whirled and tumbled. Before fully recovering he replied, "You've known all along?"

"I never told you, but my brother's a silent partner in that tavern," Bain said with half a smile. "Anyway, you think anything goes on in my district that I don't hear about?" A smile broke fully across his face.

"So then," Joe pressed on, "do you also know about the information—"

This time the senator raised his hand in front of Joe, stopping him in mid-sentence.

"You don't want to tell me what you're about to say, and I don't want to hear it."

They sat quietly for a few moments, allowing their thoughts to go their separate ways before the senator continued.

"We've both been through a lot, learned lessons about ourselves and the politics around this place. The important thing is that we're both still here. Your coming here ready to tell me all of this, and risk your job, tells me more than anything you were prepared to say."

The senator was playing the father figure, and Joe was happy to let him step into that role.

"All I know," Senator Bain continued, "is I'm still looking for ways to help my constituents, and that's what they want me to do. This recent experience showed me things about myself that aren't particularly nice to look at, but I'm willing to learn, and keep fighting through the mistakes and that will help me weather the highs and lows that come our way."

"I realized a lot of things this weekend, too," Joe responded. "Realized there are sides of me I need to learn more about, give voice to and not be afraid of, but more than anything, I realized this is what I'm made for. Doing the job of keeping the state running, but also finding ways to be fair to those who don't have much and aren't connected to those in power."

"I couldn't agree more," Senator Bain said, getting up and reaching his hand across to Joe.

Joe rose swiftly from his seat and grasped the hand extended to him.

"Let's go out there and slay some dragons," Bain chuckled.

"Let me check your calendar. I'll see if I can schedule some jousting sessions."

They laughed freely and openly. Someday, Joe and Jeff would look back at these events for the wisdom they bestowed upon them, but they weren't interested in looking in the rearview mirror right now. Instead, their gaze rested on what lay before them, the challenges to be fair and just leaders that at this moment did not seem insurmountable.

ABOUT THE AUTHOR

Fred Burton grew up in Queens, New York. He wrote fiction in his early 20s and returned to it again after his children reached their teen years. His first novel, *The Old Songs*, takes place in Queens during the 1950s and early 1960s. Although he grew up after the years covered in the book, he did experience the turbulent effects of this era and heard the stories brought forth from it. One reviewer said the book read like a "gritty Anne Tyler novel."

His latest novel, *Bountiful Calling*, is set in central Pennsylvania and was drawn from a variety of influences. While living in Harrisburg, Pa. he was involved in the anti-fracking movement. This was an excellent vantage point from which to see not only the powerful business and government forces coalescing around the economic potential of fracking but also its effects on individual people and communities.

Burton avoids easy answers, whether in the emotional interactions in *The Old Songs* or the ideas swirling about in *Bountiful Calling*. He carefully constructs situations and characters and at a certain point frees them to pursue their own destinies. He would rather place the reader within a richly textured, complex situation and let him or her decide what is important, and what rings with the sound of truth.

Burton spent his career working in the computer information world. He retired from that line of work and is now working on a new novel that expands on themes developed in *Bountiful Calling*. These ideas are set in the context of a technologically advanced culture in the very near future.

He and his wife now live in Baltimore, MD.